Resurrect the Dead

Lauren Sapala

Copyright © 2024 Lauren Sapala

All rights reserved. No part of this publication may be reproduced, stored in or introduced into a retrieval system, or transmitted in any form or by any means without the prior written consent of the copyright holder.

Copyright licensed by Lauren Sapala.

ISBN: 979-8-9881782-6-2 (Ebook)
ISBN: 979-8-9881782-5-5 (Paperback)

Cover design by John Price.

Books by Lauren Sapala

Fiction

(West Coast Trilogy)
Between the Shadow and Lo
West Is San Francisco
Enormous Forces

Nonfiction

The INFJ Writer
Firefly Magic
The INFJ Revolution
Writing on the Intuitive Side of the Brain

Contents

Preface   ix

Part I
1. February 1986   3
2. July 1969   10
3. February 1986   18
4. July 1969   24
5. March 1986   31
6. May 1970   39
7. April 1986   46
8. June 1974   52
9. April 1986   57
10. June 1974   66
11. May 1986   73
12. July 1986   79
13. September 1986   85
14. September 1986   90
15. September 1986   99
16. September 1986   108

Part II
17. January 1987   117
18. March 1987   126
19. April 1987   133
20. June 1987   139
21. September 1987   146
22. October 1987   153
23. October 1987   160
24. November 1987   166
25. November 1987   171
26. November 1987   177

27. July 1972	181
28. June 1974	188
29. December 1987	195
30. December 1987	200
31. December 1987	206
32. December 1987	213
33. December 1987	218
34. December 1987	227
35. December 1987	233
About the Author	241

*For John,
my favorite metalhead*

Preface

Writing is an act of creation, but in my opinion, it's also a process of elimination. When a writer absorbs energy from their environment, they digest that energy, and then later excrete it in the form of writing. Personally, I believe writers absorb the most energy from the environment of the era we grow up in, because we are the most open to receiving outside energies when we are young. To name just one example, Stephen King is a favorite author of mine who has given me countless intimate glimpses into the decades of the 1950s and 1960s through his stories. And so, as someone who grew up in the 1980s, it seems only natural that I should carry that singular decade with me, under my skin and in the back of my mind. It makes sense that, as part of my own elimination process, I have a somewhat obsessive need to revisit that time and retell it—even reimagine it—in my own unique way.

When I was growing up in the 1980s, the Vietnam War hadn't happened that long ago, and it was everywhere in popular culture. Movie heroes of the day like Arnold Schwarzenegger and Sylvester Stallone were frequently cast in the role of the Vietnam vet who went up against hostile, inhuman political forces that

Preface

wanted them dead at all costs. There was also the cliché of the Vietnam vet who had lost an arm or a leg and was now homeless on the street and begging for change, which showed up more in TV shows than in the movies, but ultimately came back to the same theme. There was the conquering lion and the wounded lion, but they were all lions. They had all fought their way through the jungle.

If you were a kid who grew up in the '80s, chances were pretty high that you had a dad or an uncle—or you knew someone who had a dad or an uncle—who had been in "Nam," and you also knew that they didn't talk about it. Maybe they had seen some horrible shit they shouldn't have seen, or been part of some horrible shit they didn't want to remember. No one really knew. And no one asked. If you were an intuitive kid, as I was, this weird energy around Vietnam was confusing. It felt like a locked box full of secrets that I would never be able to figure out.

When I grew up, my curiosity about Vietnam only grew stronger. I watched more movies and read a lot of history. Then I discovered the movie *Apocalypse Now*, which led me to revisit the book it's based on, *Heart of Darkness* by Joseph Conrad. In *Heart of Darkness*, the character of Kurtz is located in the Congo in the late 1890s, a land exploited by the Belgians at that time, where the civilized rules of society no longer applied. Kurtz's journey takes him into "the interior" of the country and he slowly becomes a legend to those he's left behind, while undergoing his own disquieting transformation at the same time. In *Apocalypse Now*, the character of Kurtz is located in Vietnam in the late 1960s, and experiences a similar metamorphosis. In both stories, the catalytic agent is the alien world Kurtz has entered, "the interior," a place outside of Kurtz, but also inside him as well. The farther Kurtz travels into the dangerous interior of the country, the further he also travels into the dark interior of his own soul.

Preface

The transformation of a character like Kurtz is exactly what I wanted to examine in a story of my own. Just as it does in Conrad's story about the Congo, I wondered if the experience of Vietnam manipulated people into growing in distorted directions, forcing their souls to change course in response to the environment. Conrad's Congo didn't seem like a place that was quite "real" to me, and Vietnam didn't either. It felt like both existed in an alternate reality, and once a person experienced that reality, whoever they had been before was erased. When they came back to our world, they were different. That was what I wanted to understand. How someone could start out as one person and then —as latent traits and tendencies became activated by a certain set of circumstances—gradually turn into someone else.

I thought that this process of gradual, and mostly hidden, transformation could probably happen to anyone, and that being sent to the Congo or to Vietnam wasn't necessarily a prerequisite to it happening. Maybe it wasn't about traveling to a physical place, but instead, going through an experience that *feels the same* as journeying through the interior of Conrad's Congo or the Vietnam war. Maybe this is where we bury our worst memories, in the heart of that dark jungle within ourselves, and maybe a part of us never forgets they are there, no matter what false story we layer on top of it in order to preserve our own sanity.

That was the story I wanted to write. A story that helps us think about the darkness inside each one of us. Whether we want to own it or not, no matter if it makes us deeply uncomfortable or even disgusts or horrifies us, it's there. It's there in all of us. And at the bottom of that darkness is a gut-wrenching primal fear that no one loves us, that no one *can* love us, because of what lives inside of us, in the shadows. That fear makes humans do all sorts of insane, horrible things. You will find a few of those insane, horrible things in this story. I hope you also find moments of

Preface

brightness, and a reason to believe in the power of friendship, because I wanted to explore that, too.

Thank you, dear reader, for taking the time to journey into the interior with me.

—Lauren Sapala, February 2024

Now if Christ is proclaimed as raised from the death, how can some of you say there is no resurrection of the dead? If there is no resurrection of the dead, then Christ has not been raised; and if Christ has not been raised, then our proclamation has been in vain and your faith is in vain.
 —1 Corinthians 15:12-14

One day he remarked, without lifting his head, "In the interior you will no doubt meet Mr. Kurtz." On my asking who Mr. Kurtz was, he said he was a first-class agent; and seeing my disappointment at this information, he added slowly, laying down his pen, "He is a very remarkable person."
 —*Heart of Darkness*, Joseph Conrad

Part I

Chapter 1
February 1986

Alex woke up and rolled over toward the wall that sat flush against his bed. He sat up and parted the blinds of the window next to him to peer outside. As he stared at the cloudy sky, the wind came by and rattled the thin pane of glass in its metal frame. Early morning, but Alex knew the sky would stay just as blank and gray all day as it was now. From where he sat, propped up on his elbow and running his eyes along the decaying trailer that sat next to theirs, the whole world looked gray. The balding patches of grass on the ground, the bare tree branches scraping the top of the window, everything. As far as he could tell, there wasn't one bit of color to be seen anywhere.

He had woken up because he heard Darwin's low whine, coming from the foot of his bed. It had permeated his dream. In the dream, he was hiding in the bushes. It was the same dream he had all the time. He was hiding in the bushes from someone, and as he was hiding, he was spying. He was watching something he shouldn't be watching. He couldn't see what it was in the dream, but he knew that if he was found—and worse, if he got caught watching—something very bad would happen to him. He started crying in the dream, with both hands clapped over his mouth so he wouldn't make any noise, so he couldn't be found, but it didn't work. He could hear whimpers escaping from him, no matter how hard he tried to hold them inside. That was what woke him up. Then he realized it had been Darwin making that noise, not him.

Alex rolled back over to the other side of the bed and looked down at the floor next to him. Darwin was still asleep, and he must have been dreaming too. His eyes were shut but his legs twitched. His lip was raised in a snarl, showing wet pink gums and white incisors. He growled low in his sleep and then whined softly again.

"Darwin!" he called, and snapped his fingers, keeping his voice low. He didn't want to wake up Roger if he wasn't already awake. But Darwin's eyes stayed closed. His lip twitched again. Alex tapped him on one trembling leg. Darwin jerked up, his eyes peeling open in startled terror. Then he came fully awake and looked around sheepishly. He moved to the bed and began licking Alex's hand.

"Good boy." Alex patted him on the head until Darwin's tail started thumping hard on the floor. "Shhh..." He put a finger to his lips and Darwin's tail came to rest. He knew when to be quiet.

Alex got up and pulled on the jeans he'd left folded on his dresser. He stepped softly to his closed bedroom door and then flattened himself against it, listening. A gust of wind came up and rattled his window. He waited until it passed and then focused on listening through the door again. No sounds came from the living room. He opened the door slowly—expecting the squeak of the top hinge and managing it as it came—and then stepped out. This part of the hallway led to his bedroom and the back bathroom, and it also housed their small washer and dryer. The short expanse of carpet that covered the hallway floor was particularly threadbare, and as he stepped forward, crumbs rolled like pebbles under his heels. He'd have to vacuum again soon.

Resurrect the Dead

He walked quickly to the end of the hall and looked out into the living room.

Collapsed into one corner of their sagging couch, Roger sat slumped over, quietly snoring. His mustache fluttered underneath his nostrils with every breath. Spots of food in his long black beard caught the gray light that filtered in from the window above him. A warm patch of fur pressed itself into the back of Alex's leg. Keeping his eyes on Roger, Alex reached down and took Darwin by the collar and then backed up slowly. He turned and started back toward his room.

Alex washed quickly in the bathroom, brushing his teeth and then soaping his face and armpits. He left the door cracked and listened through the splashing of the water, poised to catch any sound coming from the living room, but he didn't hear anything. When he finished washing, he returned to his room and chose a clean white t-shirt from the closet and a fresh pair of socks from the top dresser drawer. He dressed and then inspected his room. He slid two quarters sitting on the top of his dresser into one hand, and then hastily brushed away any miniscule bits of dust that may have gathered around them overnight. He pulled the one blanket on his bed up to the pillow, folded over the top, and then smoothed it down. He fluffed the pillow and set it back in its place. Finally, he cracked the blinds just slightly, enough so that he could see out of the window without anyone on the outside being able to see in. He looked everything over, satisfied with his work. Darwin sat at his feet, with one floppy black ear folded back, and seemed to survey the room as well. Alex snapped once, softly, and turned. Darwin followed.

When Alex got out to the living room, he saw that Roger was awake. He barely moved, but Alex could see him blinking against the light of the late winter sunshine coming through the blinds and outlining him in stripes. Alex walked into their small eat-in kitchen and grabbed the sponge he always kept by the sink. Right after Roger woke up was the best time to wipe down the counters. He could be present, and at the same time not run the risk of making any accidental loud noises that might trigger Roger in some way. Alex had learned that Roger was the most vulnerable immediately after first waking up in the morning, especially if it was early.

"Alex...?" Roger said, and then cleared his throat. Alex pictured an ancient gate rattling open over the abyss. "Alex...you there?"

"Yeah. I'm here." Alex stepped out from behind the counter.

Roger gave a big watery sigh and looked over at him. "Where'em m'smokes?"

"Right here." Alex slid a pack of Winstons off the end table and Roger held open one beefy red palm. He took the pack from Alex and then, fumbling, shook one out and put it between his lips. Alex lit it for him and he took a long drag.

Alex watched him for a moment, his face unreadable, and then he went back to the morning's chores.

Since nothing had set Roger off during the night, it would probably shape up to be an okay day, Alex thought. He could count on being able to do the dishes, get in a load of laundry, and mop the kitchen floor before he had to leave for school. He started in on his chores and Roger sat in his place on the sofa, smoking and watching TV. After a quick breakfast of a couple pieces of toast—and cereal for Roger—Alex grabbed his backpack, let Darwin out, and told Roger he was leaving. Then he shut the door quietly behind him, leaving it unlocked for Greg, who would be by later to check in on Roger before he left for work. Alex would be free from Roger until later that afternoon when the bus dropped him off after school.

Resurrect the Dead

As Alex walked to the bus stop, he gave thanks again to whatever God might exist that Roger hadn't had a bad night. When Roger had a bad night, Alex didn't sleep at all, and then he was up most of the following day too, waiting for Greg to come over to help out. That might happen late morning, or it might be late afternoon, depending on when Greg could get off his shift. If Roger was still freaking out, and Alex had already been up all night, he found that it made very little difference when it came to his own mental state.

Many different things could trigger Roger, but Alex had noticed that it was most often sudden, loud noises from outside. Any kind of siren going off might do it. All their neighbors knew that Roger had problems, and so when they heard him yelling they just ignored it. But Alex had often thought that anyone who didn't know the situation would think Roger was being murdered right there in his own living room. What really unnerved him though, was the way Roger would frantically point at the air in front of him, as if he were trying to make Alex see something that was standing just a few feet away. He would aim his index finger at this imaginary target and stab his hand forward, over and over, as if accusing the thing and warding it off all at the same time. Sometimes, too, while he pointed with the one hand, he groped at his mouth with the other, pulling his lips together and making a low, guttural sound in his throat, which Alex thought was somehow worse—much worse—than him yelling.

If Roger started screaming in the middle of the night, the first thing Alex did was get all the lights on, and fast. He turned on every lamp in the living room and all the lights in the kitchen, and then all the battery-powered camping lanterns Greg had brought over. Sometimes this worked and Roger stopped screaming. Then he would huddle up in a corner of the couch, silent, staring with huge eyes and pointing at whatever it was he saw across the room. In the middle of the night, this really gave Alex the willies. Somehow, the possibility of some sinister imaginary friend of Roger's being in the room with them seemed significantly creepier in the middle of the night.

Sometimes though, Roger didn't stop. He screamed and screamed and there was nothing Alex could do about it. All the lights in the world weren't going to help, and Alex had no choice but to wait it out. After a couple of hours or so, he would know the end was in sight when Roger's screams started tapering off into deep hitching breaths and long minutes of silent sobbing. He cried with one hand covering his eyes, the other hand still out in front of him, but with his finger pointing limply now, as if losing steam. Alex sat in the chair on the other side of the room and watched him quietly. He'd learned a long time ago that no matter how he was feeling inside, it was important for Roger to see him as calm and unemotional. He made his face as blank as possible and imagined he was sending waves of coldness over Roger, like a shower of freezing water that would slowly encase him in ice and finally silence him.

Whenever Roger started screaming, Darwin would hightail it to Alex's bedroom and squeeze himself into the corner by the bed. There he remained until Roger stopped howling. When the worst was past, Alex made his way back and deposited a treat by the door, for whenever Darwin deemed it was safe to come out again. Then it was back to the living room, to continue sitting and waiting. At some point, Darwin would creep out of Alex's room and sit in the kitchen doorway, watching Alex trustingly, but also ready to bolt back to the bedroom again at any moment.

Lately, whenever Alex found himself sitting and waiting for Roger to stop losing his shit and come back to sanity, he found that he was wishing that maybe something would happen to Roger, and every time he went through another cycle of it, he was wishing for it more and more. He wished for something quick and definite, something that would release Alex into some kind of new life, the details of which remained hazy and never fully imagined, because the moment those thoughts came into his head, Alex pushed them aside. He felt annoyed with himself, and also ashamed. It wasn't Roger's fault he got the screaming terrors. Alex knew he couldn't help it. But sometimes after he had been sitting there for a long time, steeling himself against another wave of screaming, watching Roger point at the air in front of him at nothing at all and grasp at his mouth over and over again, and then cover his eyes and cry, Alex felt a subtle shift in himself, like if he had to sit there for even one more minute, he wouldn't have any choice but to join Roger in his insanity. Then maybe they would end up screaming together, forever, locked in a cycle of fear and pain that was impossible to escape.

But last night had been a good night, Alex reminded himself, and so today would be a good day. He pushed his thoughts about Roger to the side and focused on walking straight ahead. He would be at the bus stop in just a minute, and then he'd soon be at school and wouldn't have to deal with Roger for at least a few hours. He reached down and patted Darwin and then breathed in deeply and tasted the cold air. It would be a good day, he repeated to himself. Right now, he could stop thinking about Roger altogether, at least for a little while.

Chapter 2
July 1969

Roger hadn't waited to be drafted to go to Vietnam, he'd signed up. It wasn't a decision he anguished over, and he didn't do it to serve his country. He did it to get out of Oregon, and away from the little town where he'd grown up and people had always given him funny looks. Roger had never been sure why they looked at him like that, but he thought that maybe if he went somewhere where all the people were different and he didn't know any of them, he might meet some people who didn't look at him like that. He also thought that going to Vietnam might make him feel more real in the world, or make the world feel more real to him. Nothing had ever felt real to him. He had always felt like a ghost, just gliding through things with no one noticing him, until he snuck up on people and then they got startled and gave him one of those funny looks. But even then, none of the people seemed real, not the people he knew or the people who were strangers. Not even his mom or dad, and he'd known them his whole life. It didn't feel to him like there was much difference between people and trees and cars. They were just there and did people things, like trees and cars did tree and car things.

Roger's mother told him once that he stared at people too

Resurrect the Dead

much. She said it made people uncomfortable. Roger nodded but was also surprised, because he hadn't been aware that he was staring. After that, he got in the habit of averting his gaze whenever he was around other people and trying instead to stare at the wall or the floor. His father said this wasn't much of an improvement and told him to just be normal for God's sake. Roger didn't know what that meant. He was being normal. It was other people he didn't understand. They got so upset by everything, and raised their voices and made faces when they talked about this or that different thing in the news. Roger didn't feel anything about any of it, not what was in the news, or anything else they talked about. Sometimes he did feel lonely, but only if he happened to hear a sad song or something like that. Once the song was over, he forgot about it. He never cried, although sometimes he noticed that his mom did.

When Roger got to Vietnam he adjusted quickly. He had discovered in basic training that he fit in well with the army. He was good at following orders because he liked following orders. Living day to day—always going through the same routine and not having to think about the next day until it came—was a way of life that suited him. He mostly kept to himself, just like he had at home, and just like at home, the other guys sometimes gave him funny looks, but that was okay. Roger concentrated on each task of his daily routine and was mostly able to forget about if anyone else was looking at him or not. He liked the way each task they were assigned was supposed to be done in a certain way, and the more complicated ones were broken into steps that everyone was supposed to follow in the same order. That ghostly feeling Roger had had all his life began to recede. Within the confines of the army's structure, he felt some kind of solid definition taking form.

One thing that did surprise him though, was that it seemed like most of the other guys couldn't wait to do their time and get out of there. Roger didn't understand that. He loved Vietnam. It wasn't just the army and the routine and the structure, it was the jungle itself. He loved that he always felt hidden there, and protected. At first, he'd thought the jungle was a place that was utterly still, until he moved further in and began to feel himself merge with it, and then he knew it was teeming with life. No one else could see this because almost everything in the jungle took cover and hid in the dark places until the men moved through. Often, when moving through the jungle, Roger felt like he might instead be on the bottom of the sea on another planet, moving across the ocean floor of an alien world. He knew there were countless creatures in the depths, hidden from the humans who bumbled about overhead, carefully camouflaging themselves so that the humans would look the other way, waiting until they passed by before they emerged back out into the light.

When Roger's first tour in Vietnam was over, he signed up for another, and then another. Sometime during his third tour, he realized that the old world—Oregon, his parents' house, the life he had lived before he came to Vietnam—had faded so far into the past that he could hardly remember it. It was like his life before he'd become a soldier had belonged to another person. This realization didn't bother Roger. If anything, it felt like a relief. He felt like he was finally somewhere that he really belonged. He wondered now and again what he would do if the war ended, but that didn't seem likely to happen anytime soon, so he didn't think about it all that much.

Roger had a bunch of different duties as a soldier, but one of the things he was best at was walking point. He didn't try to be good at it, he just was. Probably because he liked doing it so much. It was simple, and fun. There were people who hid in the bushes in front of him while other people trailed somewhere behind him, waiting for him to make it all clear so that they could keep following. To Roger, it all felt like a big game. He got the rules and he got how to play, and most important, he got how to win. It was easy.

Resurrect the Dead

You just kept moving forward, and you killed anyone who got in your way.

Once Roger had earned his combat infantry badge, his sergeant started making him the point man whenever they needed to drop into a hot LZ. Then after he proved himself through night ambush patrol, he was allowed to scout farther and farther ahead. It seemed now that he was the permanent point man—or the first point man, since sometimes he was so far ahead that they needed to send a second point man behind him just to make sure the areas he had cleared stayed clear. Roger adapted to his new role as a lone-wolf point man just as effortlessly as he had adapted to army life. He liked being on his own in the jungle, moving through the brush as if he were swimming through deep, dark water, feeling the hidden world around him fall still and then come back to life after he had passed. However, he did get lonely from time to time, and at these times he thought about commercials he had seen on TV back home, when some man and woman would run toward each other and then hug and kiss after being separated for so long. He wondered if something like that would ever happen to him.

The first time Roger saw Mary was the first time he experienced having a feeling for another person—*any* other person—ever. He had been making his way through the jungle, focused on forging a path and listening for anything up ahead, when he came out into a clearing and there she was, all alone under a tree. She was obviously hot and tired, and had probably sat down for only a few moments, to get her strength back and drink some water. To Roger, she looked like a little girl, sitting with her legs folded up and one small hand on her forehead, so quiet and still.

Roger halted right where he was and stared at her. Finding this woman here, sitting under a tree almost as if she had been waiting for him, seemed like a magical happening. She was so pretty, and so small. Her hair was beautiful. Even hanging limply around her face, it was still glossy and black and silky. She reminded Roger of an animal, with sweet big brown animal eyes. He opened his mouth but couldn't speak. He didn't know what to say to such a perfect tiny creature.

She appeared to be just as shocked as Roger was by their unexpected meeting. She became as still as a real little animal would, the only sign of life in her being a slight widening of the eyes that displayed a subtle but clear terror. Roger smiled at her. She remained frozen for a few seconds more, and then she nervously smiled back. Roger slowly walked toward her and then stood over her and she looked up at him, still smiling, but her eyes darted back and forth between him and the surrounding area. Her smile became slightly more strained.

"Hi," he croaked, finally managing to say something. He heard how rusty his voice sounded and realized it had been many days since he'd spoken to another human being. She stayed where she was, the corners of her smile now beginning to wilt a bit, and didn't answer.

"I'm Roger." He looked at her and waited, but still she said nothing. She just kept smiling at him, and looking between his face and the surrounding jungle. He tried again.

"Ro-*ger*..." This time he pointed to himself as he sounded the word out, loudly, and to this, she rapidly nodded, as if she had understood him the first time and were impatient for him to go on. He watched a delicate tendril of sweat trickle out of her hairline and down her temple. Her eyes kept darting around. He wished she would stop looking everywhere but at him.

"Who are you?" he asked. Slowly, she got to her feet, still smiling, and Roger thought that was a good sign. She might like him. He wanted to touch her. He thought, maybe, this was what love was. This was how it must feel, like warm water traveling all through his body, and a buzzing lightheadedness that wasn't entirely unpleasant. He wanted to hold her, to bring her closer to him, and this desire quickly began to feel like a need, as non-negotiable as food or water.

Yes, this was it, he thought. He must be in love.

"What is your name?" he tried asking, and also wondered if she might have a hearing problem, when suddenly she made a dash for it. She was quick, almost too quick. She skipped fast to his left and would have taken off at a run if Roger hadn't caught her arm. He pulled her back and she twisted around so she was facing away from him and then bit down on his forearm, hard. Instantly, Roger bent her forward, grabbed her head in a lock, lifted her (it felt like lifting a cat, Roger thought) and then twisted his arm to jerk her neck back toward him.

He heard a small snap. Then she went limp in his arms.

Roger propped the girl up against the same tree under which he'd first found her.

He'd closed her eyes so that she looked like she was sleeping. Her face was completely still, and her eyes didn't move between him and the jungle anymore. She could have been a fairy princess, waiting for her prince to come wake her up. He stood back and looked at her. Her head sat at an unnatural angle, but her little face was still so beautiful. He couldn't just leave her abandoned here underneath the tree, it wasn't right. She wouldn't want to be all alone. He hoisted her up over one shoulder and left the clearing with her. As he began pushing through the jungle again, he breathed her scent in deeply and felt blissfully happy with the warm weight of her swaying over his back. As he walked, he decided he would call her Mary.

Later, when he stopped to rest and to eat something, he

lowered Mary to the ground and left her there while he went to relieve himself. In the few moments that he was away from her, he began hearing the voice in his head that didn't sound like him. Even if the voice tried to imitate his own voice, he could still tell the difference, because it felt like someone else. It was like someone else's thoughts were in his head, like someone else had *inserted* their thoughts into his head. That was how he knew those thoughts weren't really his.

He'd heard this voice in his head for many years, although sometimes it seemed to be dormant, because it left him alone for long stretches of time. But here it was again, and even though he was usually able to ignore it, this time the alien thoughts formed into an idea that left him cold with fear. What if Mary wasn't really dead? What if she was only unconscious—or worse, pretending? Maybe when he was sleeping in the middle of the night she was planning to get up and leave him, and then he would be all alone again. He'd just found her, he couldn't risk losing her. He remembered her biting him, which had confused him and also hurt him deeply. Why would she do a thing like that? He had only wanted to talk to her. He had only wanted her to stay with him and not leave. But what if she didn't understand that? What if she left anyway and she got so far away from him that he could never find her again?

That was when the voice told him to cut off her head.

Roger immediately saw the wisdom in this idea. He pulled out his KA-BAR knife and got to work. As he sawed through her windpipe and then the tough little vertebrae of her neck, he whistled to himself and noticed that the alien voice seemed to have fallen silent. That was good. That meant that his thoughts were his own again. He pulled back and looked at his handiwork and decided to leave just a tiny bit of muscle and skin intact so that her head couldn't fall completely off and roll away somewhere. After all, he didn't need her head to be absolutely separate, he just needed a guarantee that she wouldn't be going anywhere. When he was all finished, he propped her up and pushed her head back where it was supposed to go and it made a noise—*thup*—like a thermos top falling into place. Later, he saw that a tacky circle of blood had formed around her throat. It gave her the appearance of wearing a necklace made of black beads that had liquefied and bled down to her collarbones.

That first night he made camp and then laid her down next to him. He whispered to her in the dark, explaining who he was, how he came to be there, and most importantly, how he had felt when he'd run into her in the middle of the jungle. After a while, he realized that he could talk to her without saying anything out loud. He directed his thoughts to her and could feel that she was receiving them immediately. He positioned her carefully, so that her head stayed on straight, and took her hand, telling her how lonely he had been before he met her. Then he moved her again so that the top of her head was buttressed by a nearby log, keeping it firmly pressed onto her body, and he made love to her in the dark. Afterwards, he lay beside her, holding her little hand and kissing it every few seconds. Her hand was cold, and she was dead, he knew that. But still, he realized that he didn't feel so lonely anymore.

Chapter 3
February 1986

Alex stood at the bus stop, bouncing lightly from foot to foot in an effort to keep warm. He shoved his hands deep into the pockets of his parka, jingling the change in one pocket, and crumpling the few dollars in the other pocket into a tight fist. He looked up at the gray sky and then down at Darwin, who whined and then happily yipped at the girl who came crunching over the gravel toward them. Her long pale-blonde hair was tied back in a ponytail, the hood of her jacket thrown back and resting just below her ears. Alex smiled without being able to help it.

"Hi, Alyssa."

"Hi." She came to a halt beside him and gave him a sideways look and a small grin. The color in her cheeks had blossomed into a delicate pale pink in the cold, the rest of her face was white as marble. She looked down and smiled wider.

"Hi, Darwin." She ran a hand behind Darwin's ears and scratched him in his favorite spot. He squinted and thumped his tail with pleasure.

"I wish it was a holiday," Alex said suddenly. "Or...I mean...I wish there was no school."

Resurrect the Dead

"Yeah, me too." Alyssa agreed, and then sighed. The two of them stood in silence for a few moments. Their mutual wish for no school seemed to undermine the relevancy of any other topic.

"Hey..." said Alex, an idea dawning. "Let's cut." He turned to Alyssa, excited by his idea and hoping she was too. She widened her eyes and nodded. They didn't need to discuss any more details. Immediately they walked, fast and together, away from the bus stop, and didn't look back. Darwin followed.

Neither Alex nor Alyssa would have dreamed of going home—as bad as school was, it was way better than home for either of them—and so Alex decided to take her to his private spot out in the woods. The woods lay just behind the trailer park where both of them lived, but as far as Alex could tell, he was the only person that ever went into them. He thought of his private spot as the place where he was left alone to live his own life, even if that life was conducted entirely inside his own head.

The brown shells of dead leaves crackled under their feet as they made their way forward on the path that Alex had forged into the small clearing. When they got all the way into the clearing, Alex introduced Alyssa to the big old log he used sometimes as a seat and sometimes as a backrest, and the two of them sat down on it, side by side. The silence of the woods surrounded them and the gray light of the sky shone through the bare black branches hanging overhead. They sat and glanced at each other every few moments, both of them smiling a little. Alyssa kicked one foot out, spraying more dead leaves over the bare ground in front of her.

"This is definitely better than school," said Alex.

"Yeah," said Alyssa, and kicked at another pile of leaves. Then, "I have some cigarettes."

She unbuttoned a small pocket in her jacket and brought out a crumpled half-empty pack of Kools and a book of matches. She looked at Alex and he nodded. She handed him one.

"Thanks." He held the cigarette, and waited until she had hers going before he took the matches from her. When she handed them over, he squeezed her fingers for just a moment and let himself smile again. Alyssa took a deep drag on her cigarette and smiled back. She flipped her ponytail over her shoulder and with a small trembling motion of her other hand she flicked off the little bit of ash that had collected on her cigarette. When she looked away Alex studied her profile, arrested by the startling red of her lips and the pink in her cheeks set against the backdrop of her pale skin.

Alex knew that most of the boys at school thought Alyssa was pretty, but hardly any of them ever approached her. There was something about her that was tough, some quality in her eyes and expression when she looked at someone that was coldly appraising. She didn't talk much. When she did, she only answered questions that had been directly asked of her, and even then, she rarely volunteered more than basic information. Alyssa was one grade below Alex, and so he'd seen her around at the junior high when they were younger and he'd known she lived just a few trailers down from him, but this was the first year they'd both had to wait at the same bus stop to go over to the high school and had started talking to each other on a regular basis.

Alyssa's mom was a haggard woman with puffy red eyes and stringy gray-blonde hair. Alex recognized her most easily by her voice—her loud, frequently yelling voice—that he could hear all the way down at his house if he had the windows open. Alyssa was the oldest of five, and the younger four were all boys. Whenever Alex said goodbye to her when they walked home from the bus stop together, he got a glimpse of a cluster of frizzy blond heads poking out of doorway of her mom's trailer, and usually a

Resurrect the Dead

couple of boys' faces lighting up the windows, more if her brothers had friends over. Her mom was always yelling at one of them, or all of them, Alex couldn't really tell. Alyssa said she had never seen her dad. She guessed he was gone somewhere and not coming back. She said her mom never talked about him.

"Do you remember your mom?" she asked suddenly, tapping her cigarette again and sending another small cap of ash flying into the wind.

"Not so much." Alex thought it over. "Hazy bits and pieces here and there, but...no, not really." He paused for a moment to take a drag and then went on. "I only really remember Roger being around when I was a little kid. I remember Greg's house and us living there for a while. But I don't remember my mom, except for...flashes. And I'm not even sure those really happened. I just remember Roger, that seems like it was the beginning." He looked at her. "How about you? What's going on with your mom?"

"Same old, same old." Alyssa sighed and rolled her eyes. "She's crazy."

"Is she really crazy? She's not *crazy* crazy...is she?" Alex had wondered about this more than a few times, but had never before had the courage to voice the question out loud to Alyssa. He had a hard time allowing to himself that Alyssa's mom was *truly* crazy.

"Yup. Crazy." Alyssa's tone of voice shut down any chance for argument, crazy was crazy. Alex nodded thoughtfully and puffed on his cigarette.

"What does she do?" he asked.

"Oh, *you* know..." said Alyssa, cutting her eyes away from him. "Gets drunk, yells. Gets *real* drunk. Acts stupid—so stupid. It's humiliating." Alyssa sighed again and finished her cigarette. She tossed it into the leaves at her feet and ground it under her heel. Then she stood up and faced him and lightly kicked the side of his foot. "C'mon. Let's go."

"Where?"

"Just let's go." She walked away and started on the path back towards the park. Alex snapped for Darwin to come, and then followed.

They ended up walking into town and going to J.R.'s Roller World. J.R.'s was an old warehouse that had at one time been transformed into some sort of rec center, and then converted after that into a roller-skating rink. The floors were cement and most of the place was as dark as a nightclub. Two bars of cold white light —one coming from the skate rental window and the other from the snack bar—acted as beacons. A disco ball that looked like it had seen better days made apathetic revolutions over the scuffed and dirty skating floor. Everyone under the age of 18 loved J.R.'s. If Alex and Alyssa had had any other friends, they probably would have hung out there with them on the weekends.

But, Alex knew, neither one of them had any other friends. On the weekends they were at home, Alex taking care of Roger and Alyssa watching her pack of little brothers while her mom sat on the couch watching TV and hitting the bottle. The only time they went anywhere like J.R.'s was in the middle of the day on a Tuesday, when they should have been in school but were cutting. The only time they did what everyone else did together to have fun, they did it alone with each other, in secret. Sometimes Alex felt like his whole life was like that.

Alex didn't care much about roller skating, but he knew Alyssa loved it, and if Alyssa was happy then he was happy. He changed his shoes for skates and then let her drag him out on the floor. Fortunately—in Alex's view—the place was empty. The two of them glided together and then skated apart. Alyssa was a better skater than Alex and spun around and skated backwards, then she laughed and turned away, skating fast until she was on the other side of the floor. Alex kept his steady pace, confident that eventually he would catch up. She came back to his side, let herself fall behind and then raced past him again. The disco ball revolved above them and spangles of light settled over Alyssa's hair, dancing like sprinkles of rain, and then jumped off again, down to the floor, then back up to her face.

Whenever she skated up close to him, Alex glanced over at her. When they were alone like this, and he could really look at her face, he realized she reminded him of someone. When he tried to put his finger on it, he could almost feel something trying to break through the surface of his mind, but then it glided away again. Whatever memory was evading him felt so faint that it must have been buried deep. Maybe it was impossible to resurrect it and ever bring it to life again. Maybe it wasn't even a real memory anyway. Inwardly shrugging to himself, he let it go. It was pointless to try to remember something that might not even be there to be remembered.

When Alyssa got tired of skating, they made their way off the floor and back to the skate rental window, where they both sat down on the bench beside it and pulled off their skates. Neither one of them said anything as they concentrated on lacing their sneakers, and then finally Alyssa sighed. "I gotta get home," she said.

"Me too. It's gonna be about time the bus dropped us off."

They walked out of the twilight of the skating rink into a bright and cold, but still overcast, afternoon. The twin doors of J.R.'s Roller World banged hollowly behind them.

Chapter 4
July 1969

Roger kept Mary with him for ten days before he had to give her up.

His unit had finally caught up with him after the sergeant sighted him while they were crossing relatively flat terrain. Sergeant Graber was a hot-tempered man who was nonetheless quite canny, and he'd let Roger get so far ahead of the unit because it was a situation that worked out well for Roger, and for the rest of the unit too. The sergeant had observed that, at best, his men reacted to Roger with a diffidence that bordered on repulsion. At worst, it appeared they were frightened of him, although they never said anything about it out loud.

Sergeant Graber had also observed that there was nothing specific that Roger did or said that seemed to provoke this reaction in others. It was just the way he was with people. He seemed almost robotic at times, his eyes going blank and unfocused, and then at other moments he gave the appearance of listening very hard to the air, like he heard someone talking to him, when no one else was there. Sergeant Graber wouldn't even fully admit it to himself, but there was something that deeply unnerved him about Roger. Plainly put, he could be spooky. However, he also

Resurrect the Dead

happened to be one of the best killing machines the sergeant had ever seen.

As the rest of the unit trailed in Roger's wake, they came upon bodies strewn here and there, some piled together in twos and threes, like logs. No one knew how Roger did it, but he *did* do it, and that wasn't up for argument. Since no one ever saw him at work though, it wasn't long before rumors spread through the unit, and within a short time the rumors took on the dimensions of legend. Roger had help from a supernatural force, he'd made a deal with the devil, or worse yet, some kind of demon had possessed him and was using him to mow down anyone who came across its path. During the day, these stories sounded ridiculous, even to the men who were telling them, but at night, in the middle of the jungle, things looked different, and all of them silently hoped that Roger was as far ahead of them as possible.

The worst possibility though, barely hinted at by the men but full-bodied and invisibly present in their conversation nonetheless, was that there was nothing supernatural about what Roger was doing. It might just be Roger. Whatever ability he had to kill that many people, that ruthlessly, and that continuously, was coming from somewhere inside of him. Whenever the presence of those thoughts came into the circle—almost totally unspoken but dancing between the minds of all the men—the conversation shut down for the night. Suddenly, it was time for everyone to turn in and go to bed. And then there would be no more talk of Roger that night.

Now, as he used field-glasses to sweep the area, Sgt. Graber spotted something in the distance that looked like a caveman. It was wearing a loincloth, carrying the standard army-issue duffel bag, and walking fast. Although the sergeant was more familiar than he wanted to be with Roger's strange ways, he still wondered for a moment if he was suffering from some sort of hallucinations brought on from the heat. He suddenly remembered all the crazy things his men said about Roger and claimed were true, and for that one moment he didn't doubt any of it.

He gave the order for the unit to speed up and get their asses in gear, *now*. They were going to catch up to that crazy motherfucker. From what the sergeant could see, it appeared Roger was setting up camp ahead of them, and this gave Sgt. Graber reason to pause. If he could see Roger from where he was standing using the field glasses, anyone else could too. It seemed to Sgt. Graber that Roger might—just *might*—be slipping. Of course, he'd known for some time that Roger was loony, but up until now he'd also decided to overlook that small detail. He had proved invaluable as a point man, if that was what they were still pretending he was. Really, he was more like a sweep-the-area-and-kill-everything man, and that had come in quite handy when moving through the type of country in which they'd been for the past few months. But still, he had to admit to himself that he wouldn't be completely disappointed if Roger was losing his touch.

When the unit caught up to Roger the sergeant saw that he hadn't been mistaken in any of the conclusions he'd already come to about the situation. Roger looked more like a savage than a man. He was beyond filthy and had discarded most of his clothes—other than the loincloth which, up close, Sgt. Graber could see was made from a large patch of cloth that could only have come from Roger's fatigues—but also, there was a skittish quality to his eyes, a subtle agitation in the way he kept blinking and wouldn't make eye contact. They stood on a small piece of land that stretched into a flat plain, with no sort of tree cover, and the hot sun fell over them like a blanket made of fire. The air was thick with heat and gnats, and something else that smelled rotten.

Roger stood where he was, facing them, without saying anything. His duffel bag was on the ground next to him and the sergeant noticed that he kept glancing over at it, as if checking to see that it was still there. The sergeant walked closer and the smell intensified. Now it was all around him, a wave of stench that smelled like cooked roadkill. He stopped and sniffed the air, turning his head in all directions, and at that moment Roger leaned down and grabbed the handles of his bag and hoisted it over his shoulder. Sgt. Graber saw a large wet stain dripping down the side of it.

"What's in the bag, soldier?"

Roger flicked his eyes right and left, and then back again. He licked his lips.

"Nothing."

The sergeant tilted his head back and took a deep breath. He fanned his nostrils open, so that Roger and the rest of the men could see him draw in the air. Then he released the breath in one long, loud exhalation and stared at Roger. Roger stared back at him blankly.

"I said...*what's in the bag soldier?*"

Roger didn't answer.

Sgt. Graber had never betrayed the fact that he had a violent dislike for Roger by any outward sign of expression on his face or change in his tone of voice. He would not have his men thinking that anyone—even if they *were* batshit crazy—had the ability to put even an ounce of fear into him. But at that moment, standing in the 102-degree heat with the sun streaming down on him like hot butter melting all over his head, Sgt. Graber got a distinct chill looking into Roger's eyes. He stood and stared at Roger gripping that bag—gripping it so tightly that Sgt. Graber could see his knuckles turning white, even in the bright sun—and he knew for certain that Roger had lost any little bit of sanity he had ever had. And that scared the shit out of him.

The moment he realized how scared he was, he did the only thing he could to defend himself. He gathered every bit of fury and hatred he had inside, and he pushed it out, screaming in Roger's face.

"I SAID, WHAT'S IN THE BAG SOLDIER???"

This time he didn't wait for an answer. Although the sergeant was a big man, he could also move fast, and he darted quickly now to Roger's side and wrestled the bag away from him. It jostled between the two of them, and the stain on the side grew larger, as if a can of soup had been spilled inside. Then Sgt. Graber had the bag and he backed up with it, still quick as could be, and Roger stood alone, panting and empty-handed. He stared at the sergeant but made no further moves toward him. Sgt. Graber dropped the bag and then squatted in front of it and unzipped it. He heard coughing from his men behind him, and a rustling as they all backed up together, but he didn't turn around and look for one moment. He kept his eyes trained on the bag, and on Roger.

The first thing he registered was that there was a dead girl inside the bag. The second thing was that her head had been separated from her body. The third thing was that she had been dead for quite some time. The smell that came out when he unzipped the bag was monstrous. It slammed into him and he knew it had the power to knock him down, if he let it. He gagged deep in his throat, without making a sound, and then stood up and backed away. Throughout everything, he noticed that Roger had remained very still. He tilted his head and seemed to be gazing on the remains of the body, some of which were now falling out onto the ground. Part of the girl's face was crushed in on one side—probably as the result of the tug-of-war over the bag, the sergeant thought—and one of her eyes peeked through the unzipped opening with one of her feet poking out beside it. Black flies, as big as large bumblebees, had begun lazily circling the bag, some of them landing on it and crawling over the wet parts. Sgt. Graber moved carefully around the bag and its contents. He moved toward Roger until he was only two inches from his face. But instead of screaming this time, he lowered his voice to almost a whisper.

Resurrect the Dead

"A *gook*? A fucking *dead gook*?"

The men who were there that day and watched everything unfold later said that was the scariest part, that Sgt. Graber became so dangerously calm before he really lost his shit. When he started screaming at Roger again, an almost palpable sense of relief washed through the unit, because even though all of them had seen some fucked up things in the war, Roger dressed up in a loincloth carrying around a bag of putrid human remains was something that fucked up didn't begin to cover. None of them had words for it, and that made all of them want to start screaming, and so when the sergeant got in Roger's face and went crazy for those few seconds, it felt like they could finally come back to themselves.

"Carrying that shit around like it's a *fucking SUITCASE?*" As the sergeant screamed at Roger, he kicked his steel-toed boot into the side of the bag and a big glop of the dead girl went flying through the field. Pieces of her also flew back and landed on the sergeant's pants. Sweat streamed from his face, which had gone a deep red and was now approaching purple. He looked down at the faint residue of slime left on his fatigues by the bits of the girl that had hit him and his eyes bulged in disbelief, and then in fury. The corners of his mouth twitched. He caught the slight movement of one of his men in his peripheral vision and suddenly turned on all of them.

"What the FUCK are you fucking shitheads LOOKING AT?"

No one said anything. No one met his stare. After a moment he turned back to Roger, eyed the bag, thought about giving it one final kick but decided against it, and then his face turned to stone. "Clean this shit up. And bury the fuckin' bitch." He squinted at Roger and shook his head in disgust. "Jesus. Show some goddamn respect." Then he turned and ordered the men to move and move NOW and they did. They marched past Roger and left him on his knees, gathering up what he could of the dead gook that had been in the bag. Sergeant Graber didn't look back, but his mind never left the problem of what Roger had become for one moment. If only they weren't all trapped out here in this hellhole and didn't need him so goddamn much, he thought, he wouldn't hesitate to get rid of the fucking psychopath for good.

Chapter 5
March 1986

In the past year or so, Alex had started to notice something funny about Roger. It seemed like sometimes, usually when Alex was least expecting it, he seemed to turn into someone else. It happened in a matter of seconds. First, a barely perceptible wave passed over Roger's face. It looked like a new skin was settling over it, molding itself onto his original face that was now hidden underneath. His eyes changed too, and so did his mouth. They were the eyes and mouth of another person, a different person that Alex didn't know and had never seen before. And even though Roger didn't do or say anything out of the ordinary, Alex could swear that he felt some change in his personality. Like there was alien inside him, entirely separate from Roger but using his body and mind all the same.

Sometimes, if he started to let himself think about it too long, he would get scared. What if Roger lost his mind entirely? What if the change Alex sensed in him was only the beginning of some sort of inevitable mental unraveling? What if they had to come take Roger away? Where would Alex live? Where would he go? Would Greg take him in? What if he couldn't? Every question he asked only increased his feeling of panic until he snapped and ordered himself to shut all lines of questioning down. Alex trusted his own brain above anything else, and he knew asking these kinds of questions was no way to think about things. Predicting the future was impossible and he could only meet each day as it came.

Sometimes it happened when Greg was around, and at these times Alex watched both men carefully. He watched Roger to see if the change was as noticeable as he thought, and he watched Greg to see if the change in Roger was noticed at all. But Greg never made any sign that he thought something was off, and that was almost worse, because then Alex questioned if he really was just seeing things. Maybe he *couldn't* trust his own brain above all else. He guessed it didn't matter though, because even if some alien thing was slipping inside of Roger and looking through his eyes and speaking through his mouth, there wasn't much Greg could do about it except call the authorities, and then Alex was right back on the merry-go-round of panicky thoughts about Roger being taken away. Besides, maybe it was nothing. Maybe Alex just thought he was seeing something when nothing was there.

He did talk to Alyssa about it, saying that it seemed sometimes like Roger was a different person, but he didn't mention anything about feeling like it might be an alien entity inside his body. It was just too weird. He couldn't risk her thinking he was crazy. Outside of Greg and Alyssa, Alex had no one else to tell. And so, since Greg didn't seem to notice anything particularly out of the ordinary, and he couldn't tell Alyssa the whole truth of his private fears, he found himself alone, asking the same questions over and over again.

Of course, Roger knew. Alex was somehow sure of that. If it was all real and Alex wasn't imagining any of it then, on some level, Roger had to know.

That suspicion was the worst feeling of all.

Even when Alex wasn't vigilantly watching Roger to see if he had turned into someone else, he still had a long list of questions that had no answers. For example, Roger would never talk about Alex's mom. Ever. Whenever Alex asked about her, he either acted like he hadn't heard the question, or he said she was an angel and that was it. If Alex pressed him on it, Roger would stop talking entirely. Alex had tried many times, in many different ways, to get any little bit of information on her out of Roger, but he had never gotten anywhere. Roger wouldn't tell him the color of her eyes, where she was from, or even her first name. As Alex had grown older, he began to formulate the theory that possibly Roger didn't actually know the answers to a lot of these questions. That was telling in itself—but of what, Alex couldn't fully articulate, not even in his own mind.

When he went over his own memories to see what he could come up with, there just wasn't much there. He thought maybe he remembered the shadowy outline of a blonde woman, always smiling, and always taking him somewhere, in a car with someone else or on a bus, always moving. But when he tried to focus in on the details, everything turned even hazier. The shadows of the memories seemed to come apart entirely, as if any conscious examination made them dissolve, like dreams do after you come fully awake in the morning.

Eventually, it became less about finding out things about his mom, and more about wanting to know what Roger was hiding. Because why else would Roger not tell him *even one thing* about her? He already knew Roger wasn't his real dad. He had called him "Roger" for as long as he could remember, and if he had called him Roger when he was still just a little kid then that pointed to the fact that his mom had left him with a man to whom he wasn't biologically related. So, Roger must have been his stepdad at one time, or in some form of relationship with his mom when she took off and left Alex with him. Of course, Alex had no way of knowing if any of what he had pieced together into this hypothetical picture had a chance of being true, but it was the best he had. Nothing else made any sense.

He just couldn't understand why Roger wouldn't talk about her at all. Was she that bad? Had she done something even more horrible than abandoning her son? Something that would make Alex hate her? Maybe that was why the only thing Roger would say about her was that she was an angel, because if Alex found out what she really was, then he would know she was actually the complete opposite. At this point though, Alex could honestly say that he didn't care what she had or hadn't done, he just wanted to know the truth.

Sometimes he could make himself focus on other things and not think about it so much, but lately it seemed like it was getting harder and harder to ignore it. Especially since Roger had been such a nightmare to deal with the last year or so. If things hadn't gotten so bad, Alex thought maybe he could have gone on as he always had before, trying to work in questions here and there, but also not expecting much and being resigned to knowing basically nothing. But now, Roger was different. He couldn't even work at the factory anymore. He just sat on the couch all day watching TV, and then had horrible meltdowns in the middle of the night. It was like living with a semi-animated robot, who sometimes had screaming fits, instead of an actual person. And because things were the way they were now, Alex felt differently about Roger's refusal to answer questions too.

As the weather got warmer, Alex and Alyssa started meeting in the clearing out in the woods every day after school. Alex brought some supplies and kept them rolled up in a piece of plastic tarp that he hid under a pile of branches. A lighter, a pack of smokes, candy, a ratty torn-up sleeping bag for them to sit on. Every day, he pulled out the bundle and unpacked everything and they made their little camp. Then he packed it all back up and replaced the tarp in its hiding place before they left every night. One day, toward the end of March, it was warm enough to take off their jackets, and so they sat in the clearing and talked even longer than usual, luxuriating in the first mild breezes of spring.

"I wish we had a car," said Alyssa. She stretched her legs out in front of her and fished a new lighter out of her pocket. She clamped a cigarette between her teeth, then passed one out of the pack to Alex and lit her own.

"Or...I wish we could hop a train," Alex said. He took a drag from his cigarette and then laid it on the log, meticulously ensuring it was fixed in place by a ragged piece of bark clinging to the wood. Then he stood up and kept moving around, tidying their little camp.

"What do you know about hopping trains?" Alyssa asked, watching him as he walked back and forth.

"Roger and Greg used to talk about it. Greg used to do it, I guess." Alex surveyed the clearing and seemed satisfied with his work. He dropped onto the log beside Alyssa again, picked up his cigarette and then sat looking at her.

"Oh..." she said, and then fell silent. Neither of them felt the need to fill the space between them with words, and so they sat and smoked for a while. Alex glanced over and imagined running a hand over Alyssa's cheek and up into her hair. She leaned forward to tie her shoe and he looked at the back of her neck, noticing the bones there. He observed how small they were, how vulnerable those little bones seemed, and he shivered. He was glad it was just him out in the clearing with Alyssa and not anyone else.

"You guys have always lived here, right?" he asked, mostly to break the silence but also to change the focus of his thoughts.

"What do you mean?"

"I mean, I always remember you guys living just a few trailers down from us."

"Well...yeah. As far back as I can remember..." Alyssa paused and thought about it. "But I was born in Cincinnati...I think. I'm not sure. It seems like my mom told me that. Anyway...it *feels* like we've lived here forever."

Alex didn't say anything. He leaned his head back and looked up at the sky.

"What about you?" she prompted.

"Hm?"

"When did you and Roger come here?"

"Oh...well...Roger brought me here when I was about three, or four maybe. He'd gotten out of the army a few years before that, I think. That's how he knew Greg. They were in Vietnam together...Roger came here because he knew Greg, I guess. And for a while we lived with Greg, when I was little. When we first got here. I told you that before."

"Do you have any idea where you lived before that?"

"No," he said, and Alyssa watched a muscle in his jaw clench. "I don't really know *anything* about what happened before we got here. And Roger won't tell me. Every time I've ever asked him about my mom, he gives me some bullshit excuse and won't talk about her. He says she was an angel. It's complete bullshit. It's like he's telling me my mom was Santa Claus. I don't know if he thinks *I* believe it, or if *he* actually believes it or what, but it pisses me off."

Alyssa dug out her cigarettes again and offered another one to Alex. He shook his head and she lit another one up for herself and then sat and smoked and continued to watched him. That muscle in his jaw was still doing its little dance every few seconds whenever he gritted his teeth.

"What about Greg?" she asked. "Wouldn't he know something?"

"I'm not sure...I don't know..." Alex looked up at the sky again, thoughtful, and then looked back at her. "I always assumed Greg knows about as much as I do. I know that he knows Roger came to Michigan because Greg said he could get him a job, and he did. He did get him that job. Roger used to work at the factory too, before, when he could still work."

"Has Greg ever asked Roger about your mom?"

"I don't know. Probably. You would think. I mean...Roger's not my real dad, you know. Not that he's ever said that, but it's... kind of obvious. I mean, I've always called him Roger, even when I was a *little*-little kid. Why would I call him Roger if he was my real dad?"

Alyssa shrugged. "Sometimes kids call their parents by their first name. There's a girl in my class, Shelly Mohler, she calls her mom Carol."

Alex gave her a look. "That's different. Shelly Mohler's a teenager. You don't call your parents by their first name when you're, like, three. That's weird."

Alyssa tilted her head and then nodded. Alex was right.

"Have you ever asked Roger straight out if he's your real dad?" she asked. Alex sighed and looked up at the sky again. His face held no expression but Alyssa could see what was going on inside of him all the same. Defeat.

"You don't understand. You don't know how it is with Roger. When he wants something locked away it's like he's a fucking vault. And the way he is now, I don't even want to mess with things. If he's having a good day, I want him to stay good. Bringing up any of this stuff is only going to get him all worked up and then..." Alex stopped and swallowed before he could go on. "Then...I have to deal with him all night long." Alyssa gave him a careful, sideways look.

"How do you mean?"

"I mean he gets fucking crazy," he said quietly. "He screams for a long time and sometimes he breaks a bunch of shit..." Alex's face had gone pale and Alyssa could see dark shadows under his eyes in the fading sun. It almost looked like he was wearing a mask. For a moment she was reminded of creepy Michael Myers from the Halloween movies, and then it was gone and he was Alex again. Just a scared, lonely-looking Alex who seemed more fragile than she'd ever seen him before. The thin white t-shirt he wore seemed suddenly too thin. The wind blew through the clearing and molded it to his ribs like wet paper.

"It doesn't matter," he finished. "Roger's just crazy is all."

"Okay," she said. "So leave Roger out of it. Go to Greg. Ask him what he knows. Maybe not directly, but get him talking, see what he remembers." She reached over and grabbed Alex's hand. "You have to start somewhere."

Darwin got up from where he had been lying down by Alex's feet and crept in between them. Alyssa smiled and rubbed his silky black ears. He licked her hand and then panted happily, his tail thumping on Alex's leg. Alex looked down at him and smiled. He covered Alyssa's hand with his own. She turned her palm over and he wove his fingers in between hers and squeezed.

Chapter 6
May 1970

"Run Through the Jungle" by Creedence Clearwater Revival was popular that year, and the lyrics frequently ran through Roger's head as he was running through the jungle himself. He ran through underbrush and thick tangles of vines and a veil of humidity so hot and heavy it felt like a wool blanket. He ran listening to his own heartbeat drum in his ears, with sweat trickling into his eyes and burning them, and his breath sounding like some sort of engine panting at regular mechanical intervals. He ran through the jungle but also *into* the jungle, journeying deeper into its dark secret heart, remembering at times that he should be frightened of what he might find there, but unable to bring himself to feel any fear, because what lay behind him was so much worse.

Behind him were his nightmares. Behind him was the man with the glass bowl, and the spiders, and all the rest of it. Each day he woke up and kept moving forward, hoping to evade them and leave it all behind him, forever. But every night it was the same. The nightmares returned and there was no escape. That was why Roger had no fear of whatever might be waiting ahead of him, because he couldn't imagine anything hiding in the shadows that could be worse than what he was dealing with now.

So, Roger ran through the jungle, and he tried not to look back.

The nightmares had started when he was a teenager. Most of the time he had them when he was asleep, but sometimes they happened when he was awake. His mother had said they were nothing more than bad dreams and that he had an overactive imagination. His father had shaken his head and not said anything but then he took Roger to see a doctor when he was 16, even though his mom had gotten upset and said he didn't need to see any doctor. Roger remembered the doctor asking him a lot of questions that he hadn't known how to answer and then he said he was having hallucinations. That was the clearest part of the memory for Roger, that word. *Ha-loo-sin-nations*. When he got home and his father had told his mother what the doctor said, Roger remembered her mouth drawing in on itself and almost disappearing into her face, like someone had pulled a string that bunched her lips up tight. Her eyes got big and wide when she heard that word even though his father's face hadn't changed at all when he said it. Roger wasn't sure why his mom's face looked like that, but he had loved the sound of that word. It sounded like a silk scarf running through a beautiful woman's fingers. *Ha-loo-sin-nations*. After that, he said it to himself sometimes, but never in front of his mother. Only when he was alone.

At night, lying on the floor of the jungle, Roger still suffered from the nightmares. He still had the *ha-loo-sin-nations*. It always started with the spiders. When he was younger, he would fall asleep, only to wake up a few minutes later and see dozens of tiny spiders streaming down the walls of his bedroom. They looked like furry raindrops, each one bejeweled with a glistening cluster of black diamond eyes. In Vietnam, the spiders had returned, but now they were bigger, much bigger. They also came closer to him,

Resurrect the Dead

some moving in so closely that he could smell their foul hot breath and taste it in his own mouth.

Sometimes the spiders faded within a moment or two, and sometimes they were with him all night. But the spiders weren't the worst of it. The most terrible nightmare was the one with the man with the glass bowl. Although Roger had never discussed the details of his nightmares with anyone else, he had listened when other people talked about having bad dreams. It sounded like maybe they also saw things that were scary, but he had never heard anyone mention anything approaching the level of the man with the glass bowl. But he also had never heard anyone else say the word *ha-loo-sin-nations* in connection with a bad dream they had experienced. It seemed that word was meant for him alone.

The man with the glass bowl was bald, and he wore something that looked like a butler's uniform. Sometimes the man's eyes glittered and sometimes they danced, and he always held a glass bowl cradled in one hand. To Roger, it looked somewhat like an empty fishbowl. The man turned the bowl out toward Roger, as if he were making him an offering, and that was when Roger noticed the other thing. The horrible thing. Something was wrong with the man's mouth. Once Roger caught sight of it, he couldn't look away. His stomach crawled and his brain locked up. After that he was only capable of thinking one thought, over and over again. *His mouth...his mouth...something's wrong with the man's mouth.*

Whenever the man first appeared, his mouth looked just like his mother's mouth had looked when his father told her about the *ha-loo-sin-nations*. It was puckered, as if pulled tight by a drawstring. But then suddenly the man's mouth changed, and it turned into something that looked like a big bloody gash. Roger could only imagine that his mouth had been stitched shut and then knifed open, from the inside. It began dripping, and then it changed again. It formed itself into the mouth of a rodent, with sharp yellow teeth, and then a pulsating red vagina that coughed out black clots of blood. The man's mouth cycled through form after form. Just as Roger settled on it being one thing, it turned into another. The eternal hellish metamorphosis of that mouth was the scariest thing Roger had ever known. Even the most terrifying rumors of what Charlie did to soldiers caught alone in the jungle couldn't hold a candle to the man with the glass bowl.

Roger had been terrorized by his nightmares since adolescence, and the man with the glass bowl, in particular, had seemed to materialize even more frequently since Roger had been in the jungle these last few years. However, once Roger had found Mary and taken her with him, the man had disappeared. That's when Roger knew that Mary must be some sort of a magic charm capable of protecting him from the man with the glass bowl, warding off the apparition of him and his terrible mouth and keeping his spirit away. The night after Sergeant Graber had discovered her in Roger's bag and desecrated her remains, he saw her that night in a dream. Her face was crisscrossed with black lines, each line representing a fracture of her broken heart. He knew he was looking at the shape of her sorrow, cut into her skin. She gazed at him for a long time. When she waved goodbye, Roger looked away. When he looked back again, she was gone.

The very next night the man with the glass bowl came back.

After what happened with the Sergeant and Mary, Roger got ahead of his unit again, and this time he made sure he stayed ahead. During the day he channeled himself into an animal existence that focused on nothing more than the path he was forging and the need to keep moving, always moving. When he finally came to rest, he sat immersed in the dark and humid night and concentrated on keeping his eyes open until he couldn't anymore. In those moments right before sleep, he saw Mary again. It was as if she were sitting with him, her cold little hand in his, waiting for him to tilt her head so that it would sit where it was supposed to on her neck. He thought maybe it was her spirit that had come back to visit him, since she knew that she couldn't protect him from the man with the glass bowl anymore. But if he accidentally jolted himself awake again, Mary would disappear. It seemed that she couldn't stay all the way in this world if Roger were fully in it himself. In order to see her, to even feel her presence, he had to have at least one foot in dreamland.

That was when he decided to build the mansion.

Every night, Roger waited until full dark, and then he lay on the ground and focused on breathing along with the jungle until he felt like he was inside the heart of it. Then he imagined the mansion coming into form. First, he saw the path. Made of large, flat stones, it was set deep into the earth. Some of the stones were half-buried, as if they had been abandoned for ages, and every time Roger walked across them, he noticed that a couple had disappeared entirely into the dirt. He followed this path to a porch that wrapped around the first level of a grand house—dilapidated and rotting, but grand all the same—and he saw that this porch framed a set of old wooden doors.

He pushed open the doors and entered a great hall, and it was there that Mary was always waiting. She was alive and smiling, standing by the entrance to the dining room and holding out her hand, beckoning him forward. She took his hand and led him to a long table laid with silver dishes. He smelled roasts and potatoes and hot bread, and when they sat down, plates appeared magically before them, along with silverware. Roger never saw the people who brought these items to them, but he also didn't have time to think of that, because he noticed that every time he looked across the table at Mary, she seemed farther away than before. The details of her face blurred together and her hair looked as if it were floating around her head. He glanced at the platter nearest to him and saw that it wasn't a platter at all, but a giant seashell. The table itself was sand. When he pushed away from it, it dissolved under his hands. He looked up and saw that what he had taken for a chandelier suspended from the ceiling was actually an enormous carcass of something that had tentacles at one time, and a large and sharp black beak.

Then Mary rose from the table and she looked like herself again. She gestured for him to follow her and led him outside, to a spacious veranda in the back. Two chairs and a small table were waiting for them and the table held drinks with ice in beautiful crystal glasses. Mary settled herself as gracefully as a cat, taking one of the glasses and drinking from it as if she were dying of thirst. Roger watched the delicate movement of her throat as she swallowed. They had a view of the path to the house and Mary shifted her eyes to it now and again, but Roger felt no fear. No guests were coming. The stones of the path were half-buried, and impossible to see in the dark. Anyone who tried to find them here would lose their way, or they would fall.

Roger watched Mary drink again, and this time he noticed a thin black line around her neck that seemed to be leaking. She greedily gulped more out of the glass she held, and suddenly Roger could hear the jungle breathing. It panted raggedly, sounding like some huge hidden monster lying in wait, somewhere out there in the dark. The air became heavier, thicker, almost textured with moisture. He reached for Mary's hand but now she batted him away, intent on pouring more liquid down her throat even though none of it seemed to be making it past her neck.

That's when Roger knew that guests had come anyway. It didn't matter that the path was hidden and half-buried, or that they shouldn't have been able to make it over the steps in the dark. They had still come, and there was nothing he could do about it. They had come to find him and Mary. They had come to take her away from him again.

When he turned around, he saw that the mansion had

changed now, too. The walls fell in on themselves, crumbling into dust, and the tiles of the porch had cracked, right under his feet. Long streaks of soot decorated the exterior, as if there had been a fire. Inside, through the open doors, he saw cobwebs swaying from the ceiling. When he glanced back at Mary, he saw that she had finally put down her drink. She looked at him and smiled and he saw that her bottom teeth had turned black. As he watched, one of her cheeks sunk and then caved in. Her left eye clouded over.

Every visit to the mansion ended like this. Every time he pulled himself out of the vision it felt like sliding out of warm water into the cold night air. An instant chill enveloped him and left him shaking. When he looked around, he realized he was back in the jungle, alone, and then he remembered how it always happened that way. He was never allowed to stay there. The mansion always fell into ruin in front of his eyes. There was nothing he could do to keep it intact. And Mary always had to stay behind.

Chapter 7
April 1986

One afternoon, Alex came home from school and found the house torn apart. It looked like a tornado had ripped through it. The two chairs that usually sat at the kitchen table, and the coffee table in the living room, were overturned. The pantry shelves in the kitchen were bare. Cans of food spilled across the floor, and the linoleum was crisscrossed with trails of flour, syrup, and milk. The refrigerator door hung open, and a jug of orange juice lay on its side on the bottom shelf, dribbling a thin stream of liquid out of the fridge and down onto the floor, where it pooled into a big sticky puddle.

Roger sat quiet in his usual place on the couch.

Alex picked his way through the mess and grabbed one of the chairs lying on its side. He righted it and sat down and faced Roger. He felt calm, but he also felt a headache starting up behind his eyes.

"What happened Roger?"

"Wrecked the place," Roger grumbled.

"Yeah, I know. I see." Alex sighed. "Why?" He ran a hand through his hair and pressed his lips together.

Resurrect the Dead

"You know why," Roger said, without looking at him. Although he didn't move, he sounded almost as if he were cringing away from something. Alex couldn't quite put his finger on what it was, but he could hear it in his voice. Roger suddenly sounded like a little kid who was afraid of the dark.

"I do?"

Roger nodded, and then he finally looked up and glared at him. "You know why," he said again. "Because that...*man* ...won't leave me alone," he said, and then his voice broke. He stared down at the floor again and Alex could see his chest hitching as he tried to get his breath. He got up and found Roger's inhaler on the side table and handed it to him. He heard Roger take a few puffs from it as he turned away to survey the wreckage.

Although it looked bad, he also saw that it wouldn't take that long to restore everything to order, as long as Roger stayed calm and didn't need anything. He went over and switched on the TV and dialed through the channels until he found a rerun of *M*A*S*H*. He turned up the volume, made sure Roger's attention was caught by it, and then quietly backed out of the living room and started cleaning up the kitchen.

As he worked, he thought about what it had been like when he was younger, when it had been Roger taking care of him, instead of the other way around. He couldn't remember anything from the time before he was with Roger, but he did have a few clear memories of being a little kid after that. He remembered the two of them walking to the store, his own small hand swallowed up in Roger's larger one. He remembered Roger waving goodbye to him as he climbed the steps of the school bus for the first time. He had a random memory of Roger fixing him a sandwich, and then another one of him showing him how to brush his teeth the right way. He guessed he was probably five or six years old in these memories, and he was 15 now. That meant Roger had been a completely different person less than ten years ago. To Alex, it felt more like 50 years. The memories he had of those times felt ancient, as if they had happened centuries ago.

Alex wondered what he would feel like if the memories he had didn't belong to him. Like, if he were watching a movie, and the hero of that movie was remembering these things, he would probably find them touching. Or if someone else told him about memories they had like the ones he had just gone over in his own mind, he'd probably think: *Well, there you have it, you did have good times together after all. Your dad took care of you.* But when it was his own movie, when he was the one telling himself the story, when he was the hero and the hero's father was Roger, then he felt nothing at all. Or sometimes, he felt deeply, despairingly sorry for Roger, but also that Roger was a stranger to him, like a homeless man he'd just tripped over in an alley or something. He felt like they weren't related at all, and never had been.

Sometimes he thought that if Roger died tomorrow, he wouldn't care, and sometimes he wished he would get better, that he would be how he used to be, someone who never talked much and who was slightly strange at times but someone you could count on all the same. When Alex thought of him sitting in that same spot on the couch, day after day, with his wet gravelly cough and matted black beard, he couldn't help but shudder. Maybe Roger had never been the best substitute for a dad, but at least he'd been more like a regular person before. He was repulsive the way he was now. Encased in flab, tortured by his failing lungs, and haunted by the imaginary terrors of his own mind, it seemed to Alex that Roger spent his days living in a kind of prison. He had just about lost every shred of freedom. And the worst part of it was, Alex knew he was trapped with him. Because of some fucked up choice someone had made years ago, he was chained to Roger, and there was no way out, no escape.

But it wasn't me who made that choice, thought Alex. *It was*

Resurrect the Dead

my mom, right? She was the one who decided to leave. Did she really never want to see me again? Then his mind went back to the memories he had just reviewed. Roger had been different back then. Maybe his mom had thought she was doing the right thing. Maybe, as Alex had suspected before, she'd done something so horrible that leaving him with Roger was actually the best choice she could have made. Alex looked over at Roger sitting on the couch and felt a stab of guilt deep in his chest. It wasn't his fault he was the way he was, he couldn't help it.

"Roger?"

"Yeah."

"Do you remember back when I was a kid? You know, when I was like...five. Maybe six. You remember?"

"Mm-hm...yeah."

Alex thought it was likely Roger hadn't really heard the question. *Gilligan's Island* had come on, and he was staring at the screen as raptly as if he were listening to the President address the nation. Then he surprised Alex.

"I remember," he said, shrugging his shoulders, as if he could feel the weight of Alex's look and wanted it off him.

"What do you remember?"

"We had fun. Did stuff. I used to drive..."

Roger rumbled the phlegm at the back of his throat and then gave a wracking cough. His upper body shook and his eyes squeezed shut. Alex watched him until the spasm passed, noticing that the edges of his beard looked like the frayed tassels on an old rug.

"We used to go around," he said, when he stopped coughing. "We used to go places. I took you up to the ice cream place so you could get a cone. Chocolate. You liked chocolate."

With those few words, it was like Roger had opened some sort of door, and a flood of images filled Alex's mind. He remembered being with Roger at the park and Roger waiting for him at the end of the slides because he was scared to go down. He remembered going to Roger in the middle of the night because he'd wet the bed and Roger patting him and then changing the sheets, hugging Alex to him when he began to cry. He remembered Roger checking on him when he'd been really sick with a high fever and he'd had to miss a whole week of school in the second grade, and he remembered the model airplane Roger had gotten him one Christmas, and then helped him build. In that one moment, he remembered *all* of it, and the weight nearly crushed him. He couldn't move, and he couldn't breathe.

He didn't want Roger to die, he loved him. But he didn't want to feel trapped with him anymore, either. He was tired of taking care of Roger, sitting up with him in the middle of the night when he had his screaming spells and cleaning up after him and helping him to bathroom and all of it. He was so tired. And he wanted to know why his mom had left. He didn't care if she had done something horrible, he just didn't want to feel like he was in the dark all the time. There were big pieces of his life that had always been shrouded in darkness and he was tired of that too. He had a right to know where he had come from and who his mom was and what had happened to her. And if things went on like this with Roger for the next couple of years and he had to wait until he was 18 to get out and find a place of his own and a job, he thought he would probably just snap and go crazy.

He thought about all of this in the few seconds after Roger said that about taking him to get an ice cream cone. In fact, he had almost forgotten Roger was there completely until he spoke again.

"I remember, Alex. We had fun together. You were always my little boy."

Roger made a low choking sound in the back of his throat and Alex realized he was crying. He turned away before Roger could see that he noticed and went back to cleaning the kitchen. For some reason he had a lump in his own throat. He swallowed it

Resurrect the Dead

down and focused on what was right in front of him. He had to get this floor clean. He pulled out the mop and less than a minute later he found he couldn't remember what he and Roger had even been talking about before he had started mopping.

Oh well, he thought. It couldn't have been that important.

Chapter 8
June 1974

Greg's wife Irene had died of cancer when he'd been in Nam and when he got back, he'd come home to an empty house. Her mother had gotten Irene's key and cleared out most of her stuff. *What a shame*, Greg had thought to himself, looking around the bare rooms of the trailer Irene had decorated so well when she'd been alive. She'd had pictures up and a tablecloth on their table that she'd sewn herself and even flowers out on the front steps. Now, almost everything was gone and only a few empty boxes remained, strewn here and there in the living room and kitchen. Irene's mom had obviously gone through the house and kicked his stuff to the side as she grabbed her daughter's things. Well, she had never liked him anyway, so it wasn't a big surprise that she'd picked the house clean like a vulture, just to spite him.

When he'd come back to his house with no Irene in it anymore, and none of Irene's things, he realized that his life was nothing but empty, and underneath that empty feeling was another feeling. It was a slippery black dangerous feeling that told him the *best* he could hope for was to feel empty, because at least that was just a shade away from totally numb. If he started to move in the other direction—if he started to become *less* numb—then he would really have problems. Faced with that, Greg started drinking every night. He'd been lucky enough to get his job back at the factory, and every evening after his shift ended, he stopped by the party store and grabbed a couple of six packs. He went through both of them as he killed the rest of the night sitting in front of the tube. He watched all the sitcoms and by the time the 11 o'clock news rolled around he was cracking open that last can, and then it was off to bed, where he slept like a log and had no dreams. Or at least, he didn't remember any of them, which was as good as the same thing.

The mornings were a little rough, but he was able to get through them okay. But then he started bringing home a six-pack *and* a bottle of whisky every night, and that was when his mornings started going to hell, until he figured out that downing a can of beer as soon as he got up served most effectively as a hair-of-the-dog remedy that quieted the nastiest of his hangovers. Pretty soon he was drinking that one can every morning, and then he was keeping a bottle of whisky under the driver's seat of his car for the afternoons.

It went on for a while, and for the most part, he was able to keep it together. There was no one around to notice or comment on his drinking anyway. After Nam and after losing Irene, he'd lost everyone else too, all his old contacts, all his old friends. All he had was his trailer and his job. So, the day his boss pulled him into his office and screamed at him for being drunk on the line, Greg knew he was close to losing damn near everything. Not only had he endangered himself, his boss raged, but he'd endangered his coworkers. With a drunk operator handling that type of machinery, someone very well could have lost a limb, or their life. Greg had never felt as shitty as he did standing there that day with his boss yelling at him all red in the face and looking at him like he was the worst piece of shit on the planet. He wished he were dead.

That was when he knew he had to quit drinking. He went to an AA meeting the very next day, and then to another one the day after that. For the first few weeks he felt awkward and out of place. He didn't have anything to say. But then, after a while, he started talking, and he could tell the people at AA really listened. He could see it in their faces. No one had ever listened to him like that before. It was a feeling he didn't want to give up, and so he kept going, every day for a long time, and then three times a week after that. He helped make the coffee and set out the chairs and then stack them back up again at the end of the night's meeting. He got a sponsor and he got to know everyone else in the group. After a few months, he realized he felt at home.

When he wasn't at meetings or at work, Greg spent his time writing letters. He wrote an old high school sweetheart and got no answer, and then a couple of cousins he had grown up with, but after one letter back they stopped writing. Everyone seemed to be like that. Whenever Greg ran into someone he used to know, he could feel an unexplainable distance between him and them. Almost everyone who had known him before treated him strangely, as if they recognized him but didn't believe it was really him underneath his face. He felt oddly naked in front of them. Naked and strange. But he had to talk to someone, he needed a friend outside of AA, a friend who understood what had happened to him. Nam—and everything that went with it—well, it wasn't something you could explain to other people, not if they hadn't been there. He needed someone who knew what he was talking about, someone who wouldn't look at him like he was crazy. Someone who had been there.

He started writing to guys he'd known in the war, and Roger was the one who wrote back. Although he didn't write long letters,

Resurrect the Dead

he did write regularly. Greg had started writing him at the address Roger had given him back in Nam—the address for his parents' house—but when Roger responded Greg saw that he'd provided a different address. In the letter he said he wasn't at his parents, that he'd been committed to a mental hospital in Pennsylvania. Some people might have judged him for it, but in Greg's mind there was no possibility of judgment, not when it came to what had happened over there and what it had done to people. Greg had first-hand experience with that. He just hoped they weren't going too rough on him in that place. Roger mentioned he'd gotten a Section 8, which wasn't surprising if he was locked up in some sort of hospital now, but Greg wasn't sure of the details beyond that. What he did know was that being in Vietnam was like doing time in prison. You didn't go prying into the details of another guy's business after he'd come out of either situation.

After Roger had shown up at Greg's front door with Alex in tow, the two of them moved in and lived with him for about a year. Greg got Roger the job he had promised him at the plastics factory in town and they worked side-by-side for a while, before Roger's health went downhill a few years later and he went on disability. Lung problems, heart problems, you name it, Roger had it. During that year though, Roger was able to work full-time, and so he and Greg would leave Alex with the woman next door, who had a bunch of kids of her own and didn't mind one more as long as Greg and Roger gave her a few bucks when they had it. She also smoked Kools, which was the same brand Greg smoked, and so sometimes he'd pay her by bringing her a couple packs when he got off work and picked up Alex and that suited her just fine too.

When Roger finally had enough money to move out, he moved himself and Alex into their own trailer, just down the lane. Greg was happy for them, but underneath that he felt that old empty feeling coming back again. He would miss them. Things had been good that year when they were all together. At night, when the three of them had sat around the TV and ate dinner, Greg had felt like they were a real family. He realized years later, after Roger was dead and Alex long gone, that he never got that feeling back again after that year.

He tried never to think about that though, because every time he did it damn near broke his heart.

Chapter 9
April 1986

Alex got off the bus one afternoon and was surprised to see that Darwin hadn't come to meet him. He didn't know what to make of it. Darwin always came running to meet him out by the road. But today he wasn't there, and Alex saw he wasn't at the trailer either when he got home a few minutes later. Roger, of course, hadn't strayed from his habitual place on the couch. When Alex walked in, he was sitting and watching TV as usual. He appeared to be absorbed in an episode of a Transformers cartoon, which didn't surprise Alex. He had observed that Roger would watch anything, as long as the picture changed every few seconds.

"Hey, Roger," he said, speaking mostly on autopilot, his mind still on Darwin. He scanned the living room and then the kitchen, bending down to check underneath the table. No Darwin. He wasn't in the bedroom either. Alex even looked in the narrow space between the wall and the washer and dryer—although he seriously doubted Darwin could fit there even if he wanted to—but he didn't find anything.

Darwin wasn't anywhere in the house.

"Roger, have you seen Darwin?" he asked, walking back into the living room.

"Huh-uh," Roger muttered, shifting his weight slightly on the sagging couch. Alex stood and watched the cartoon on the screen for a few seconds, thinking. Megatron threatened to crush Optimus Prime with his bare hands, his voice sounding like it came from an evil old wizard locked up in an abandoned tower. *Really?* thought Alex. *With his bare hands?* What an odd line to give a robot. Megatron was made of purely mechanical matter, even if that matter was, in this case, possessed with a murderous rage.

He put all thoughts of Megatron aside and walked outside again, calling for Darwin as he trudged back and forth past the row of trailers on his and Roger's side of the park. He circled around and then went out to the main street, calling louder. When he'd almost made it back to his place, he ran into Alyssa as she was coming home. When he told her he couldn't find Darwin she started walking with him and calling Darwin's name over and over again too. Over the next two hours, they walked all over the park. They knocked on doors and asked anyone who answered if they had seen Darwin. No one had. Finally, twilight started to turn to full dark and Alyssa said she had to get home.

"He'll turn up," she said.

"I don't know." Alex looked past her, over her shoulder, as if he could see something out there in the dark that she couldn't. Alyssa shivered. "I have bad feeling about it," he said. "A really bad feeling. Something happened to Darwin...I think...I don't *know* but...I just have a bad feeling." Alyssa nodded. She'd had those kinds of feelings before, and she knew they were almost always right. "Thanks though," Alex said. "For helping..." He hugged her clumsily and kissed her cheek. "I know you love Darwin too," he said.

Resurrect the Dead

"I'll help you tomorrow again," she said.

"Nah. Don't worry about it." Alex stood back and chewed his lip, thinking to himself. "I'll get Greg to help me."

The next day both Greg and Alyssa ended up helping him search, without finding anything new. There wasn't one sighting from anyone, not one clue. It was like Darwin had just vanished and no one had seen anything. As the days went on, Alex stopped asking people if they had seen him, but he couldn't stop himself from peering up and down the street every day when he got home from school. He couldn't stop listening for Darwin while he lay in bed next to his open window every night. He heard a lot of dogs barking, but he never heard Darwin, and he knew he would have recognized Darwin's bark if he'd had to pick it out of a pack of ten million dogs. Night after night he listened, but not one of those dogs he heard barking was him, and Alex didn't expect that would change. It was like he'd said to Alyssa, he'd had a bad feeling, and that hadn't changed either.

He was pretty sure Darwin was gone for good.

After Darwin disappeared, Alex started going back to his room every night after he finished up dinner with Roger and washed the dishes. He lay on his bed and thought about things while playing his favorite tape, Maiden's *Number of the Beast*. Through song after song, he stared at the ceiling with dry, burning eyes, his hands clenched into fists. He had to get out of here. He had to get away from Roger, somehow.

It wasn't just the way Roger was now. If it had been *only* that, Alex knew he could have handled it. He could have just waited out his time with Roger and then left it all behind on his 18th birthday. But it was more than that. He didn't belong with Roger.

He couldn't say why he felt that, but he did. It was a certainty. With every day that passed, he felt the sure knowledge of that truth grow stronger within him. He didn't belong *to* Roger, and he didn't belong *with* him, and he never had. Some mistake had been made, some freak accident had happened long ago and it had cost Alex the life he should be living. Whether that life was with his mom or not, Alex couldn't say, but it didn't matter. What did matter was that he was in the wrong place and—he increasingly felt—perhaps the wrong time, too. Because lately, he felt out of step with reality at the oddest moments. Like he was struggling to keep up with a song, but kept missing the beat. Whenever he noticed it happening, it disturbed him so much all he could do was drop his head into his hands and press on his temples with desperate force, until it passed. Although he didn't have words for the thing that was moving through him, he could sense what it was —a pure shot of despair, traveling at the speed of a bullet, right to his heart.

He had to get away from Roger.

But he didn't have any money, he didn't have a job. He didn't even have a driver's license. So how was he supposed to get away? Sometimes he thought that maybe he could find his mom and she would be all right. Maybe she would be glad to see him again and she would take him in. Maybe, maybe, maybe. Alex had a lot of questions, but no answers. On these nights, lying on his bed and staring at the ceiling, he listened to Bruce Dickinson sing about six, six, six, the number of the beast, and he pressed his fists into his closed eyes until he saw starbursts against the black.

One night, without thinking about it, Alex got up from his bed, moved down to the foot of it, and then got on his knees on the floor. He tented his hands and closed his eyes but he didn't know what to say. He didn't know the Lord's Prayer. He didn't know any prayers, in fact. He had never been to church. But, Alex figured, if God was really listening then what could he say that was not already known? Because if God didn't already know what was in Alex's mind and heart, well then, he couldn't be God. In light of that argument, Alex decided to let God come to him. He knelt there and listened to the song and waited. After a while he got lost in the music and forgot he was waiting. He let himself fall further into the pounding rhythm of Maiden's passionate call. It vibrated under his skin, pulling him toward a different time that made him think of heroes and towers, and dragons that waited in a cave at the very end, unaware they would serve as a sacrifice in some final test of strength and courage.

After that night, Alex started praying every night, always while listening to Maiden's Number of the Beast. It felt fitting. He was sure the energy of God was in heavy metal. It probably wasn't all that different from the teachings of Jesus, he thought, even though he had only the vaguest sense of what those teachings might be. But if he was uncertain about Jesus's message, he was crystal clear on the meaning of the Number of the Beast album. And in Alex's opinion, it wasn't too weird to think that Maiden was up there with Jesus, because he figured that any true messenger from God showing up in the modern world would have to come bearing a name that had darkness in it, otherwise people wouldn't listen, because it wouldn't mean anything to them. God couldn't be all heaven and doing good and ignoring all the shitty things that came along with life. That version of the world wasn't real.

After he finished praying, he always felt better. It was like he'd shared a secret part of himself with the song and cleaned out his head in some way, and now he could think clearly again. He could move forward into whatever was waiting for him. That was when he got up and brushed off the knees of his pants. He turned off the tape and got undressed. Then he lay on his bed, staring at the ceiling again and thinking for a long time, until he fell asleep.

At the end of April, Alyssa walked out to the clearing one afternoon, looking for Alex, and found him there, pacing. He walked in circles, his hands shoved deep in his pockets, only pausing to look at her when she showed up at the entrance before he resumed walking again.

"It's Roger," he said, without any prelude. Alyssa walked over and then slowly lowered herself down to the log. She sat there, quiet and pale, looking at him, waiting. Alex completed a few more circles and then stopped and stood before her. He shook his head and ran a trembling hand through his hair, then opened his mouth and closed it again. Finally, he sat down on the log beside her, but he didn't look at her. He just sat and stared straight ahead.

"He has these...waking nightmares. In the middle of the night. And he screams and screams. It's been going on a long time. Years...I don't know...a long time." And then Alex said the thing he had never shared with anyone else, not even Greg. "Sometimes he...cries. He cries about a girl...he says she's been taken away from him or something. And...sometimes...he talks about a man. 'The man with the glass bowl,' he says. It's just...creepy. It's so fucking *weird*." Alex slapped his open palms down on his thighs and wiped them down his jeans and Alyssa saw that his hands were shaking. "I don't know what to do," he said in a small voice, and then he started to cry. "I just don't know what to do, is all." Carefully, Alyssa moved closer and then put her arms around him and held him. He leaned into her and shuddered, crying harder. Then he pressed into her, almost knocking her over, and they moved off the log until they were sitting on the ground together. "I don't know what to do," he said again, and then he kept saying it, over and over.

"Sssh..." she said. She didn't know what to do either.

She looked up at the leafy crowns of the trees that circled

above them. The warm weather had turned cold during the last week and droplets of rain scattered down on them as they sat huddled next to each other. Patches of gray light filtered through to the clearing and Alyssa could hear the wind shriek like an old woman caught up in the trees. It gusted through the clearing again, lifting her hair and making it dance across her eyes, a feathery blonde veil that blindfolded her for a few moments. Alex's sobs finally subsided but he stayed where he was, leaning on her, catching his breath. She had worn a knee-length denim skirt that day, and in the cold air the dry white skin on the calves of her legs goose-pimpled.

Slowly, Alex reached over and circled a hand around her ankle. Alyssa didn't say anything, but watched the hand to see what it would do next. The hand squeezed. She looked into his face and saw that Alex was staring at her ankle, transfixed, as if the ankle weren't a part of her anymore but instead some fascinating but deadly creature that had accidentally crossed his path. Gradually, he widened the circle of his thumb and forefinger, and slid his hand from her ankle up her leg. When he got to her knee, he laid his hand across it and then squeezed, hard. Alyssa kept watching but didn't make a sound. His fingers began to turn white. When he dug his nails into the thin flesh over the bone, she finally cried out a little. Then she fell into him.

The clearest memory Alyssa had later was of the vacant look in Alex's eyes. He didn't look like himself anymore. He started kissing her, but in a weird way, like someone who was really drunk or halfway to drowning and didn't understand what he was doing. Then he stopped trying to kiss her and simply clung onto her, and she could feel how desperately afraid he was, like an animal that had suddenly found itself in a trap. He flailed his arms and she thought he was going to push her away but then he forced her down onto the ground and reached up her skirt. He tore into the crotch of her panties.

"No, Alex. Don't," she whispered. She couldn't see his face, it was buried in her neck, but she could hear him breathing raggedly, and crying, and then crying harder as he thrust himself into her. There was a small explosion of burning pain and then a stretching ache. She gasped and opened her eyes wide to the gray sky. She pushed back against him, but he had her wrists pinned to her sides, up by her ears. Other than that one small act to contain her, he seemed to have forgotten she was there.

It lasted less than five minutes. When it was over Alex sat up and looked around as if he didn't know where he was. He had the same look on his face that Alyssa's mom had in the mornings when she woke up on the couch after going on a bender the night before. Stunned, and confused. As if she'd woken up in a different year or a different body than she'd expected. He swiped his dirty palms up his wet cheeks, and looked at Alyssa as if she were another object that was cause for astonishment. Alyssa wonderingly touched the skin on her own arm. Maybe she had dematerialized, and then reappeared. Then she pulled her skirt down and sat up too. Her panties were ripped, but nothing else, and she was wet between the legs. She knew she was bleeding without looking to see, but any actual pain had faded. She looked up and saw that the clouds had been ripped to shreds by the wind. All she could smell was mud.

Alex stared at her, stricken, shame flooding his eyes, which also seemed to reflect the cold gray light of the sky above. "Are you...okay?" He rubbed his face again, leaving streaks of dirt. Alyssa laughed a little and it sounded broken and she liked that. It seemed to reinforce the unnamable feeling that was coursing through her.

"Yeah, I'm fine." She sniffed and offered Alex a tight smile. She wasn't faking it, she realized. She was fine. She had entered something new, something dark and treasured that he could never understand. She had done something for him, although she wasn't sure what, only that it was a kind of debt that would connect them, maybe for always, and she knew that even if Alex didn't understand, he would never forget either. "I'm good," she said. She looked off, through the trees. The gray light was turning blue in the cold dusk. She wiped her nose with the back of her hand.

"I'm good," she repeated.

Chapter 10
June 1974

After getting a Section 8 discharge, Roger was sent to Oak Meadows, a large gray building that looked like a mix between a hospital and a factory with a large pale green lawn planted stolidly in front of it. It was a place his parents had chosen and it was situated right outside Pittsburgh. Sergeant Graber had alerted his parents to some of the more disturbing facets of his activities in the army over the past few years and, rather than bring him back home after his discharge, they had elected to have him committed somewhere that "he could be sure of staying safe," as his mother put it in her monthly letters to him. He spent two years at Oak Meadows before his parents ran out of money and then found out that Roger wasn't eligible for VA benefits due to his Section 8 status. Overnight, Roger went from the insulated and ordered world of the institution, to being out on the street with one cardboard suitcase and nowhere else to go.

In her last letter to him—which had sounded horribly apologetic, but also firm in the pronouncement that Roger would not be allowed to return home—his mother had included a money order for $200. The day that Roger got out of the hospital, he called a cab to come pick him up and take him to the bus station. He already knew where he was going, he just needed a ticket and he'd be on his way. While he'd been at Oak Meadows, there had been only two people he'd received letters from regularly. His mother, and Greg Richards. His relationship with Greg was the closest Roger had ever come to experiencing anything that approached a real friendship. He knew Greg wouldn't turn him down if he needed help, and he needed help now. If there was anything in the world that he knew to be true, it was that Greg owed him one.

In one of Greg's letters, he'd said that if Roger could make it to Michigan, he'd have a place to stay, and he could probably get him a job too. So, Michigan it was. He got to the bus station and wasted no time in buying his ticket, and then he sat down on a bench to wait. After he'd been waiting for about 20 minutes, a young woman made her way over to the same bench and smiled at him and asked if he minded if she sat down. He turned to look at her and he froze.

It was like seeing Mary for the first time all over again.

Granted, this woman looked much different—she was taller, and blonde, with pale skin and light freckles, her face almost coltish—but the *feeling* Roger had, it was the same. He flushed and felt warm all over, and slightly lightheaded. She was one of the most beautiful women he had ever seen. As he stared at her, she smiled again. She covered her mouth and giggled and then asked what his name was. He managed to get out a clumsy introduction, and then she said her name was Linda and she was on her way to Philadelphia. She said she was coming from California, where she'd been living with a group of people for the past few years out in the desert. She spoke as if she was out of breath, sometimes talking so fast that her words jumbled together, as she started telling him all about the people she'd been living with and how beautiful they all were, and how they had all become free together. They had broken their ties to this world, and now they were as one. Sometimes she trailed off and seemed to lose her train of thought. But Roger didn't care, he just wanted to sit beside her, forever. It was okay if she couldn't remember what she was going to say, he just wanted her to keep looking at him.

She wore a long red and yellow dress, and a light green eye shadow that sparkled in the light. Her golden hair was long and loose too, and to Roger, she looked like a goddess. As she talked, she shifted around on the bench, her hands flying around her face as she described the beauty of the desert sunsets and the cold desert nights. It was then that Roger noticed she had a little boy with her. He had light brown hair, and brown eyes that matched hers, and he was so silent and still that he almost startled Roger when he finally noticed him. He must have been about three, or maybe he was four. Roger couldn't really tell. He hadn't been around any kids in a long time.

Linda asked him more questions—where he was coming from and where he was going—and Roger saw the little boy move closer to her and then reach over and grab her hand, silent but watchful. His little hand in hers looked sticky, and slightly grubby. The boy looked at him with large, solemn eyes. He seemed to examine Roger's long black hair and beard as if he were carefully taking stock of a great shaggy beast that might be slow to rouse but full of wrath after being goaded wide awake.

When Roger said he was going to Michigan, Linda's eyes danced and she smiled even wider. She dropped the little boy's hand and clapped, once, and then clasped her hands together, so tightly that Roger could see her fingertips turning white. The little boy looked up at her sharply, and Roger saw that watchful look on his face again, as if he was on guard and waiting for something. But then it was gone and the boy looked like any other kid Roger had ever seen in his life.

Linda repeated that she was on her way to Philadelphia, which was where she was taking her little boy. She was going home to see her parents, but just for a while. They would be surprised, she said. They didn't know about her son, who had been born in the desert with only the people she'd been living with to help her through the birth. She'd never even registered him for a Social Security Number, she added. She refused to tie him to the establishment, she said, wrapping her arms around herself and shivering. Roger saw a wariness come into her eyes. Children were pure, she said. Adults were the ones who ruined them.

"And then I'm going back to California..." she whispered, as if to herself. Roger didn't like the way she said those last words, as if she might leave at any moment and never come back. He had to think of something to keep her here. He looked around wildly, searching for anything in the environment he could comment on, anything around them that might distract her from leaving. His eyes landed on the little boy.

"What's his name?" Roger touched Linda's arm and then pointed to him, and for a moment, her reverie was broken. Her eyes refocused and she looked at the boy beside her, and then back at Roger with a wide smile.

"Alex."

Roger looked at the boy and the boy stared at him. Linda laughed and they both looked at her, and then back at each other. The boy's face held much the same expression of wonder that Roger's did, as if Linda were some sort of magical apparition that had unexpectedly materialized in his life too, and he didn't know what to do with her either.

He also looked as if he were just as afraid of losing her.

When Roger showed up on Greg's doorstep with a bundle of his letters and a little boy that he said was his son, Greg's first thought had been that the kid needed a bath. A dusting of grime coated his face and his little fingernails were caked with dirt. Greg was also struck by the boy's eyes, which held a quiet, serious expression, even though he also looked tired and unhappy, and frayed around the edges, like he'd been dragged there from a thousand miles away. Greg asked what his name was and Roger paused as if trying to remember something. Then he said, "Alex." Greg asked where the kid's mom was but instead of answering his question, Roger asked him if he was serious about helping out an old friend and if that job at the factory that he'd talked about in his letters was still available. Greg nodded and said, yes, of course it was, and he owed him didn't he, of course he could get him work, and of course they were welcome to stay with him. He would never forget what Roger had done for him.

That night, Greg put Alex to bed on the fold-out cot while Roger took a shower. As he tucked him in, Alex looked up at him, concentrated and grim, as if he already knew the answer to the question he was about to ask, but needed to hear it anyway.

"Did you know my mom?" he asked, and Greg suddenly felt cold inside, although he didn't know why. He saw Alex's eyes glance rapidly back and forth between his face and the bedroom door, his dirty little fingernails digging into Greg's palm. Something was wrong with this, with all of it. The way Roger had just shown up with this kid out of the blue and the way Alex's face looked right now, it gave Greg a weird feeling. But then, he thought, he really couldn't trust himself. Not since Nam. Maybe he was sober, but his mind was still broken in places. He'd seen a lot of things—or thought he did—that turned out not to be true. He misinterpreted signs and misunderstood situations. He thought people were joking when they were dead serious. He had also contemplated blowing his brains out or walking in front of a train, and both of those options had seemed like good ideas at the time. If he hadn't been too scared to do either he'd be dead now.

So, when Alex asked if he knew his mom, Greg felt the weird

feeling and then he pushed it aside. He hesitated for only a moment. Then he smiled and ruffled Alex's hair, and skirted the question. He wasn't sure what had gone on between the boy's mother and Roger, but that was Roger's business and it wasn't his place to pry into it. He told Alex it was time to go to sleep and he would see him in the morning. Then, without a backward glance —because if Greg had learned anything in Nam, he had learned that backward glances were dangerous—he turned off the light and shut the door. He waited out in the hall a second or two, to see if Alex would start crying, or maybe call out that he needed a glass of water or something like little kids do, but he didn't hear anything, and so he started for the living room and a few moments later had forgotten all about it.

That night, Greg and Roger stayed up late and caught up on the last few years. Mainly, Greg talked and Roger sat and grunted in agreement every now and then, but Greg didn't mind. Roger had always been a man of few words and he didn't expect him to change now. He did manage to get a few more details out of him about the kid's mom though, and what had happened to her. In his terse, unemotional way, Roger told the story of meeting Alex's mother, whose name he said was Linda, at a bus stop in Pittsburgh. They had been talking and she said she was on her way to California. When the bus pulled up, Linda got on without saying goodbye, without even waving at him after she'd found her seat, way at the back. Roger had watched her sit down, right on the side with the windows that faced him, but she didn't look in his direction again, not once. It was like after she boarded that bus he had ceased to exist, forever. After the bus had pulled away and was down the road and out of sight, Roger said he realized that her little boy was still standing right beside him.

"What?" Greg couldn't help but interject. "She just...abandoned her son? Left him with you?" Roger nodded. "But Roger... you have to get a hold of her. You can't just...just keep him." Greg shook his head, disgusted. What kind of woman would abandon her little boy at a bus stop with a stranger?

Roger let out a long gusty sigh.

"Tried. She'd told me her name. I looked her up. Found her parents. Called them."

"What'd they say?" Greg stared at Roger, unable to imagine how Linda's parents must have reacted to her abandoning their grandson with an unknown man at a bus stop.

"Said he was better off with me. Said he was a bastard kid. And Linda was crazy. Had always been crazy. She had..." Roger paused, as if trying to think of the word. "Hall-loo...hallucinations." Charlie sat back in his chair and stared blankly at Roger. The way some people were in this world, it was horrible. That poor kid Alex. Thank God he'd landed with Roger, a truly good person who had it in him to save the life of others.

"So...what are you going to do?" he asked the question hesitantly, as if unsure if he should have asked it in the first place. Roger sighed again.

"Adopt him, I guess. 'Bout all I can do."

That was all Roger said on the subject. It was clear he was done speaking and so Greg stopped asking questions. After an uncomfortable silence, he cleared his throat and changed the subject, filling Roger in on his own life and all that had happened since they had last seen each other. After that night, Roger never brought up Linda again, and Greg didn't either. He wasn't one to pry into another man's business.

Chapter 11
May 1986

One night, when Greg came over for dinner and then stayed to help clean up afterward, Alex knew he had his chance to talk to him alone. The two of them were in the kitchen, separated from the living room by the eat-in counter in between, and Roger was on the couch as usual with the TV on and the volume turned up loud. Alex had calculated this distance, between where he was in the kitchen and where Roger was now, many times. He was completely sure of what Roger could and could not hear, and he knew that with the TV on that loud and the water running in the sink, it was all clear.

"Hey Greg?"

"Mm-hm?" Greg turned from the sink where he'd been doing the dishes, a wet plate in one hand and a towel in the other.

"I want to find my mom."

Greg stared blankly at him for a few seconds, but as Alex's meaning began to fully sink in, his expression changed and his eyes grew wary. "Um...I...uh...I don't know if that's such a good idea."

"Why?" Alex kept his voice low but refused to look away. "Is she a bad person or something? Did she do something?"

Greg shot a worried look toward the living room. "I don't know. Honestly, Alex. I don't know. I don't know anything about your mom."

"He's never said anything?" Alex cocked his head in Roger's direction. Greg didn't answer, but Alex could see guilt written all over his face. "You know something," he pressed. "I can see it. Please. You have to tell me. Whatever you know, you have to tell me. Please, Greg. There's no one else, I need to know—"

"Okay!" Greg held up a hand. "Shit...I guess you're old enough. Roger probably should have told you this by now anyway." He sighed deeply, glanced up at the ceiling as if sending a silent message to God to see him through this, and then continued. "I really don't know much. I know her name is Linda. And I know Roger met her in Pittsburgh. Seriously—" He put up a hand again as Alex opened his mouth. "That's all I know. When Roger first showed up with you, he said he was taking care of you because Linda—your mom—ran off. He said the last time he saw her was in Pittsburgh and then the two of you came here. Honest to God that's all I know Alex...and I've said too much already."

"Thank you, Greg." Alex's face didn't change but he felt more hope than he had in a long time. "Seriously, thank you. You don't know what it means—"

"Okay, okay," Greg said shortly. "Just forget I said anything, okay? Really. I don't feel good about this Alex. Just don't do anything stupid with that info, okay?" He turned back to the dishes and started washing and drying again, and when he did, he missed Alex slowly nodding to himself. He didn't notice that Alex never answered him.

~

That night, Greg went home and thought back over the conversation he'd had with Alex and he couldn't help but worry.

Resurrect the Dead

He had already known it was only a matter of time before Alex came to him and asked questions about his mom and how she fit together with Roger, but he still hadn't been ready for it when it actually happened. He felt guilty for saying anything at all because he knew Roger didn't want to talk about it. Even when Alex was still a little kid, Roger had been reluctant to share anything on the subject, but in recent years, he'd clammed up about anything to do with the past like some sort of secret agent. Greg couldn't blame him. Most of the guys he knew who'd been in Nam, himself included, didn't relish talking about it, and there were some that made it clear it wasn't a topic to be spoken of, ever, in their presence. Roger had become one those secretive, tight-lipped men that never would talk about the war, or even a lot of the things that had come immediately after it. Greg knew what it was like, and if that was how Roger wanted it, well, he could respect that.

But Alex's mother...that was kind of a different story. It wasn't just that she was part of a vague past history that Roger refused to talk about, it was that she had walked out on her kid. She had left Alex behind without so much as a backward glance. It was no wonder Roger didn't want to talk about her, and didn't want Alex to know about her, either. How would Alex feel when he found out the truth? That his mom couldn't care less about him. That she was probably mentally unstable. That she had abandoned her son with a total stranger, and had never so much as even made the attempt to find him again.

Of course Roger didn't want Alex to know all that, and Greg didn't either. But at the same time, Alex was only getting older, and someday he would be old enough to try to find her on his own, and probably then he *would* find out the truth. Greg could only hope that it wouldn't absolutely shatter him. He thought back to the pleading desperation he'd seen in Alex's eyes when he'd been asking about his mom, and he knew that the truth couldn't be held back forever. Someday, whether Roger liked it or not, Alex would know about her and what she had done, and when he thought about it like that, he also thought that maybe he was being too hard on himself. After all, he had told Alex everything he knew, which honestly wasn't very much, and probably Alex would later find out that same information anyway. Because, whether or not Alex believed him, that really *was* all he knew of the story.

Except, of course, for the part about Roger being in a mental hospital.

To be fair though, Alex hadn't asked him any direct questions about that. Roger being in that place didn't have anything to do with Alex's mom, and as far as Greg had figured it, it seemed like Alex's mom hadn't been right in the head, either. She must have had something wrong with her, to just leave her kid at a bus stop with some guy she'd been talking to for less than ten minutes. In Greg's view, leaving Alex with Roger was actually the best thing she could have done, because at least he'd had someone to raise him who was relatively stable and could hold down a job, for a little while anyway. Alex had a roof over his head. He had food on the table and he wasn't starving. He wasn't being beaten black-and-blue. That was more than Greg could say for his own childhood. Greg liked to think that he and Roger hadn't done such a bad job of taking care of Alex as best they could, and he would bet they had done way more for him than his mom ever could have, being the type of person she'd been.

Sure, Roger had his problems, but that was how it was sometimes for guys who came back from Nam. His health wasn't great, but he wasn't a bad guy. And besides, Roger had saved Greg's life —once upon a time and long ago out in the jungle—and he had saved Alex's life too after his crazy mom decided to run off to God-knows-where and leave her son behind. If it wasn't for Roger, Alex would have ended up in some kind of foster home. And if it wasn't for Roger, Greg himself would be dead. He'd never forget that.

Now, when it came to Alex, that kid was tough. Greg had known him almost his whole life and he'd never seen him break. Alex had always maintained the quiet and serious expression Greg noticed the first second he laid eyes on him. But recently, it did feel like things had changed between Alex and Roger. In the last year or so, a coldness seemed to have infused the way they were with each other, like an invisible barrier had taken root between the two of them. When Greg was over at their place, he could sometimes feel it as intensely as if it were an actual pocket of cold air that shifted around according to their positions in relation to each other. Of course, it wasn't fair that Alex had to deal with Roger, how he was mostly immobile and sunk into that couch, only getting up to use the bathroom and wash up occasionally. Alex was a 15-year-old kid and he needed a parent, but with every day that passed, Roger drifted further away from being any kind of father to Alex anymore. Instead, Alex was now the one who took care of him. No kid should have to deal with that, thought Greg.

Not even one as tough as Alex.

Alex told Alyssa what Greg had said about his mom, which wasn't much, but as Alyssa pointed out, at least it was something. It was a place to start, she said, and Alex made a face. Not really, he said, shaking his head. You never know, she said, sometimes the smallest clues lead to something big, and I bet we could find your mom, just don't give up on it. What I really need to do is get out of here, away from Roger, Alex said. Go somewhere far away and never come back. Yeah, but your mom, Alex, you can find your mom, she's out there, and Alyssa pushed him on it until he finally half-heartedly agreed, saying he would think about it.

They still met every day in the clearing in the woods after school. The weather had gotten warmer as the weeks went by until finally the clearing was hemmed in on all sides by walls of green and the air was soft and smelled like flowers. During these long warm afternoons, Alyssa sat next to Alex on the ground and they both leaned back against the big log. She sat and folded blades of grass to give her hands something to do and sometimes she made suggestions or asked questions but mostly she just listened. And even years later, when she thought back to those golden days, she could still remember almost everything he said.

Chapter 12
July 1986

Alex's 16th birthday happened at the beginning of July, and it was about a week later that Greg decided to give him driving lessons.

He knew better than to ask Roger about it. He either wouldn't really hear him, or he would say no and it would set him off in some way and then Alex would have to deal with him having a bad night later. Roger had always been possessive of Alex, and while Greg understood being protective, he also felt that Roger needed to give the kid some freedom. Alex hardly had any friends at all. None really, except for that Alyssa girl that Greg had gotten to know over the last year, because she was always with Alex. They hung out together somewhere in the woods in the evenings. Greg had seen them come walking out from the overgrown trail that led back there more than a time or two. In Greg's opinion, that was just fine. Alex was a teenager, and if he had a little girlfriend, that was great. Alyssa seemed like a good kid, and Alex couldn't be expected to just have him and Roger—two worse-for-the-wear old Vets—as his only company. He needed other kids, and if Roger couldn't see that, well, there was just something wrong with the way he was thinking.

Although Roger technically owned a car, it didn't work anymore. It had turned into a big rusting hulk of metal that sat to the side of their trailer in the driveway, slowly disintegrating through the seasons. Whenever Alex needed a lift somewhere, Greg drove him in his 1975 Ford Pinto, which rode well enough and was still in pretty good shape, all things considered. It was also a good car for Alex to learn on, and there really was no harm in teaching him, Greg told himself. He was 16 and that's when a kid's supposed to get his license to drive. It just made sense. It made so much sense that Greg was almost able to push away the troubling feeling that kept coming up in him, the feeling he had that someday Alex would *need* to know how to drive, and if he didn't know when that day came then things would go very badly for him. That was at the bottom of it, if he was honest with himself. He wanted Alex to be prepared.

Part of it, Greg thought, was that lately he'd noticed that maybe Roger was getting worse. A lot of the time he was just like a zombie sitting there all day on that couch. He hardly spoke and his face carried a weird spooked look, like he didn't quite know where he was. For the most part though, Greg was able to shrug it off and forget about it. Roger had always been a little odd. Maybe he *was* getting worse, but he could still sign his SSI checks and take his medication. The numbness in his legs and feet probably wouldn't improve, and neither would his lungs, especially with him smoking a pack a day. Roger had been in Nam for over three years, and with all the shit they were exposed to over there, Greg was just glad that he could function at all. Even though he was sure the government would never fess up to it, everyone knew that a lot of the soldiers who were lucky enough to come back alive had still ended up with something that would probably kill them off slowly, and Uncle Sam had conveniently fixed things so that no one could find anyone to blame.

That was the way the world worked. You think you've gotten

away from one thing, only to get hammered by another. That was why Greg vowed he would always stick by Alex. It was a hard world and that kid had struggled enough. Greg loved Alex like he was his own son, and even if Roger was slipping further downhill with every day that passed, once upon a time he'd risked his own life to save Greg's, and Greg wasn't one to forget.

Late one evening after dinner, before he took off for home, he drew Alex into the kitchen, out of Roger's hearing. He asked him if he wanted to go driving the next morning.

"Uh, sure," Alex answered. "But why?"

"Because... I want *you* to do the driving," Greg said in a low voice, eyebrows raised.

Pensiveness shadowed Alex's features and his eyes went blank as if he were looking far away inside himself for a couple of seconds. Then he revived, and nodded slowly. *O-kay,* he mouthed, and then he gave Greg a small grin. *O-kay,* Greg mouthed back, making the sign with his thumb and forefinger pinched together in a circle. He left, more excited than he had expected to be about the next day.

Alex met Greg in his driveway at 9:00 am. First, they sat in the car together with Alex in the driver's seat. "Okay," Greg started. "Here's your ignition. Here's your gearshift—down there you got your gas and your brake—"

"Um, Greg?" Alex interrupted. "I know that stuff."

"Oh. You do? Okay, well, um...how do you know all that?"

"Just from watching. I've been in a car before, you know."

"Oh, well, yeah. Makes sense. So, uh, well, what don't you know?"

"I've never actually driven a car," Alex said quietly. "And you said you wanted to go driving. Do you want me to drive?"

"Yeah. Yeah, why don't we do that." He tossed Alex the keys. "Start her up."

Greg was a little surprised at how good of a driver Alex was, especially if it was true that he hadn't ever driven a car before. He noticed that Alex handled the car with a certain careful confidence, and a surety that usually only comes from experience. He drove like someone who had been driving for years and had already been in a few accidents and already made all the stupid mistakes, not like a kid of only 16, who to Greg's knowledge hadn't yet made a single one. Alex drove them around for about an hour, and after that Greg said they should be getting back. He'd told Roger they were running out to the store, so he didn't want to stay out too long.

By the time they pulled back into Greg's driveway the sun had climbed into the middle of the sky. It was going to be a warm and sunny day. When Alex killed the ignition, they both sat there, neither one of them making any move to get out of the car. Alex stared out the windshield with an unreadable expression on his face, watching a stray cat move in and out of the shadows around the steps to the front door of Greg's trailer.

"Is Roger getting worse?" Alex blurted the question out as if he hadn't planned on saying anything, as if it was as much a surprise to him as to anyone else, although Greg had felt it coming all the same, and to be honest, he'd felt it coming for a long time. He sighed.

"I don't know," he said.

Alex didn't say anything and his face didn't change, but Greg knew he was thinking it over. He got the feeling that Alex had taken his answer—with all of its unspoken implications—into himself, and was now busy squirreling it away somewhere private, somewhere secret, for deep consideration later. A moment later, they both got out of the car, without mentioning Roger again.

Greg started giving Alex driving lessons every day in the late afternoons. Roger never asked where they were going or what they were doing, and after a while, they both stopped worrying about it. On their drives, Greg talked a lot. He told Alex about his wife Irene, and how he still missed her sometimes. He said it went better for a man if he was married. Sometimes he shared the gossip he'd heard from other guys who lived in the park, the men who came down occasionally to watch him when he worked on his car in the evenings. Alex didn't know any of those guys by name, and when Greg mentioned Bill or Jack or Mike, he didn't try to keep track of who was who. He didn't really care. But he nodded along as Greg talked, and he put in a word now and then, to show he was listening.

Alex stayed mostly quiet. He didn't talk about Roger, or how he was praying in his room every night to find a way to escape from him. He didn't talk about Alyssa or what had happened between them out in the clearing. It didn't occur to him to talk about those things or anything else in his life. There was nothing Greg could do or say to change the situation, and there was no new information that Greg might have that would help Alex, so there was no need to talk about any of it. Alex would figure it out on his own, or not, just like he always had. It was generous of Greg to teach Alex how to drive, and he appreciated that. He had realized a long time ago that Greg was lonely, and so listening to him talk about his dead wife and the other guys in the park was something he knew he could do to repay him.

After his daily driving lesson was over, Alex usually followed the trail into the woods and met Alyssa at the clearing. He most often found her sitting on the sleeping bag on the ground, smoking a cigarette and waiting for him. A couple of weeks after he had started driving with Greg, she asked him when he was going to go get his license. He paused and thought about it.

"I guess I won't be getting it, not anytime soon," he said slowly. "Roger would have to take me to apply. He's my legal guardian.

And fat chance of that. But it doesn't matter, I don't need it. I know how to drive now."

"But you don't have a car," Alyssa said, taking a last hit off her cigarette and then grinding it into the dirt.

"Doesn't matter. I know how to drive. And I know where Greg keeps his spare set of keys. He told me. If I need to, I'll take them."

"Why would you need to take them?" Alyssa asked, but Alex didn't hear her. He was looking out into the twilight, lost somewhere within himself. She gave up talking then and stared up into the evening sky. The stars sparkled through thin clouds, the first fireflies of summer lighting up in glimmers all around them as they floated through the warm air. When Alex finally looked back at her again, he smiled and then took her hand and squeezed, and she smiled back.

They sat there holding hands for a long time, safe in the darkness together.

Chapter 13
September 1986

When school started at the beginning of September, Alex started his junior year. It was only two weeks later that he came home one afternoon and found Roger slumped over on the couch. Although he didn't stop to think about it at the time, he later realized he was surprised at himself. Surprised he reacted so quickly, that he so efficiently began to put things in motion, without pausing to question his actions for even one second. It was as if he'd been preparing for that exact moment for a long time. In a way, he thought, that was true. He had been preparing a plan all along. It was just that the conscious part of his brain hadn't been aware of the plan until things started to happen.

He moved to Roger's side and looked at him flopped over on the arm of the couch, his head fallen forward, his chin nesting in his matted black beard. He could see his scalp showing through his black hair, white and exposed, like the rind of a melon. He stretched one arm forward, almost touching him with the fingers of his left hand, but then he froze. He took a step back and let his hand fall back to his side. He breathed quietly for a few seconds, continuing to watch Roger, waiting for any sign of life and not seeing one. Then he turned and grabbed his backpack off the floor where it had fallen when he'd first come in and discovered him like that. He ran for the bedroom.

He eased his closet door open carefully, trying not to make any noise, only dimly aware that his exaggerated caution was an automatic behavior that probably wasn't necessary at the moment. Rapidly, he scanned the contents of the closet and then ripped three shirts from their hangers. He snatched his second pair of jeans—he was wearing the first pair—and a couple of pairs of underwear out of the bottom dresser drawer. He only took two minutes more to rummage through the hallway closet and the kitchen, gathering a bag of Oreos, a flashlight, batteries, and his old winter coat that was frayed but warm. He didn't need anything else, not from this house at least. Then he was out the door. Greg would be at work, and Alex knew he didn't get off until 5:30. On Tuesdays he normally got a ride to and from the factory with one of the guys in the park that worked his same shift. That meant the Pinto would be sitting in his driveway. It also meant Alex was left with approximately two hours before Greg came home.

He pulled the straps of his backpack tight around his shoulders and breathed deep to steady his thundering heart. He started walking toward Alyssa's trailer, putting up a hand against the late-afternoon September sun that seemed to be fighting to get into his eyes and blind him. He saw a figure coming down the lane toward him but he could barely make it out and then he realized it was Alyssa. She waved but he didn't wave back. As he got closer, he saw that the smile that had started to turn up at the corners of her mouth faded. She didn't bother with questions. She just stood there, looking at him, waiting.

"Do you want to go with me? I'm taking off."

"I'll go," she said immediately.

"Get your stuff. Not too much. Just basic things. Important

things. We need to go. Now. Fast. Meet me at the clearing in 10 minutes." Alyssa nodded and then gave him a sharp questioning glance, love and anger all mixed up in it.

"Did he...do something to you?"

Alex shook his head. "No. I'm fine. Get your stuff." Alyssa nodded again and then ran off toward her house. Alex watched her make it inside and then turned in a different direction. He had one more stop to make.

When he got to Greg's trailer he crept up to the front door, even though he was already sure no one was at home. He had never broken into someone's house before. While he wasn't nervous about the moral implications of breaking into Greg's place —it was a necessity that canceled all argument about whether or not he should do it—he *was* nervous that he wouldn't be able to jimmy the lock right, and that he'd spend so much time fumbling around that he'd attract attention. Even though almost everyone in the park had probably seen him around with Greg, and wouldn't think it odd if they saw him going into Greg's house, he still didn't want to deal with any of them being nosy about it right now.

He slid the small piece of card stock he'd saved from an art class he took sophomore year, and had been keeping in the bottom of one of his dresser drawers ever since, into the crack between the lock and the door frame. Nothing happened. He stared at the lock and thought for a minute. He slid the card back in, now at a different angle, and then tilted the other half of it back toward the door handle. When he bent it the opposite way again, he felt it slip under the bolt and he leaned into the door. It swung open.

Once he was inside, he found Greg's spare set of keys easily. They were right where Greg said they would be, in the empty coffee can on top of the refrigerator. But then he spent nearly 30 minutes searching for the other thing he needed, because even though he was sure it was in the house, he didn't have any idea where Greg would have stashed it. He checked the cupboards, and then the drawers. He looked in the freezer. It was when he was turning over the couch cushions and his glance snagged on the outline of the springs underneath his hands, that he got an idea, and suddenly, he knew where Greg had hidden it.

He walked fast to the bedroom, got to his knees next to the bed, and then lay down on his side on the floor. He stuck one arm out, his palm flat and fingers tensed, and felt around between the mattress and the box frame. Within moments he found the slit. He slid his hand into it and located a small bundle. He pulled it out and counted. 500 bucks. Good. It would last a while. He got to his feet and dusted himself off. Then he shoved the wad of cash down into the bottom of his backpack.

By the time Alex and Alyssa finally got in Greg's car and took off, the heat of the day had begun to fade and a cool evening breeze had started up. Alyssa could smell autumn in the air. Alex took the back roads that led to the highway out of town. As they entered the on-ramp Alyssa held her breath. If they were going to be stopped, now would be the time. She nervously checked the side mirror, already imagining swirling red and blue lights, but when she looked, she saw nothing. The road was empty behind them. She glanced over at Alex, expecting to find him as nervous as she was, but instead she was surprised. She had never seen him look so peaceful. His eyes were tranquil and bright, focused on the road ahead.

"Do you know where we're going? I mean—which direction?"

"Mm-hm. 69 South," he said. "We'll get on that and take it to 80 East, or 90. Or...I think 80 turns into 90." He smiled to himself. "I'll figure it out."

He sounds so confident, she thought. All her fears about

flashing lights and sirens coming up behind them vanished, and she stopped checking the side mirror.

"Alex...what happened?"

"Hm?"

"Why are you running?"

A few long seconds passed. She had just decided that he probably wasn't going to answer, when he gave a deep sigh and then started talking.

"It's Roger. I think he's dead, or...I'm not sure. I came home. He was...collapsed, kind of. On the couch. I didn't check to see if he was breathing. I didn't want to touch him. I just wanted to get out of there as fast as I could. So...I did. I ran and got you, and then Greg's car and...that's it. Here we are." Alyssa nodded slowly, trying to process it all. If Roger died, then Alex really would be on his own. Except, Greg would take him in—of course he would—and Alex knew that. So, why was he running? It didn't make sense. Unless Alex didn't believe that Roger was actually dead. In that case, he would have felt he had only a brief window in which to get away, just the sliver of a chance, and when he saw that sliver of a chance, he had taken it.

And so, as Alex had said, there they were.

Chapter 14
September 1986

A few hours later they were in Ohio, and by midnight they had passed the Cleveland area. Sometime after that, Alex pulled off at an exit and into a gas station planted parallel to the freeway. He filled the tank, went up to the little window and paid the cashier, and then got back into the car. He slammed the door shut, bringing a wave of the chilly night air with him, and Alyssa suddenly felt worn out, and lonely. If she was by herself, she'd probably start crying, she thought.

"You okay?" As he looked over at her, the cold fluorescent light from the gas station streamed in through the car windows and lit up his face, making it look for a moment like he was wearing a mask. She felt more alone than ever before, as if he were a total stranger. She looked away, pushing down that awful sensation until she couldn't feel it anymore, and then when she looked back at him, the lighting had shifted and he looked just like Alex again.

She shrugged.

"All right," he said, and started the engine. "Let's go."

Instead of getting back on the freeway, Alex drove around the area surrounding the gas station. He said he wanted to find somewhere to eat. After making a complete tour of the little commercial strip and finding only dark streets and shuttered businesses, they had to agree that everything was deserted. Even the McDonald's was closed. As they approached the freeway again, Alex pointed out a neon sign on the other side of the road. It was the truck stop they had passed when they first pulled in. Now, they both realized that it was the only thing around that was open. Alex turned into the parking lot and found a spot right in front of the small restaurant.

"After we get something to eat, we can come back and sleep in the car."

"Okay," Alyssa agreed, and they climbed out. The restaurant turned out to be a diner attached to a convenience store, guarded by a row of diesel pumps. They made their way inside and a waitress pouring coffee at the counter gestured for them to sit wherever they wanted. They walked to a booth in the back and as soon as they sat down, the same waitress came over and deposited two scummy plastic menus on the table.

"Coffee?" she asked. Alex nodded, and then she was gone again.

Alyssa looked around. The place wasn't that big and it was grimy, bright from the buzzing lights overhead, and busier than she would have expected. Various men—most of them middle-aged and overweight from what she could see—sat pulled up to the counter, and two more sat talking quietly in a booth across from them. All the men seemed to be trudging through gelatinous stacks of pancakes or apathetically sipping coffee as they picked through sections of discarded newspapers scattered around on the counters. They all looked old to Alyssa, and every one of them tired. Except for the guy sitting at the end of the counter. He was younger than everyone else in there, but probably a couple years older than her and Alex. He had a full head of thick jet-black hair and he didn't seem tired at all. To Alyssa, he looked wide awake. As she stared at him, he turned and looked at her.

"Hey. There's a guy over there," Alyssa said, barely moving her lips.

"Where?" Alex was faced away and couldn't see the guy. He didn't move and his expression didn't change, but his eyes told her that he was on high alert.

"Not a cop. Not like that. Just a guy. Like us. But he's older."

"And?"

"I don't know. He looks interesting."

Alex seemed to consider this information but didn't say anything, and then the waitress returned with coffee. He ordered bacon and eggs for both of them and handed the menus back to her. When she walked away, he pushed the dish of sugar packets over to Alyssa's side and took a drink of his coffee, grimacing. "Hot," he said. He put the mug back down and started drumming his fingers on the table.

"Alex..." Alyssa looked over his shoulder, her voice tight. "He's coming over."

A second later, the guy with the jet-black hair—and jacket to match, Alyssa noted—was at their table. He glanced at Alyssa warily, before fixing his gaze on Alex. He cleared his throat and then took a breath, as if he'd been rehearsing what to say and was determined to forge ahead no matter what kind of reception he received.

"Mind if I sit?"

Alex looked at him for a moment and then slid over to the wall to make room. He motioned for him to take a seat. The guy sat down, looking relieved, but still awkward in some way Alyssa couldn't quite define. His eyes and mouth didn't match, she realized. His eyes had a pleading look to them, almost hurt, as if she and Alex had already taken an unspoken vote and rejected him, but then his mouth looked actually cheerful, as if he were waiting for the punchline to a joke. For some reason, Alyssa found she instantly trusted this volatile boy with his pale face and black hair and clothes, and his nervousness that they would turn him away and not want to talk to him, all of it revealed by an innocence she found incredible to believe, but could also see plainly in his eyes.

She wondered if Alex felt the same way.

"What's your name?" Alex asked.

"Joel." The boy's eyes flickered between the two of them and Alyssa saw that he wasn't as old as she had first thought. He might only be a year older than Alex. The waitress came with the bacon and eggs, and a serving of toast, too. She slid the hot dishes onto the table and then hovered, staring at Joel.

"Another plate?" She looked to Alex and he nodded.

"You guys smoke?" Joel asked, flipping a pack open toward Alyssa and then to Alex. Alyssa took one and laid it neatly beside her plate. Alex put his hand up and shook his head. Joel shrugged and lit up as Alex started in on his eggs. "I'm not from here either," Joel said, and then chuckled as Alex looked at him thoughtfully and chewed. "I knew you were wondering. I can see it all over your face. And yours too." He flicked his glance toward Alyssa and smiled at her, but with just one corner of his mouth, then he turned back to Alex and was serious again. "So...you guys are gonna get back on the highway...when? Now? Tomorrow morning? Doing some big on-the-run thing, huh? That's cool. That's cool. You gotta tape deck in that car?" He jerked his thumb toward the window, gesturing toward the parking lot, where the Pinto sat waiting for them.

"Why?" Alex paused with his fork in mid-air, waiting for Joel's response.

"I wanna come with you." Joel dropped all playfulness and stared at Alex. "I wanna go...wherever you're going."

"What if we don't know where we're going?"

"Doesn't matter." Joel shrugged. "I need to get out of here."

He straightened up abruptly, took a drag from his cigarette, and then hunched over the table again. He looked up at them from underneath lowered brows. "Seriously, let me come with you." His gaze on Alex, and that pleading look again, Alyssa saw. Alex took another bite of eggs and chewed. He looked over at Alyssa and then he looked down, as if he were deciding something within himself.

"Okay," he said finally, to Alyssa's surprise, and then he did a funny thing. He stuck his hand out like a businessman cutting a deal, and Joel grabbed it and shook it and laughed. The waitress glided by and slid Joel's hot plate under their joined hands, and then Alex picked up his fork again and nodded at Joel's food.

"Now eat."

Joel was from Ohio. He said he'd gotten a ride out to wherever they were now—which as far as any of them could tell was the edge of BFE—with some guys he knew from school. They'd been on their way to a concert, and they were pretty much assholes, but they had a car. Joel had jumped in with them for the ride, but then they'd dumped him.

"Just as well," said Joel, in between mouthfuls of bacon, eggs, and toast. "Their music sucked. Fuckin' Duran Duran. Girl shit. Just awful." Then he glanced at Alyssa and blushed. "Sorry. I mean...you know." Alyssa laughed.

"I don't like it either," she said.

Joel smiled at her and pushed his plate away. He sat up and tapped his fingers rapidly on the table, glancing back at Alex again. Alyssa had already noticed the pattern of Joel looking to Alex after he finished every sentence, as if waiting for his unspoken approval to continue. "What do you guys listen to? What do you like?

Music's pretty much my life so I'd, uh, like to know." He cleared his throat and suddenly seemed a bit fussy, almost embarrassed, as if he felt like he was asking for too much too soon.

"Slayer. Judas Priest. Lately it's been Maiden." Alex sounded completely indifferent and scanned the door as he answered, but Alyssa could tell he was more present than before Joel's question. She could feel some sort of emotional charge coming off him, like static electricity.

"Maiden, eh? That's cool. They're rad," Joel said. "Got any tapes?" He looked at the door and then back again at Alex, hopeful.

"In the car." For the first time since Joel sat down, Alex smiled.

They decided not to sleep after all. After Joel climbed into the backseat and Alex started the car it somehow felt like a party with just the three of them. Both Alex and Alyssa got a second wind, and Joel said he had never been tired in the first place. Alex pulled the car back onto the highway, going east. "This is good," Joel said. He leaned forward from the backseat, folding his arms and planting his elbows on his knees, his black coat draped around him. Alyssa glanced over and thought to herself that he resembled a big crow, perched on a branch, huddled up under its wings. "Maiden's good," he clarified, snapping along to the beat. "I like the stuff they sing about. Feels like ancient times. I like that stuff... stuff from centuries ago."

"Yeah? Like what?" Alex asked, cracking the window and taking the lit cigarette Alyssa handed him.

"Rome...the gladiators...Socrates and shit...all that stuff. It's good." Joel closed his eyes and rocked along to the song. Then his eyes snapped open again. "You guys heard of Julian?" He stopped rocking. "Emperor Julian? You guys heard of him?"

"Um...I don't think so," said Alex. Alyssa shook her head.

"No shit? He was rad. *One bad dude* was Julian. He was the emperor, but man, like...also a gangster...kind of. Like, he got to be emperor because he pulled all this political revenge shit on the emperor before him—who was responsible for murdering his family. Then when *he* got to be emperor, he pretended to everyone he was a Christian, but he was really *anti*-Christian. Like, he hated those guys. He was really into the *old* gods—Zeus, Apollo, you know. So he was a pagan, and if the Christians woulda known they woulda totally come down on his shit, thought he was evil and stuff."

"Wow. That's cool," Alyssa said, lighting up a cigarette of her own.

"Fuckin-A. You got that right. Julian was a fuckin' *bad ass*. He hated the Christians. I can't stand those fuckers either—I mean—hey, you guys aren't Christian, are you?" He suddenly sat up straight, his eyes wide.

"No." Alyssa shook her head.

"I don't think I'm anything," said Alex.

"Oh." Joel relaxed again. "Well, good. Neither am I. Obviously. But my mom is Christian, hard core." He let out a tight hiss from between clenched teeth. "Man, I can't *stand* that shit."

After that they talked about music, and movies—Alyssa discovered that both Joel and Alex were horror fans and had it especially bad for Nightmare on Elm Street—and Joel's mom and how he couldn't stand living with her anymore and how that was why he left. Alyssa didn't say anything about her own mom, and she noticed Alex stayed conspicuously silent on the topic of family, so for the most part she just listened to the two boys talk, with Joel doing most of the talking. That was all right, she thought. There was something comforting about Joel and the way he filled the silence. He seemed not to notice that she and Alex didn't say much, or he didn't care. Whenever Joel exhausted one line of conversation, he then followed a new one effortlessly, and whenever she or Alex did choose to say something, he paused and listened raptly, hanging on their few words.

It was nice, Alyssa decided. For some reason, even though he'd only known them for a few hours, it felt like she and Alex mattered to Joel. Like they were real friends.

Around 5:00 am, they got off the freeway and Alex found a Kmart and parked the car at the edge of the parking lot, out by the road. Joel said it would probably be fine to stay there for a few hours and sleep, because Kmart usually didn't open until nine or ten, and even so, it was a big parking lot. No one would notice their little car. Alex and Alyssa reclined the front seats back and Joel stretched out almost underneath them, all along the backseat. When they woke up it was almost noon and it was raining. After digging the sleep out of their eyes, they made a run for it across the street to a gas station where they picked up chips, candy, and more cigarettes. Then Alex pulled back onto the highway again.

The rain picked up speed until it was coming down on the car like bullets hitting the windshield. It fell off for a bit and then started again and repeated that cycle for the next hour. Finally, Alex pulled off at the next exit. "We're getting a room. I can't drive anymore in this," he said. Alyssa stared at his profile in the gray light coming through the windows and saw how tired he was. He looked like an old man. She realized she felt unbearably tired too, and limp and cold. She suddenly wished Joel would go away.

"That's fine. You guys can get a room and I'll take off," Joel said, almost as if he'd read her mind.

"You'll stay with us," Alex answered, and Alyssa knew it was decided. In the backseat, Joel flicked his lighter to a cigarette. Alyssa heard the dry windy way he inhaled and noticed again how his fingernails were chewed to the quick, and for no reason at all, she felt sorry for him. Suddenly she felt sorry for all of them, and all her previous irritation vanished.

"Besides," said Alex. "You're the only one who's 18. You gotta rent the room." Joel made a snuffling sound through his nose which Alyssa took as agreement. A minute later, they pulled into the parking lot of a Super 8 and Alex leaned forward and let Joel climb out of the back. He and Alyssa watched as Joel tented his thin black coat up over his head and ran to the office, slanted lines of cold rain beating down on him. He was back in 15 minutes with a wide grin and a set of keys, which he tossed to Alex through the driver's side window. She and Alex got out of the car and the three of them jogged to the room. When they got inside, Alyssa noticed the room smelled like cigarettes and the carpet was threadbare, but it was warm and dry. She immediately collapsed on the bed.

They spent the rest of the day watching TV.

Chapter 15
September 1986

They went to sleep late that night with Alyssa and Alex in the bed, and Joel on the floor.

All through the day, Alyssa and Alex had taken turns telling Joel different pieces of their story. Alyssa said her mom was probably too drunk to notice she was gone, and if she did notice, she doubted she would even miss her. Alex explained how he had taken Greg's car, and the wad of money found in the mattress. They also told him about Roger, and about how he was, but not about what they thought might have happened to him.

Of course, Alyssa thought to herself, they couldn't really be sure of what *had* happened. If they never had to go back, they might not ever know, not how Roger had come out of it, or if he had come out of it at all. Maybe he was dead. But no matter what state Roger was in, she knew she and Alex couldn't stay gone forever. Sooner or later, they would have to go back. Dealing with her mom wasn't such a big deal, that wasn't what she was worried about. It was Alex. She had a feeling that if they went back—*when* they went back, as they would have to at some point—that she would lose him then. Forever.

Alyssa lay in bed, staring at the wall, chewing over these

thoughts for what felt like hours, though when she rolled over and checked the clock it had only been 45 minutes. Soon after that she drifted off and then dozed in and out of a thin, troubled sleep. Finally, around dawn, when the velvety black darkness of the room became a soft gray, she woke up and knew she wouldn't be able to fall asleep again. She didn't turn over, but stayed facing the wall. She listened for Alex. He was still right beside her. She could hear the rhythmic rise and fall of his breath. She turned onto her back and stared at the ceiling. Alex turned over, and then he turned over again. Alyssa froze, for some reason apprehensive that he would wake up, but he didn't. He settled back on his side and began breathing evenly again.

She thought about how Alex was the person she was closest to in all the world, and how sometimes she also felt like she didn't know him at all. It was like he was two people. There was the Alex that she knew, the one who was her best friend and whose eyes lit up, just a little, every time he saw her. That was the Alex she always felt safe with, the Alex who would never betray her. But then there was a second Alex. She felt that Alex more than saw him, in some way she couldn't define. He left traces, but never tracks. When she caught that Alex looking at her, it was like he didn't recognize her. The expression in his eyes was cold, unfeeling, sometimes even dark. That was the Alex who had forced her down onto the ground in the clearing.

Alyssa wondered if there were other people who had a second invisible person inside of them. Maybe she did too. She guessed she really couldn't say for sure. But then she thought of Joel. He was only one person. She could already tell. And even though he was different than her and Alex—wildly different—he also seemed to fit with them. She had been surprised to see how Joel had gotten Alex to relax and even laugh a few times in the car, because she had never seen Alex laugh with anyone besides her. When he had sat down with them at the diner, it had been weird, but also oddly perfect. She'd felt like a knot had been tied, or a contract signed. She sensed that, without saying anything at all, the three of them had come to an agreement, and there was no going back.

She had no idea what they were doing and she didn't know where they were going, but she trusted Alex and she knew she was right to trust him. There was something in Alex that other people didn't understand, something even she didn't understand, and she trusted that unnamable thing in Alex more than she trusted herself. It was Alex who would lead them, just as it was Alex who had decided Joel was not to be left behind and that Roger was. It was Alex who had some sort of plan in mind —and that he *did* have a plan, Alyssa was sure—even if he wouldn't talk about it. Alyssa took a deep breath and then slowly let it out. She knew it wasn't up to her to decide the next move. That was Alex. She didn't know what he had in mind, but whatever it was, he had a reason for it. Alex would drive them east, and then whatever was supposed to happen, would happen.

That morning, Joel checked out of the room—paying for it with the cash Alex gave him—while Alex and Alyssa took their few things to the car and then pulled up in front and waited. When Joel came out, Alex leaned forward and let him climb into the backseat and a few minutes later they were back on the highway.

"So, where to now folks?" Joel asked.

"I don't know," Alex said.

"Don't you have any idea?"

"Not really."

Joel sighed. It looked like getting answers out of Alex today wasn't going to be any easier than it had been yesterday.

"Listen," said Joel. "I don't want to step on any toes here. I know it's your car and all, but shouldn't we have at least the *idea* of a plan?"

"We do," said Alex. "We're driving east."

"Okay man. Whatever." Joel turned his attention to the window. "I guess it is your car."

A couple hours later they stopped for gas. Alex went in to pay and grab some sodas while Alyssa and Joel stayed in the car and waited for him. They sat there for a few moments in silence before Joel broke it.

"Hey, Alyssa?"

"Yeah?" she said, without turning around. She kept her eyes on Alex through the window. She could see him inside at the counter.

"Do *you* know where we're going?"

"Why would I know where we're going when not even Alex knows where we're going?"

"Well, who says he doesn't know?" Joel answered back. "He keeps saying east, like there's something there he sort of expects to find or something. He doesn't even slow down past the exits, or talk about how many miles to here or there. It's like he knows exactly where he's going, but he won't let us in on it."

Alyssa fought for a moment with herself about how to explain Alex to Joel, or if it was even possible. What Joel said was true—it *was* like Alex knew exactly where he was going, and some part of her knew that he really did. But the way Alex operated was also sometimes impossible to understand. He saw farther than other people, or maybe deeper was a better way to describe it. But there was no way she could communicate this to Joel just by telling him about it. Alex was a person you had to experience over time to really get it. She turned around and looked at Joel, and then glanced back at the store. Alex was walking back toward the car, a convenience-store bag in his hand.

Resurrect the Dead

"Alex just knows," she said quietly. "He knows what he's doing."

Joel fell silent. When she looked back at him again, she saw he was looking down at his hands and chewing his bottom lip. Then he raised his eyes and met her gaze.

"Okay," he said, and nodded. "If you say so."

The driver's side door opened and Alex got in, looking at both of them and smiling. Without a word, he handed each of them a can of Coke and a packet of Skittles. "Yes!" Joel pumped his fist in the air and immediately opened his soda and took a long swig, all previous worry apparently forgotten. Alyssa smiled at the two boys and resumed staring out the window.

Then Alex started driving again.

An hour or so later they started passing signs for Pittsburgh. Joel leaned forward and tapped Alex.

"You know, there's a big Priest concert tonight in Pittsburgh. It's gonna be fuckin' rad."

"Really?"

"Yeah. We should go," said Joel.

"We don't have tickets," Alex said.

"That doesn't matter."

"What do you mean? You don't need tickets to get in?"

"Nah. You *definitely* need tickets to get in." Joel snorted. "But we could hang out in the parking lot. It's almost as much fun. Especially with a band like Priest. Everyone hanging out is really into it."

"So...we just go and stand around in the parking lot all night?"

"Yeah. I mean..." Joel sighed loudly and slapped his palms on top of his thighs. "If you don't wanna go just say so. I know it sounds stupid. But it's fun. I swear. I did it before. It was actually one of the most fun nights of my life if you want to know the truth. Go ahead and laugh."

"It does sound fun," Alyssa said. "We should go."

"Okay," Alex looked over at her and shrugged. "We'll go."

"All right!" Joel rocketed forward from the backseat and sent the packs of cigarettes that had been stacked on the middle console flying.

"Where do we get off? What exit?"

"Just wait," said Joel. "I'll show you."

A few minutes later Joel pointed out where Alex needed to get off and soon after that they got to the venue and found parking just a few streets away. Now the three of them stood on the fringes of the crowd that had gathered in the lot right outside of the entrance. Joel was right, the people there were excited, and ready to party. It seemed that everyone was giddy about Judas Priest, whether or not they would be getting into the actual concert. It was obvious they weren't the only ones without tickets, as they saw different guys and girls—single, paired up, or in desperate clusters—who were trekking around the parking lot bleating their cry for tickets like lost sheep. Occasionally, one of a number of anonymous-looking men answered the call, scurrying out of the crowd, doing business with them, and then scurrying back into the mass of people and getting lost again.

A lot of people were already drunk, Alyssa saw. Some of the guys swayed on their feet as they yelled about how great the show was going to be. They leered at Alyssa as she passed, and the eyes of the girls who were with them followed, shrewdly evaluating her figure and profile. A lot of the girls looked like the girls from Alyssa and Alex's high school, with bangs sculpted into a frozen cascading waterfall of hair with Aquanet, and frosted eyelids in shades of electric blue. Their mouths hung open as they laughed at their boyfriends, who threw empty beer cans on the ground and stomped them as if they were a hated enemy's skull.

Resurrect the Dead

When they reached the end of the parking lot, they found a cameraman there, and a guy with a microphone. The two of them were moving from group to group, picking out different teenagers, asking them questions, and then filming their answers, interview-style. They didn't look like news people, Alyssa thought. More like just regular guys. She wondered who they were and where the film would end up. They started talking to a guy nearby and she saw the guy repeat the performance of crunching an empty can underfoot and heard the girl he was with say something about blowing one of the band members.

The man with the microphone noticed her and Alex and Joel passing by and suddenly turned away from the two he had been interviewing. He poked the microphone into Joel's face, and she saw Alex instinctively take a step back. Silently, she joined him, letting Joel handle it as the two of them faded into the background.

"Are you here to see Judas Priest tonight?" The guy asked Joel, sounding breathless and cheerful. He's as excited as everyone else, thought Alyssa.

"Uh no...well...I wish I was. We just came to...uh..." Joel suddenly seemed unsure of himself. He looked over the guy's shoulder and his eyes connected with Alex, who nodded at him, encouraging him to go on. "We don't have tickets," Joel said, and now he smiled. "Me and my friends. But we came to check out the antics in the parking lot."

"And are the 'antics' living up to your expectations?" The cameraman maneuvered around to get Joel fully in the shot and Alex and Alyssa took another step back. Joel looked over the crowd and spotted a girl lifting her leopard-print tube top to reveal two large, cream-colored breasts that contrasted starkly against her dark tan. The group of guys in front of her clapped and whistled and she undulated her torso until she jiggled like a waterbed that had just received a crash landing. Joel looked back into the camera.

"Yeah," he said, and laughed. "I think the antics so far are pretty A-OK." He looked over at the girl and gave two thumbs up. The guy with the mike laughed too and clapped Joel on the back.

"I'll agree with you on that!" he said, and then he was gone, onto the next group and the next question, with the cameraman trailing behind him, swiveling around to capture every moment of craziness that he could.

They stayed for the next hour, until the doors opened and most of the crowd was funneled inside. The only people left outside were the others like them, the people who didn't have money for tickets or who had been unsuccessful in finding them. The anonymous men who had been scurrying in and out of the crowd now scurried away for good. Dusk turned to full dark and it started to get cold. The three of them headed back to the car.

"See? It was fun, huh?" Joel said. "I told you guys it would be fun. And I was right. It was totally fun."

"Yeah, it was," Alyssa said, and even though he didn't say anything, both of them knew Alex was in agreement.

As they walked back to the car, Alyssa thought about the new side of Alex she'd seen emerge in the last day or so. It was like she was seeing a part of his personality that had always been there, but had also remained completely unknown to her before. Alex had smiled, and laughed—almost always at jokes that Joel made—and he'd even joked around a little bit himself. At first, she thought it must have come from hanging out in the parking lot. She knew he had probably loved being in a crowd that adored one of his favorite bands just as much as he did. But then, the more she thought about it, the more that didn't seem right, because the change in Alex had happened before they'd even gotten to Pittsburgh. It had started last night, at the diner, when they met Joel.

So, it wasn't just that Joel was some sort of a missing piece for both her and Alex, but that he also had something specific—and important—with Alex alone. That thought stung her just a bit. She couldn't help feeling jealous that Joel had been able to open up Alex in a way that she herself had not, even though she'd known him for much longer, and they were a lot closer. But she also had to admit, all jealousy aside, that she liked this new side of Alex. She liked it a lot, in fact. It was nice to see him smile for a change.

As they approached the car, she stole a glance at Alex walking beside her. He looked just like the Alex she had always known, expressionless, and impenetrable. Then suddenly Joel ran up from behind, all she saw of him was a blur of black jacket and black hair. As he passed them, he flicked Alex on the ear and they heard him howling with laughter as he kept running. It was a cry she had heard from many boys before, most frequently from her little brothers. For some reason she couldn't fathom, boys loved to hurt each other. The way Joel was laughing right now meant *I got you a good one*. Alex would be silent but furious, she supposed. But when she turned to look at him, she was shocked. He only rubbed his ear with one hand, and she saw he was smiling to himself in the dark.

Chapter 16
September 1986

That night they stayed at another motel just outside of Pittsburgh. They were only up for an hour or so before the three of them crashed on the bed together, and they all slept soundly until the maid jiggled the lock the next morning to get in to start her cleaning duties. After hurried showers they checked out, and then they were on the road again.

As they pulled out of the motel parking lot, Joel leaned forward from his by-now-customary place in the backseat and asked, "Hey man, where are we *going*?" He kept talking before Alex could even begin to answer. "And don't tell me that you don't *know*, because you obviously know something. I have no idea what's going on, but it sure seems like you do. So where to, huh? Are you gonna let us in on it or what?"

Alex met Joel's eyes in the rearview mirror and he smiled.

"I do know," he said, and then he didn't say anything else.

Joel sighed loudly and then flopped back onto the seat and Alyssa covered her mouth to hide her laughter. She already knew that getting anything out of Alex before he was ready to tell was impossible. She wondered when Joel would figure that out too.

The day was mostly sunny but had also turned cold. The sky

shone bright and blue, with clouds blowing across the sun every now and then, turning the world gray for a moment, making it feel as if summer had happened a long time ago and winter was on the way. The atmosphere in the car had grown noticeably colder too, Alyssa thought. Joel hadn't said much since Alex shut him down. They drove back through the city of Pittsburgh, and then, not far beyond it, Alex pulled off at an exit. He turned into a gas station and parked the car.

"I'm getting directions. I'll be back."

Then he was out of the car, slamming the door behind him. Alyssa turned and glanced at Joel, who rolled his eyes but didn't say anything. Within five minutes, Alex was back. He started the car and pulled out onto the street, but instead of getting back on the highway, he took another couple of turns and seemed to be looking for an address. He slowed down until they were moving at a crawl. Then he pulled over and got out of the car again.

"Alyssa—" Joel hissed from the backseat as she turned to look back at him. "*What—is—going—on?*" he whispered through gritted teeth. "What the hell is he *doing?*"

They both looked out of the windshield at Alex, who was pacing back and forth in front of the car, as if he were thinking. Then he walked out to the street, looking first one way and then the other. Alyssa had no idea what he was looking for, the street was empty. The sunlight glinted off his hair, but she knew he must be cold. The wind had picked up and Alex wore nothing but a thin t-shirt, although he didn't appear to notice the temperature. He looked all around him and then squinted at the street sign just ahead.

"I don't know what he's doing," Alyssa answered truthfully.

"But...you still trust him. Right?" Joel said, his voice softer now.

"Yes."

"Yeah," said Joel. "You know what's really crazy? I do too." He dug a cigarette out from his pack and lit it. The air inside the car turned a faint blue and for some reason Alyssa felt strangely comforted. She let her eyes rest on Alex's profile and she and Joel stayed like that, silent and watchful, waiting for Alex to figure out whatever he was going to figure out. Then Alex came striding back toward the car.

"He's coming back," she said, and Joel dropped back onto the seat and averted his eyes, as if he'd been looking out the side window the whole time without a care in the world. Alex got in but didn't take notice of either of them.

"Wrong street," he said, as if he were mostly talking to himself. "Should have gone left, not right…"

"Alex?" said Joel.

"Mm-hm?" Alex kept his eyes on the street, paying only the slightest attention to Joel.

"What are you looking for?"

Alex didn't answer. He turned down a street, looked back and forth between both sides, and then appeared to be satisfied. Then he turned down yet another street, drove for a while, turned again, and then finally pulled over.

"I need you guys to get out," he said, turning and looking at Alyssa expectantly, as if he were asking the most normal thing in the world.

"You need us to *get out?*" Joel repeated.

"I want you guys to take a walk," Alex said. "Or stay here. Whatever. But I need you to get out. There's something I have to do. I'll come back for you." He paused, as if thinking something over carefully. "I don't think I'll be very long," he added.

"Are you serious?" And now Joel's voice sounded thin, and wavering. Alyssa couldn't look at him. She knew Alex would be back, but Joel didn't, and there was no way she could convince him of that, not right now anyway. The moments stretched out between them, Joel waiting for an answer and Alex not giving him one, and she could hear Joel breathing and was suddenly afraid he might start crying, and embarrass all of them.

But Joel didn't start crying. He just blew a long angry breath out through gritted teeth and then finally said, "Okay, yeah. All right." Alex got out and pulled the seat forward so Joel could get out and Alyssa followed on her side, shutting the car door firmly behind her and then backing up onto the sidewalk. They were in a residential part of town, she saw, looking around. Boxy brick houses with patchy little yards lining streets that were pitted with cracks and potholes. She couldn't imagine what she and Joel would do here. Walk around until Alex came back, she guessed.

Then Alex was gone. He pulled away from the curb and drove off without even a wave or a glance in the rearview mirror. Alyssa wasn't surprised, that was Alex, but when she turned and looked at Joel, she could tell that he had been waiting for something. Some sign that showed Alex realized he was leaving them in the middle of nowhere. Joel stood staring after the car as it moved into the distance, squinting against the sun and watching as it turned the corner. Then he looked at Alyssa.

"Where to now, kid?" he said, trying—unsuccessfully, Alyssa thought—to sound like he couldn't care less about Alex leaving them. He looked away quick but Alyssa still caught the young, scared look that passed over his face. She gave him a couple seconds to recover, to find his cigarettes and light one, and then finally look back at her again.

"We walk," she said. She kept her eyes down, trained on the ground. She didn't need to see his face. Watching his shadow told her everything she needed to know.

For the next couple of hours, Joel and Alyssa walked around and talked, mostly about Alex. Joel still seemed a little pissed off, and a little scared, but he started to calm down the longer they walked together and killed time with conversation. Alex was like a wall, Joel said disgustedly, and Alyssa nodded and agreed. But he also really liked him, he added hastily, and he knew that he'd liked him —him and Alyssa both—the moment they'd stepped through the front door of the diner. Because even though he'd been on his own for a while, and even though he'd been sort of desperate for a change, he wasn't *that* lonely. That wasn't why he decided to walk over to their table, he said, looking intently at Alyssa, concern making him look almost weary, and older than he really was. She could see it was important to him that she believed what he said, although she wasn't entirely sure why. He wasn't mad at Alex for leaving them, he went on. Not even close. The truth was, if he could have picked anyone for a friend, he would have picked Alex. But that didn't change the fact that he wanted to strangle him right at this moment.

"Alyssa, what's he doing?" Joel asked, and Alyssa heard exhaustion in his voice, and possibly defeat. He kicked at a pebble in front of him and it went skidding off down the sidewalk.

"He's being Alex. This is what he always does." Then she said, "What about you? What are you doing? Do you always do this?"

"What do you mean?" Joel threw a hurt look her way and then went back to staring down at the sidewalk.

"I mean, do you always have to know what's going on all the time or what? You seem like you're really stuck on having a plan."

"Well, what's wrong with having a plan? What's wrong with that? I don't know Alex like you do...I don't know what he's going to do."

"Yes," said Alyssa. "You do."

"What? Know what he's going to do?"

"No," she sighed. "You know him as well as I do."

Resurrect the Dead

They were just about to make another circle around the block when Alex pulled up next to them. He didn't look over, and he didn't get out. He just pulled up and waited. Alyssa opened the door and flipped the seat toward the front so Joel could crawl into the back. Then she got in herself. From the moment she entered the car she felt it. Alex had changed. Something in his eyes had shifted. She could feel some sort of invisible wave of energy forming a wall around him. She flicked her eyes toward Joel.

"Hey man, where you been?" Joel asked, trying to sound indifferent, but it came out sounding like he was hurt anyway. She could already tell that Joel didn't see it, he didn't understand there had been a change in Alex. He didn't know.

"We're going back," Alex said, ignoring Joel's question. He sat staring straight ahead, his small white knuckles gripping the steering wheel. Joel lit up a smoke and stayed silent while Alyssa looked out the window. Everything was over. She felt it as clearly as if she'd just gotten confirmation that someone had died. Wherever Alex had gone when he'd left them, whatever had happened to him there, had killed whatever he'd been before.

She glanced over and studied the set of his jaw for a moment more before turning away from him again, fixing her eyes on the pavement outside, feeling dimly like her heart was dying inside her. She wondered briefly if she would ever see her old friend Alex again.

# Part II

Chapter 17
January 1987

Telly had always been good at fixing things—anything mechanical, and everything electrical. As a kid, he had started trying to build machines from the time he could talk. He'd never liked books because he found them too slow and boring, but he loved any kind of instruction manual. By the time he was old enough to go to school, he had established the one golden rule of his life, and it was this rule that determined whether or not a person earned his respect. They had to know more than him about how to take something apart, or how to put it back together again.

Telly's dad drank a lot when he was growing up, and fought with his mom all the time over it. Telly didn't understand why she didn't just leave him alone. She'd had enough black eyes and busted lips to know better. Sometimes he felt bad for her, but at other times he wondered if maybe his mother wasn't all that bright, because by the time Telly was nine years old, the pattern with his dad was clear to him. Every few days his dad went out and got drunk, and then he came home and waited for someone to cross his path. Once they crossed him, he let them have it. It was the same routine every time, with zero variation. Telly had learned long ago that the only effective strategy was to stay out of his dad's way, so he was baffled as to how his mom kept walking right on into it, and every time, with all the sobbing and the screaming she did, it seemed like she had forgotten about all the other times in the past when the exact same thing had happened. Like somehow, she felt it had never happened to her before.

By the time he was 14, he had largely stopped caring. He stayed in his room and stayed quiet, reading old copies of the Radio Amateur's Handbook that he'd checked out of the library, studying each edition carefully. He was determined to build his own radio and had little time for the predictable cycle of melodramatic hysterics he often heard from his parents outside his bedroom door. As a result of his frequent trips to the library, he'd also come back around to books and guessed some of them weren't half bad. He got interested in history—especially Arnold Toynbee—and science, and the faintly discernible yet timeless patterns he could see woven throughout both. Just like with his dad's routine, he could see that history moved in cycles. Every cycle appeared to be worse than the last, more intense and more deadly. Case in point was World War II, which had occurred just a few years before Telly was born. Once that one was settled there was another war, and then another after that, and nuclear weapons to worry about too. Anyone with enough power could push the button at any time and that would be it for everyone. Telly thought about his own parents and their screaming matches—somehow absurdly stupid and dangerously insane all at the same time—and he wondered who exactly were the people in power who had access to the button.

Telly decided it was safer for a person to keep to themselves. After all, he'd gotten through most of his childhood by locking himself up in his room and using the time to study up on electronics, which was in his opinion one of the only real avenues that seemed to be moving the human race forward in any way. As a result of all his studying, he landed a scholarship to the Illinois Institute of Technology, where he stayed for almost four years, mostly to get out of going to Vietnam. Telly had no illusions about patriotism or serving his country. He knew the mess in Vietnam was nothing but another version of the absurdly stupid and dangerously insane fights his parents used to get into and probably were still getting into—Telly didn't really know since he'd ceased to go home to visit his parents after he left for college—and he had no intention of getting himself killed because the people in power said that was a good idea for what he should do with his life.

After he got out of school he worked a string of different jobs, but he quit every one, much of the time because he found them to be too much like school, which he had never liked. Following instructions that came from people who knew less than he did was pure torture. In every instance, Telly would look at the situation from all angles and find that he already had all the information he needed, without needing any input from the person in charge, so it was a total waste of his time to be forced to attend meetings or act like he needed to wait for any sort of manager to approve his course of action. So, one after another, he quit them all, and then he drifted. He finally ended up getting a job at a machine shop in a factory in Michigan, and unexpectedly, this turned out to be the place where Telly was a perfect fit. He had a manager but his manager didn't care what he did or how he did it, just so long as he fixed whatever problem was brought to him, which Telly did, every time.

Although Telly still never said much, over time all the guys he worked with learned to come talk to him if they were looking to fix a TV or a radio, or figure out anything electrical. When it came to that sort of stuff, Telly was a genius, they said. When it came to anything else about him, there was no comment. This suited Telly just fine. He'd long ago gotten used to being alone, and going unnoticed. After a few years at the machine shop, he was able to buy his own trailer and could easily afford the lot rent at the park where he lived. He had his job—which he enjoyed, relatively—he had his little ham shack he'd made out of the back bedroom of the trailer, and he had the time he needed to pursue his passion for radio.

Telly had been a serious ham since the early '70s, getting his license in '72. Most evenings after work, he sat in the only chair in his house, a large wooden chair he had built himself, and searched for whatever broadcast he could find that sounded interesting. He never knew what he might discover and that was part of the fun. Some nights he ended up having conversations with other hams about nothing much, some nights he didn't find anything at all good, and other nights he might find someone doing their own version of some kind of eccentric radio show.

That was how he found the Preacher.

He never identified himself by name. He said listeners could call him the Preacher—which is how Telly came to think of him and after a while he couldn't even imagine the Preacher having a real name—and he said was based out of Ohio, somewhere around the Cincinnati area, sometimes adding that he'd originally come from Tennessee. He seemed to know a lot about history. A staggering amount, in fact. But what immediately caught Telly's attention was that the Preacher talked about the same thing Telly had noticed, the cycles. The Preacher said that each time the bad part of a cycle came around, a plague of violence consumed humanity. He also said that each cycle was always worse than the one that had come before, and that matched Telly's observations too.

Most nights the Preacher talked about history for a while, and then he talked about the Bible. Telly had never been much interested in religion, but he found himself intrigued nonetheless. The Preacher tied certain periods of history to certain passages in the Bible, laying it all out like it was a collection of puzzle pieces, or a treasure map. Clue that led to clue that led to clue. The Preacher

Resurrect the Dead

said that if humanity could figure it all out—all these clues that fit together to complete the puzzle that formed a map—then possibly they could be saved. He said that Jehovah had provided these clues because he wanted humanity to be saved. Or, at least, some of them. The Preacher said that Armageddon was coming soon, and only those who were in the truth would be saved. Human society as it was today was morally corrupt and under the influence of Satan, and so although 144,000 people would be selected to go to heaven in the current time period everyone else would have to wait to be resurrected by God to a cleansed earth after Judgment Day. Once they were resurrected, they would live forever.

Telly didn't know about 144,000 people being sent to heaven, or Jehovah resurrecting the dead, or living forever. But he did know about the cycles, and he was convinced that what played out on the global scale paralleled the psychology of individuals, as if human beings were microcosms of the larger landscape. He would never forget his dad's old pattern—go out, get drunk, get mad, and then find someone who happened to get in his way. Wasn't that the same thing that happened with warring countries? Was there any real difference between the fights he'd witnessed between his mom and dad and what had happened in all the wars that had been fought since the beginning of time? Telly didn't think so. How could humans—who were able to invent the radio and the airplane and the telephone—be so stupid as to fight each other to the death in the mud like animals? It was obvious that it was all madness. The Preacher's theory about Satan influencing society started to make sense, thought Telly, when you looked at it like that.

Telly had always known no one could be trusted. He was always aware of who was coming and going in the machine shop, who was inspecting his work, and who was observing him when his back was turned. What had always comforted him more than anything else was the assumption that he knew more than other people about how things worked. It made him feel prepared for anything. But now, listening to the Preacher, he wondered if there were gaps in his knowledge of the world that he hadn't been aware of before. The possibility that he had maybe been overlooking something valuable—something that had been right under his nose all along—gave him a hot panicky feeling in his chest. Without noticing it, he began to move his chair closer to the radio each evening, and he began to listen more carefully to the Preacher, and to take mental notes on all that he said.

The Preacher explained that those who would be saved from Armageddon, which would be the last big cycle, were those that would put themselves out there to save others. Anyone who worked to spread the message was on the side that would survive the second death and make it to heaven. Although Telly thought to himself that he wasn't so sure the Preacher could really know the details on that—it didn't seem possible that anyone could—he also didn't care about pleasing God, or making it to heaven. It was the cycles that were important to Telly, and about the cycles, the Preacher was absolutely right. He was also right about the stupidity of humanity. And so, he put an idea into Telly's head, an idea about spreading the message. If Telly got the message out, like a seed that could take root somewhere and grow and spread other seeds, then maybe he could help with balancing the cycles.

Telly knew he couldn't trust the media for help with this. Journalists and lawyers and government guys, they were all evil and corrupt, all of them liars. All of them carried the same poisonous mindset found so commonly among his fellow men that had started off the cycles in the first place. If he tried to take out an ad in the newspaper, it would be censored. If he tried leaving fliers in mailboxes, he would be arrested for messing with the government's mail. Nothing straightforward like that would work. He would have to go around the direct routes and carve out his own way. He needed to find a method no one else would use. He needed to think of something that most people would never think of at all.

First, he started thinking about his radio. That was how he had discovered the Preacher—and his message—and if he hadn't built that radio then he never would have known that there was someone else out there in the world who had also noticed the pattern of the cycles. He didn't want to just start doing his own broadcasts, though. No, the Preacher was already doing that and he was far better at it than Telly could ever be. Telly couldn't imagine talking for hours on end—truthfully, he couldn't imagine talking for over two minutes—to the faceless masses, delivering a message with charisma and style like the Preacher did. No, it would have to be something that didn't involve talking to people at all. Something that would allow him to spread the information, while also remaining silent, and anonymous.

He sat and thought about this while staring at his set-up, remembering how he had pieced it all together, how he'd had to climb up onto the roof of his trailer to secure the giant antenna. That might be something right there, he thought. If he had a big enough antenna—and he knew he could build another one, easy—and a portable set-up, he could move around from place to place and broadcast a signal directly into different houses. It wouldn't be that hard to hijack a television signal using a portable handheld, and then transmit his own frequency. Of course, he wouldn't be able to interrupt the regular broadcast signal for very long, and it would depend on how close he was to the house to be effective, but he could probably grab the signal long enough to send his own short message about the last big cycle that was coming. If he was able to catch people off guard while they were watching TV, he might likely also be able to scare them into taking the message seriously.

The more he thought about it, the more the idea began to take shape. He could start with his neighbors and then gradually increase the scope of his efforts. He would need to work out a method of getting data to see if the strategy was working, but he could worry about that later, and even if he couldn't figure out a way to get hard numbers, that was probably okay too. Spreading the message might be like scattering seeds. He may need to toss handfuls of them into the wind and hope they were growing somewhere, without ever seeing tangible evidence of any actual plant pushing up out of the soil.

For now, though, he would start with the antenna, and once that was built and ready to go, he would turn to the message itself. He glanced down at the notepad he kept by his radio and read the address he scribbled down a few days ago, not sure at the time why he had felt the need to record it but making a note of it nonetheless. Every night, at the end of his broadcast, the Preacher gave out the address where listeners could send a letter to request their very own copy of the New World Translation of the Holy Scriptures. He always said that once his listeners had their copy, they could check everything for themselves, and they would see that every word of what the Preacher said was absolutely true.

Telly dropped his letter in the mail the next day and eagerly looked forward to his copy of the book arriving. When it did, he started sitting with it in his lap as he listened to the Preacher in the evenings, and he made notes whenever the Preacher mentioned passages about Armageddon or the Resurrection. Those were the themes that Telly felt tied in most strongly to the idea of the cycles, and would also probably make people sit up and pay attention. He used a tape recorder to record himself reading different passages and then played them over, experimenting with different voices that were clear and comprehensible, but that also didn't sound like him. He worked on the antenna and the recordings for some days until he felt ready, and then, as he was putting the finishing touches on the portable set-up, he had a realization.

Resurrect the Dead

For the first time in a long time, he was excited about something. It was like he was a kid again, figuring out how to build his own radio in his room, the voices of his parents muffled outside and him safe in his own little bubble, figuring out how to do something that was worthwhile, something that made a difference. He hadn't had that feeling in such a long time that it felt almost alien to him, as if this was the first time that he had ever felt it. He smiled to himself, and then he began to hum a little. He sat back in his chair and looked out the small window of his trailer, waiting for the sun to set so he could make his first test run around the park.

He couldn't help but feel that it was going to be a good night.

Chapter 18
March 1987

As soon as the worst of the winter passed, Alex started going out to the clearing again. Even though the weather still hovered around freezing some days, every afternoon he crunched through the snowy woods and made his way to the log that he and Alyssa had used as a backrest during the hot and humid days of last summer—days that felt like they had happened a lifetime ago—and there he sat, huddled and shivering, until the sun went down.

One night he heard the faintest strain of music floating on the cold night air and he realized it was coming from the park. As isolated as he felt sitting in the clearing, it reminded him that he wasn't actually all that far away from his own trailer. He listened closely and finally identified the song. It was a bubbly pop song that was currently popular on the radio. Hearing it from such a distance, and while he was sitting out in the dark, cold woods, gave it a different feel. It sounded sad and raw, almost sinister, and not at all like the dumb happy song it was in the daytime. Then again, he told himself, he was probably imagining it. He'd been imagining a lot of things in the last year, and most of them were dark.

From the day the three of them had gotten back last fall, Alex

Resurrect the Dead

felt like he'd been dropped into the middle of a war that he hadn't even known was going on, a war with invisible soldiers and no clear objectives. After what he'd found in Pittsburgh, he knew he would have to take action, but then when they got home and he saw Roger again everything got all muddled up in his head. Instead of executing a rational strategy, he second-guessed himself at every turn, and even though he always came back to the truth, he couldn't seem to make himself go one way or another on it. Days went by, and then weeks, and now here it was months later, and he felt like all he'd done for all that time was sit on this stupid log out in the woods, not even putting up a fight as his own thoughts went to work on eating him alive. Then, somehow, things had gotten worse, so much worse, and any illusion he might have once had of formulating an actual plan had collapsed into nothing more than a day-to-day bid for mental survival.

The day they got back, Alex had dropped Alyssa and Joel off at her mom's place first, and then he went to find Greg. He had no idea what might be waiting for him in terms of Roger, but that hadn't seemed important, not at the time. All he could think about was what he had done to Greg. He'd stolen his car *and* his money. Even though he couldn't imagine that Greg would ever forgive him, he at least had to try to talk to him. But Greg wasn't home. No one answered the door. When Alex peered in the windows, he didn't see anything out of the ordinary, and he knew that Greg should have already been home from work. That left one place he could be. Although he couldn't think of anything he wanted to do less at this moment, Alex made himself turn around and march down the lane to the trailer he shared with Roger. He walked up the few steps to the front door, tried it and found it open, and let himself in.

He found both Greg and Roger sitting in the living room. Roger didn't react at all. It seemed that he thought it was the most normal thing in the world that Alex had just come through the front door, as if he'd only been out getting something at the store and had now returned. He looked at Alex and blinked and then went right back to staring at the television. Alex drew a deep breath and looked around. He smelled cigarettes, and old carpet, and Roger's sour breath. It smelled like the home he had always known, but now he felt like an outsider in it. He suddenly knew how it would have smelled to Joel or Alyssa, or a cop or paramedic, anyone who was setting foot there for the first time. It smelled like a strange house, and like it had nothing to do with Alex anymore.

Greg also looked at him when he walked in the door, but unlike Roger, he kept looking. He blinked a few times, as if he had something in his eyes, but he didn't say anything. Alex walked past him and pulled a chair out from the kitchen table. He turned the chair to face Greg and then sat down. "Greg, I'm sorry." He took a breath and waited a second. "I brought your car back." Greg's face seemed to stiffen and then it cracked. He got up and came over and dragged him up out of the chair and hugged him. Alex stood there, limp, until he finally let go.

"Jesus Christ, are you okay?" Greg asked, looking hard at him and searching his face. Alex saw that Greg's thin sandy hair looked thinner, and grayer. The wrinkles at the corners of his eyes looked sadder. He looked older. Alex knew that he had done this. He was the one who had aged Greg in just a few nights.

"I'm okay. Really, I'm okay," Alex said, rushing through the words just to make Greg stop. He couldn't take him staring at him like that. "I'm okay," he said again. "Greg—the money—" he started, but then Greg grabbed him again and hugged him so hard Alex ended up coughing and choking against his neck.

"It's okay, Alex, it's okay. You're a good kid...a good kid. Roger...he...he had a heart attack, you know. Almost died. I found him when I came here looking for you, after I saw my car gone. Jesus. It was bad...really bad. But...it could have been worse..."

Greg let go of Alex and turned away. He ran a shaky hand through his hair and stood watching Roger. Alex gritted his teeth. Roger was still alive. He didn't realize until he saw him how desperately he had been hoping that Roger had died. But no such luck. He was sitting right over there, in his place on the couch, just like always. Sort of a person. Sometimes. But never someone Alex had understood.

After talking to Greg for no more than five minutes, Alex realized that he most certainly didn't know that Alex had found Roger *before* he took off with Greg's car. He felt shitty about letting him believe that, but there was no point in telling him the truth. Because as familiar as Greg was with Roger's state of affairs, Alex had noticed that he also seemed to have an odd but distinctly defined blind spot where Roger was concerned. He would go only so far and no farther when it came to understanding the true nature of Roger's problems. From certain things Greg had said in the past, Alex got the feeling that Roger had done something for Greg a long time ago, something important, and Greg still felt liked he owed him one. Whatever it was, it didn't matter. Alex knew it would be useless to try explain what had really happened.

Over the next few days, Alex maintained a steady silence about where he had gone and why he had taken off, and Greg didn't press the issue. After a week had passed, it was like nothing had even happened, and he knew that Greg would never ask him about it. He went back to school and started going out to the clearing in the woods in the late afternoons again and life pretty much went back to normal. Only this time instead of meeting Alyssa after school, it was usually Alyssa and Joel.

Since they had gotten back, Joel had been living over at Alyssa's place. Alyssa said she had asked her mom if he could stay with them for a while and her mom said no at first but then he crashed on their couch the next couple of nights anyway and her mom didn't say anything. A few weeks later, Alyssa kicked her little brothers out of the bigger back room so she and Joel could take it over. She said her brothers were now stuck with her old room and laughed as she described them fighting over the tiny closet in it. Joel smiled as she was telling the story, but he didn't say much. He looked over at Alex now and again with a puzzled, uneasy expression, as if he couldn't understand how he'd ended up with Alyssa, who he'd thought was Alex's girl, or how he had come to be sitting with the two of them here in this moment either, as if he hadn't planned any of this at all and he only hoped that Alex didn't blame him for it. Alex noticed Joel's expression but he didn't acknowledge it, he was too tired, and after a while, he stopped noticing it altogether. He was preoccupied with other things.

As the weather got colder, Alex saw Alyssa and Joel out in the clearing less and less often. Finally, after heavy snows at the end of December and the beginning of January, he stopped going out there himself. It was too much work to clear a path through the snow to the woods, so he gave up and stayed home during those winter nights, spending most of his time in his room.

It was during those dark, cold months that he first heard Roger talking in the middle of the night. He had just gone to bed a couple of hours before when he woke up because he heard Roger's voice on the other side of the wall, the wall that his bedroom shared with the bathroom in the back of the house. His first reaction was surprise. It was hard for Roger to get up off the couch and move around, and he usually needed help to get to the bathroom. The fact that he had gotten up and made his way back to the bathroom on his own was strange. Alex was still trying to process this new development when something else caught his attention.

It sounded like Roger was talking to himself. He heard a series

Resurrect the Dead

of grunts, followed by what sounded like confused mumbling. But then he heard something that chilled him to the core and also brought him entirely awake. Roger laughed, and Alex had never heard Roger laugh before. Then he started talking again, but now it didn't sound like he was talking to himself. Now it sounded like he was talking to *someone else*. It sounded like he was asking questions, and then there were heavy pauses, as if he were waiting for answers. But there was no one else in the house. It wasn't possible that there could be. The only person who ever came over was Greg, and he had gone home hours ago.

Alex strained to hear through the wall. Now Roger sounded animated, almost chatty. This was a side of Roger that Alex had never seen. For as long as he'd known Roger—which felt like his entire life—Roger had been stoic and unemotional, almost robotically monotone at times. The voice he heard through the wall sounded like it belonged to a completely different person. He sounded like he was at a cocktail party, engaged in sparkling conversation with...who? An invisible entity? Some hallucination from his own mind that only he could see? Alex had no idea who or what he was talking to, but he didn't like it.

He didn't like it at all.

Alex lay there, unmoving but still listening, trying to shut out whatever was happening in the bathroom by sheer force of will. After a while he gave up. He would just have to wait here until it was over. There was nothing he could do about it right now, except hope that whatever insane thing was happening to Roger would stay mostly contained within him and leave Alex alone, at least for tonight. With these thoughts anxiously swirling in his head, he waited until Roger concluded his conversation with whatever was on the other side, and then listened as he shuffled back out to the living room. When he heard Roger begin to snore from the couch, he was finally able to fall back asleep.

But he didn't sleep well.

Now, as the last of the winter passed—with the skies still dumping snow some days even though it was the beginning of March—Alex sat on his log and thought about things and couldn't help but feel that he was right back where he had started. He was trapped with Roger, with no way out, and now, Roger was even crazier than before. The midnight talks in the bathroom hadn't stopped, in fact, they had only gotten longer—and weirder—Alex thought. He still couldn't make out what Roger was saying, but that didn't reduce the creepiness factor by one bit. It was obvious now that he really did think he was talking to someone else, and what was even more strange was that Alex would swear that this invisible person was giving Roger orders. It was something about the tone of his voice. Even though he mostly mumbled, Alex could hear a note of subservience in everything he said, as if Roger were conversing with someone he felt was his superior.

He had to get his head straight and put together a plan, and he had to do it as soon as possible. Roger's nightly ramblings had stretched his nerves to the breaking point. Maybe that meant he would drop out of school and take off. Or maybe he could get a job and stay around, but find somewhere else to live. Either of those options would get him out of Roger's house. But getting out of Roger's house wouldn't solve what was really eating at him. It couldn't erase the truth, or dissolve the cold paralysis that gripped him whenever he thought about doing something with what he had found in Pittsburgh last fall. No, getting out of Roger's house was only a superficial step toward illusory freedom, because no matter how far away he got from Roger, he knew that it would never be far enough. Roger had taken something from him that he could never get back.

Alex sighed and looked off into the dark woods and thought about how, sometimes, he just wanted to die.

Chapter 19
April 1987

If the voice was going to visit him, it always happened around midnight or 1:00 am, usually after he had dozed off on the couch, and it always came through the TV. The first time it had happened, Roger hadn't understood what he was hearing. He'd been sleeping with the TV on, which he always did. He was so used to the background noise of commercials and canned laughter that it never woke him up. But the voice didn't sound like a TV voice. It sounded like a real voice. It sounded scratchy and earnest and like whoever it belonged to needed to clear his throat. The voice was also louder than the normal volume of the TV, and accompanied by a low buzzing drone and sharp bursts of static. It was one of these crackling pops that woke him up the first time it happened.

On that night, Roger struggled up into a sitting position and stared at the screen of the TV. The picture was doing something weird. It was fading in and out, obscured by those wavy rainbow lines that took over the screen when the antenna went on the fritz. But the antenna was in the same position it always was, and he was sure Alex hadn't been fucking with it. He never did. The TV was solely Roger's domain, there was no reason to believe that Alex had come out here and messed with the antenna while he'd been asleep. And even if he had, that didn't explain the voice.

Then he heard it again. Raspy, almost whispery, as if the person who was talking hadn't spoken in a long time. The voice was speaking English, but the words sounded so sinister, and somehow archaic, that it felt vaguely like some message beamed in from aliens on the other side of the universe, a message that had been traveling across space and time for millions of years to warn humans of some hazy—but certain—future doom.

Look out that nobody misleads you...you are going to hear of wars and reports of wars...these things are a beginning of pangs of distress... Then people will deliver you up to tribulations and will kill you, and you will be objects of hatred...

Roger sat all the way up, paralyzed by cold fear, facing the TV and barely breathing, as if he were listening for the muffled noises of an intruder breaking into his house in the middle of the night.

And I saw the dead...and the sea gave up those dead in it...and death and Hades gave up the dead in them...this means the second death...and then the end will come...

A loud burst of static punctuated the last statement and Roger jumped a little. He stared at the TV so fixedly that if anyone else had seen him, they would have thought he was hypnotized.

Keep on the watch, therefore, because you know neither the day nor the hour...

Then it was over, as suddenly as it began. The picture came back and the sound returned to normal and Roger saw that it was only Johnny Carson on the screen, interviewing some TV star, a woman with honey-blonde hair and a shy smile. She reminded him of someone but he couldn't remember who it was she resembled. He could barely think of anything right now, not after hearing the voice and its doomsday message. He ran a hand over his forehead. He was sweating. He swiped at his beard, brushing off the crumbs from dinner, and then fumbled for his cigarettes sitting on the side table next to him. He got one out of the pack and lit it, drawing the smoke deep into his lungs and then slowly exhaling.

The next thing he knew, he was standing in the bathroom. But he didn't remember how he had gotten there. And he realized he'd been staring into the mirror. Except, it wasn't a mirror anymore. It was more like he was looking through a window and that window gave him a view of a long dark tunnel, with a pinpoint of light all the way down at the very end of it. The tiny dot of light grew until it filled the window, and then the silhouette of a person appeared. What began as a shadow slowly took on more detail until he could see that it was a woman who was standing on the other side of the window where the mirror had been before, and she was looking back at him. Her eye sockets were dark, and her mouth a black hole, but he couldn't miss the delicate bone structure of her face, and he recognized the way her head tilted to one side. It was Mary. Roger stared at her. How had Mary ended up in the mirror? She had been left behind in the jungle all those years ago. But no, here she was, right in front of him. He would have known her anywhere. And then, as he kept his eyes fixed on her, she repeated the message he had heard come through the TV.

I saw the dead...this means the second death...and then the end will come...

Roger nodded. He knew now that the message was true, and Mary smiled with her dark gaping mouth, satisfied that he understood.

Then she began giving him instructions.

As the weather warmed up, more people opened their windows at night, and when Telly drove by slowly in the dark, he could hear the buzz and crackle of their TVs as the signal was interrupted. Sometimes, he could hear the recording of his own voice, floating on the night air, delivering a message that now sounded more ghostly than he had intended when he made the recordings. But that would probably work just as well, he thought. It would be more memorable.

He had started doing his "drive-bys," as he called them, when he'd finished building the antenna for his car in February, and that sense he had of doing something important, something with purpose, had only grown with the passing of time. Every time he got in the car with his homemade portable broadcasting station, he experienced that feeling of being on a mission, and that good feeling stayed with him all through the night and into the next day. Even so, he also had moments where he doubted himself. He wasn't sure the TV messages were enough. He needed to figure out another way to wake people up. He had been deep in the middle of trying to solve this problem when, just as he had before, the Preacher unknowingly gave Telly his next great idea.

That night, he'd been sitting and listening to the Preacher's show as usual, and the Preacher mentioned that—just like people could write him and request a free copy of the New World Bible—people were always free to request a stack of pamphlets that they could distribute door-to-door if they wanted to spread the word. Telly didn't want to go up to people's doors and hand out pamphlets—he never would have done that even if he did fully believe in the Preacher's idea of the coming Armageddon—but it gave him an idea all the same.

He could make his own kind of pamphlets. More like fliers, really. All he would need was a mimeograph machine. He was sure he could get the parts and build one himself, easy. Then he would just have to come up with his own message and print as many copies as he wanted. As long as he wasn't stuffing them into people's mailboxes, he could avoid the attention of the government, and he would still be free to distribute them all over the place. A lot of people wouldn't take them seriously, sure, but maybe it would get some people thinking. It was worth a shot anyway, and also the idea of building a mimeograph machine—which Telly had never tried before—sounded like fun.

Shortly after that, Telly was talking to Ed at work, one of the only guys there that he was truly friendly with, and he mentioned that he was looking for a place that sold old office machinery for parts. Ed smiled and said he could probably root around in the storage closet in the back room of the machine shop. There were a few broken things that had been chucked back there and probably forgotten about. They'd been sitting in that closet for years at this point, he said. No one would miss a thing if Telly harvested whatever he found for parts. And that was where Telly found exactly what he needed. An old mimeograph machine, busted for sure, but Telly knew within two minutes of looking it over that he could fix it.

He was right. Within a few days he had that old machine in good working order. Now he just needed the message he would put on the fliers, which would take a little more time. He wanted to think about it carefully. It was important that he crafted something different than the recordings, but something that went along with them all the same, so that the two messages worked together and didn't just repeat each other. The best time for pondering this, he'd found, was when he was doing his regular rounds, driving around town, pausing at this or that house to interrupt someone's nightly show and plant the seed with them—spread the word, the Preacher would have said. That was too religious for Telly's taste, but he guessed it was all the same anyway. Seed, word, whatever. The important thing was that he kept at it and he didn't give up. He'd been working hard at this whole thing for over three months now and he was sure he would get some sign one way or another soon that his plan was actually working.

As he drove around and thought about what he would put on the fliers, he cranked down his window to let in the breeze. It was a warm spring night, he had good hard work ahead of him, and he was feeling fine. He put on the radio and sang along to it a little. The night was young, and he still had a lot of driving to do.

Chapter 20
June 1987

After Joel moved into Alyssa's mom's house with her last year, Alex had asked Greg if he could get Joel a job at the factory. Greg said yeah, they were always looking for people and you didn't have to be a high school graduate, so it would be a piece of cake. Once Joel was working, he started contributing a sizable portion of his paycheck to bills and groceries and that was when Alyssa's mom realized it wasn't such a bad idea to keep him around. Joel said he didn't mind the work either, a job was a job and as far as jobs went, it wasn't a bad one, so it worked out all around.

Alyssa had turned sixteen a couple of months ago, and then Alex had turned seventeen, and Joel would be twenty soon. But even though they hadn't yet known Joel for a full year, it seemed to her that all of them were so much older than they had been back then. It felt like eons had passed since they got back from Pittsburgh, like they'd known Joel for so long that she almost forgot how they met. But she never forgot how Alex had changed. She missed the old Alex, she missed everything about him. And now those days when he had been her best friend and first love seemed like they had happened forever ago.

It was easiest when all three of them were together and Joel could act as a balancing point between her and Alex. It wasn't lost on Alyssa that most boys would have felt some sort of animosity or competition with each other over her, but with Alex and Joel, it was the opposite. She often felt as if *she* were the one who was left out, as if they had a bond with each other that had already been cemented before she'd met either one of them, even though she was the one who had known Alex first.

Maybe it had something to do with the feeling Alyssa had that her ending up with Joel hadn't been her doing—or Joel's either—but more like something that Alex had orchestrated. She knew she had no rational justification for feeling that way, but she felt it all the same. Alex had never said one word about her and Joel being together. He'd never acted jealous, or awkward, or angry. In fact, he'd never shown any feeling about it at all. When the three of them hung out together it felt as natural as it had when they were on the road to Pittsburgh. But she had that weird feeling all the same, and it was a feeling she couldn't ignore. When they had picked up Joel, she'd been with Alex, and then somewhere along the line—somewhere between Alex leaving them on the sidewalk and then picking them up again and deciding to return home—she had been handed over. The transfer had been invisible and unspoken, but it *had* happened. She was sure of it.

The change in Alex was something she struggled with every day, too. Whenever she thought about it too deeply, a pain started up in her chest and then it was hard to breathe. She was terrified she would forget the way Alex used to be. The sound of his voice, or the shy way he used to look at her. She was scared she would forget all of it and then it would be just like it had never happened. Because the Alex she knew now had a hard edge to him and he wasn't shy at all. He rarely smiled, and when he did, it never reached his eyes. He always seemed to be somewhere else, like he was just going through the motions with her and Joel, just killing time with them while waiting for something else. But for what? What could he possibly be waiting for?

Alyssa didn't know, but she thought Alex—the Alex she knew now—had some idea.

For some reason, that scared her too.

One evening toward the end of June, after Joel had gotten off work, the two of them headed out to the clearing. When they got there, it was deserted. Alyssa looked around, irritated by a mosquito circling near her, and also by the fact that Alex wasn't there. She slapped at her ear to kill the mosquito and felt tears start to her eyes when she slapped too hard. She realized she'd been expecting Alex to be there, as if he'd agreed to meet them at a certain time and hadn't shown up, when of course he hadn't done any such thing, and that made her feel stupid and even more annoyed than she already was. She sat down on the log, rubbing her ear and feeling like she might cry.

"You okay?" Joel asked, coming to sit beside her.

"Have you noticed he's been different?" she said suddenly, knowing her question would seem like it was coming out of the blue at this moment, but also not caring either. She'd been holding back her fears for too long and the tension was killing her. She had to know if Joel noticed it too.

"Who? Alex?"

She nodded.

"Different how?"

"Different. Like, not himself. Not how he used to be."

Joel paused and thought about it. "I don't know. I guess I... well, I didn't really know him before. Before I met you. And him. So...I don't know how he was before. Was he different then?"

Alyssa stayed silent for a few moments. It didn't seem there was any way to talk about how Alex had changed. He had been a different person ever since that day he had left them on the sidewalk in Pittsburgh and disappeared for two hours. When he'd come back, the Alex she knew was gone and another Alex had taken his place. But it was impossible to explain that to Joel, because she couldn't even explain it to herself.

She shrugged. "I don't know," she said. "It's not important, I guess."

As if he'd sensed them talking about him, Alex appeared at the entrance to the clearing. Joel immediately smiled at him but Alex didn't smile back and Joel didn't appear to notice. Alyssa only watched him, studying the expression on his face. He was tensed, waiting. She could see it. He always looked that way now. He never relaxed, not even for a second. Maybe that was one of the things that had changed, Alyssa thought. Before, Alex had smiled and his smiles had been real. He had let his guard down, sometimes.

"Hey," he said.

"Hey man. Wanna smoke?" Joel waved a pack in one hand and Alex shrugged. He held it out to him and Alex came forward and took one, but didn't light it. His glance flickered toward Alyssa.

"Thanks," he said. He stood, watching them, holding the cigarette and bouncing it on one palm.

"What's up man? Sit down, take a load off," Joel said amiably. He moved down to the ground, flopped back against the log, and stretched his legs out in front of him. Alyssa thought she saw Alex relax, just slightly. Part of her felt hopeful, but then another part of her spoke up fast and killed that hope. *So maybe he can relax, at least a little...but what does that prove? He's changed and you know it.*

Alex sat down on the other end of the log and looked over at Joel.

"What's going on?"

Does he think he sounds casual? Alyssa thought. *Does he think I can't tell?*

"Not much man, not much. Same old. You know...living the good life up at Alyssa's mom's..." Joel took a deep drag on his cigarette and then made a fair attempt at blowing smoke rings up into the canopy of leaves above them.

"Is she still a bitch to you?" Alex asked, turning his gaze now to Alyssa. He looked at her expressionlessly, waiting for her answer without a trace of feeling. Alyssa looked at him, and then glanced between the two boys. No, Joel really didn't notice any change in Alex, and for some reason she was suddenly sad that he had hardly known any other Alex than the one sitting before him at this moment.

"Aw, she's not that bad," Joel said softly, looking at Alyssa, who remained unmoved. She was more concerned with what she saw on Alex's face than with anything he might say about her mother. Was Joel really the only remaining bridge between them? Was it because Joel was the one who still had the heart to reach out to both of them, when she and Alex could only sit frozen inside their own minds?

"What are you guys going to do?" Alex asked suddenly.

"What do you mean?" said Joel.

"I mean...what are you going to do? Get married or something?"

"What? Why would you say that?" Joel looked flustered, and confused. Alyssa sat and watched. She stayed frozen.

"Just wondering." Alex lit his cigarette and looked away. Alyssa continued to examine his face but she couldn't read what she found there. There was nothing in his expression. Not curiosity, not envy, not anger. Nothing. He looked as if he were distractedly checking the sky to see if it would rain.

"Well shit, I don't know," Joel said, and he looked back at Alyssa again, but she, too, had nothing for him.

"Who cares?" she said sharply, hurling the words at Alex like a challenge. He held her gaze for a moment, taking a drag and blowing smoke out of his nose.

"I just think you guys have this idea, you know," he said quietly. "That life will get better someday. Like...like it has to or something. And that's not true. It doesn't have to. It's very possible that this is it. This is all there is. And it's not going to get better."

It was more words than she'd heard him say all together in months, and while she was still processing their meaning, she saw the truth that she hadn't been able to read on his face before. She and Joel could have been here or not have been here and it would have been all the same to him. The old Alex was really gone, and there was no feeling in this Alex that applied to either her, or Joel. The dialogue he was having with them at this moment, was only something he was talking out with himself. It had nothing to do with either of them.

"What are you talking about?" said Joel.

"Everyone's searching for something but no one ever finds it. Everyone is looking for something different, and they spend their whole lives chasing after it, but none of them ever *find* it. Everyone thinks things are going to get better. Someday. That they have to get better. But they don't...that's all I'm saying." Alex looked past her and Joel as if he were looking right through them. "They don't."

"Find what? What the fuck are you talking about, Alex?" Alyssa heard the edge of anger in Joel's voice and she knew that Alex had hurt him. "What are all these *things* everyone is chasing after that you're talking about?"

Alex looked at Alyssa, and that was when she saw the old Alex—just for a moment, just a glimpse—and it was enough for her to see that he was still in there, trapped and in pain. He wanted to get out, but like her, he was frozen too.

"Doesn't matter," he said, and now looked away again, apparently unable to meet her or Joel's eyes. "It's all the same thing."

Chapter 21
September 1987

Roger's nightly conversations in the bathroom hadn't stopped, but as time passed Alex realized he had somehow grown more used to them. It was still weird, for sure, but his fear that Roger might be talking to some entity in the bathroom had fallen away. Alex knew that was impossible, and also, there *was* a rational explanation that had been obvious from the very beginning. Roger hadn't been mentally stable for years. Him getting up and talking to himself in the middle of the night was just one more symptom of that. So now, instead of lying awake in bed gripped with panic, whenever Alex heard Roger's voice come through the wall, he only opened his eyes briefly before he settled back into bed under the covers and fell asleep again.

But then one night Alex came awake on his own, without hearing anything from Roger. The house was silent, except for the low drone of the TV out in the living room. Suddenly, Alex heard a sharp burst of static, and then a voice. He got out of bed, crossed silently to his bedroom door, and pressed an ear to it.

Keep on the watch...

Keep on the watch? Was that some show Roger was watching?

Resurrect the Dead

It sounded really strange. He heard a burst of static again. Something must be going on with the TV reception, he thought. Then he heard the same voice talking again, but he couldn't make out what it was saying. It sounded distorted or something. Like a public service announcement made by someone doing a weird solemn fake voice. Then he caught a few words.

I saw the dead...

Alex's stomach dropped. He had definitely heard that, and what he was hearing wasn't coming from any TV show. *I saw the dead....* What did that even mean? It was so creepy it made him feel a little ill. Like he was inside a horror movie. *I saw the dead.* The words, and the voice itself, kept repeating in his mind. Had it come out of the TV? He was sure it had, and that was somehow even more awful. It sounded like some...*thing*...was in the TV, like in *Poltergeist*.

Then he heard another noise from the living room. Roger had started to move.

He unglued himself from the door and dove back into his bed. He faced the wall, away from the door, and made himself lie perfectly still. He heard Roger shuffle down the hall, move past his bedroom, and then go into the bathroom. The door clicked shut behind him and then Roger started talking. After a few minutes, he moved back out to the living room. Alex heard springs creaking and he knew Roger was settling himself back onto the couch. He didn't think Roger would come back to the bathroom soon, but even so, he didn't move from his position in bed. He didn't feel like he could. That voice coming from the TV was easily the creepiest thing he had ever experienced—and after what he'd found in Pittsburgh last year, he'd thought nothing else could ever creep him out again.

He now realized he'd been wrong about that.

What seriously frightened him, though, was a question that had popped into his mind the moment he heard Roger stop moving, just a few moments ago. *What if none of this was really happening?* He desperately hoped that wasn't true, because if it was, then sometime in the last few minutes, he had crossed over into Roger's terrain. That meant he was the one who was hearing voices. Maybe Roger had been out there on the couch the whole time, sleeping, and nothing weird had even happened with the TV. Maybe something in Alex's mind was broken, and he was imagining all of this. Maybe he couldn't trust anything that seemed real. After all, if he was going crazy, then how would he even know that his mind was making all this shit up?

He quietly turned over so that he could lie on his back and stare at the ceiling, and he started going over the facts that he thought he knew. He had heard Roger talking to himself in the bathroom at night. Or, he had *thought* he heard Roger. This had been going on for months. Or, he *thought* it had been going on for months. Tonight, he had also heard a voice coming out of the TV. Or, he *thought* he had heard a voice coming out of the TV. The voice coming from the TV had sounded strange and sinister, and like it was issuing some kind of warning. The voice from the bathroom sounded like Roger, but it also talked a lot and sounded emotional. No one else had ever witnessed any of this, and Roger had never mentioned anything about it. And—Alex couldn't help but take these facts into account too—during the day, when Roger was being his version of normal, he hardly talked at all. He mostly grunted or said one or two words to ask for things. Even on a good day, even back when Roger had had continuous good days, he'd never been a talker. For as long as Alex had known him, Roger had always been sorely lacking in the communication department. But the Roger who Alex heard talking in the bathroom was someone who talked nonstop. That was a version of Roger that Alex had never known.

If he looked at the situation as if he were on the outside—as if someone else were telling him about all of this and he was trying to evaluate just exactly what was going on—he would be forced to admit that the person who said he was hearing these things was probably losing it.

He thought about what the voice from the TV had said. *Keep on the watch...* It wouldn't be that far-fetched to assume that might be coming from his own mind. He'd been keeping on the watch ever since he and Alyssa and Joel had gotten back from Pittsburgh. And the other phrase he'd heard: *I saw the dead.* That made sense too. In the past year, he'd felt so tired and pushed to his limit, he wouldn't doubt it if he was starting to crack up. When he looked at everything that way, he had to acknowledge that it was possible he was losing his grip on reality.

Alex rolled over and faced the wall again. He wanted to think about it more, he really did. He wanted to figure this out, tonight. But his whole body suddenly felt heavy. It was hard to think about anything. Finally, exhausted, he gave up and fell into a deep, dreamless sleep.

Since last fall, Alex had been helping out around Greg's place. In the past few months, he'd been mowing the little lawn Greg had at the back of his trailer, and also pulling up weeds, fixing his shutters, and helping to clean out his garage. Although they never talked about it, they both knew he was doing the work to pay back the money he had stolen. Greg wasn't keeping track of hours, but he did notice how hard Alex was working to pay back the debt, and he appreciated it.

He had also noticed that Alex seemed to be different since he'd gotten back from running off with his car last fall, in some way that he couldn't quite define. He was a little colder, a little more quiet. Or maybe it was just that there was something about him now that felt out of reach. Sometimes he could tell he was only half listening, like his mind had gone somewhere else. There were also moments when it felt as if Alex were watching him. But as soon as he looked up and caught him staring, Alex looked away. Then he felt a bit silly. Alex was a good kid. Greg had never doubted it. He was embarrassed to think that—even for a moment—he'd felt like Alex might have been looking him over in any kind of calculating way, evaluating him with that same dangerous neutrality that he'd seen in the expressions of some of the men he'd known over in Nam—men who had come out of the jungle changed from what they had been before, and not for the better—well, that was just crazy. It was wrong to even entertain that notion.

Greg was also well aware that Alex was seventeen now. He was growing out of being a teenager and into a man. He hadn't had the easiest childhood, either. Life had been hard on him, Greg knew that. He didn't know where Alex's mother had run off to or why, but he did know that for the past few years Roger sure hadn't been able to act as much of a father.

Greg had all of this in his mind on the day that Roger started walking again, really walking. It had been a warm day, even though October wasn't far off, and Greg had been over at their place, sitting in the recliner watching TV with Roger, who was on the couch as usual. Alex had left the front door open and a mild breeze blew through the screen door and into the house and Greg could hear the faint tinkling music of the windchimes on the porch of the trailer next door. Alex had just gotten out of school and was sitting in the kitchen, at their small table that butted up against wall, doodling something or studying maybe, Greg didn't know. But when Roger suddenly stood up and walked to the front door, they both stopped what they were doing and stared. Roger opened the door and went out onto the front stoop. He stood and looked around a moment, blinking in the bright sunlight like a man surfacing from the bottom of the ocean. Then he walked down the steps and Greg lost sight of him.

He turned and exchanged a puzzled glance with Alex, then he got up out of the chair and walked over to the door to peer out to see what Roger was doing. He was still in close proximity, Greg saw, and appeared to be walking around the little plot of grass that served as the lawn to the side of the house. It wasn't the fact that Roger was walking that shocked him—and Greg realized all in one second that shock was really what was hitting him as he stood at the door and watched—but the way Roger was walking. He wasn't shuffling and it didn't seem at all like every step pained him, the way it had for the past couple of years or so. Instead, Roger seemed to be almost striding through that little side yard, walking upright and purposeful, like he had a mission.

Greg didn't know what to make of it, but for some reason he suddenly didn't want Roger to see him at the door, watching him. He backed up fast and got himself back into the recliner just as he heard Roger walk back up the steps. A couple of seconds later he was back in the house. He walked back over to the couch and sank down into it with a groan, as if the effort had tired him out, and then he went right back to watching TV, as if nothing had happened.

Later, Greg thought it was funny that Alex never said anything. It was as if he had picked up on Greg's sudden feeling of trepidation at the door and immediately understood. It should have been a hopeful moment—apparently Roger was improving—but the way Greg had felt at the door, watching Roger walk around the yard, it didn't feel hopeful. Instead, he felt some vague sense of unease, as if things had gotten somehow worse when he wasn't looking.

Within a matter of days, Roger wasn't just making trips outside, he was going down to the end of the lane and checking the mailbox. Then he was sitting out in the driveway, in a faded old lawn chair that they found for him in the garage. With each day that passed, Roger steadily made progress, and Greg knew he should have been pleased, and he was. He *was*. But he also felt nervous, and he couldn't say why. He didn't know what was wrong with him to make him feel that way. Roger was finally up and around again and that was great.

It was only that, sometimes, late at night after he'd gone home and was thinking about it all, deep down he felt nothing but scared, and he had the nagging sense that maybe Alex did too. But before those thoughts could even fully form themselves in his mind, he pushed them away. He was the one with the problem. He couldn't believe he wasn't more excited about Roger getting better. Boy, he really needed to get himself back in line. After everything Roger had done for him, and here he was, almost doubting if Roger's newfound mobility was a good thing. Obviously, Roger was improving and, obviously, he was happy for him, and for Alex.

It was only in the middle of the night, when he suddenly awoke from dreams he couldn't remember, that fear filled his heart again, and a little voice in the back of his mind whispered to him, and he knew what his gut had been trying to tell him. Roger's "improvement" wasn't something to celebrate, but something to fear. But always, after this thought, he fell immediately back asleep, and he never remembered what had happened during the night when the morning came again.

Chapter 22
October 1987

When Joel came home from work one night and said he had cut out early because he wanted to go see the latest Nightmare on Elm Street movie playing at the theater in town, Alyssa rolled her eyes. The last thing she wanted to do was go see a movie. But when she tried to protest, he said, "It'll be fun," in the tone of voice he only used every once in a while that said he was set on something and there was no talking him out of it. So, she resigned herself to it, and told herself she could use a little distraction anyway. Lately, she couldn't stop thinking about Alex. She hadn't seen him at all in the past few weeks. A month or so ago, she'd seen Roger outside, walking around, which had surprised her because she had thought that he was barely able to walk and relatively housebound. Since then, she'd walked by their trailer a few times but she hadn't seen anyone again. The blinds were always down and the house seemed deserted.

"Can we take Alex?" she asked quickly.

"Yeah, of course." Joel paused, thinking about it. "I miss that guy. I haven't seen him in a while." He looked at her and chewed on his bottom lip and Alyssa could see that he meant it, he really did miss him, and it would never occur to him to not let it show all over his face. He was so different from Alex. At that thought, a pang of sadness rose up in her that was so sharp it was almost physical, like something stabbing her in the chest. She nodded and turned away, not giving him a chance to read her face, and walked fast out the door.

When she got outside, she started up the lane toward Alex's place, eying the pumpkins that decorated the stoop of every other trailer she passed. She noticed witches made out of black construction paper taped up in one window as she squished through a pile of brown leaves. It had been raining for the past few days and the night was cold, puddles in the cracked pavement reflected the moonlight in glimmers here and there on the ground. She began to walk faster and then realized how keyed up she was. Finally, she had an excuse to knock on Alex's door and get an inside view of exactly what was going on in there. She didn't know why, but it felt important, crucial even. Part of her felt silly for thinking that, but another part of her knew it was true.

Suddenly, she saw a shadow coming toward her out of the darkness. Alex. She felt her chest tighten. Would there be any chance that she might see a glimpse of the old friend she knew? She felt like she hadn't seen him in forever.

"Alex..."

"Hey." He had seen her before she had seen him. He stood now with his hands in his pockets, on guard, waiting.

"Uh...do you wanna go to the movies?" she blurted out. "Me and Joel are going. We're going to see Nightmare on Elm Street. The new one..."

Alex shook his head.

"No," he said. "No...I can't."

"But why not?" she said, and cringed at the sound of her voice. She sounded disproportionately disappointed, as if she were a small child who had been hurt, and that was what it felt like too, as if Alex had injured her in some way that she couldn't name, but that had wounded her deeply nonetheless.

"Alyssa, I can't. I have to go..." He sounded tired now, and like he just wanted her out of his way. He moved to go around her.

"No," she said, and stepped up to him fast. Before she could think about it, she drew back her hand and the side of her palm connected with Alex's face. His head turned with the force of the hit, and for a moment he left it that way, as if he had just casually turned to look at something in the bushes. When he looked back at her again, his eyes were blank. It was like nothing had even happened.

"I'm sorry Alex...I'm so sorry..." It sounded so stupid. She thought that she had never felt as awful as she did in this moment. When she started to cry, she dropped her head and pressed her hands to her eyes until they hurt. Then she felt Alex's arms around her. He was small enough that she could lay her head perfectly on his shoulder, and so she did and they stood like that. She let him hold her and she cried like her heart was broken. After a minute or two, she calmed down and pulled away. She stepped back and looked at him.

"I got your t-shirt all wet."

"It's okay," he said, and he looked at her and for a moment Alyssa saw the Alex she had always known. He was there for that one second. She could see it in his eyes and hear it in his voice. The Alex that she loved was back.

"Alex? Will you come with us?"

"I have to go," he said, and then he was gone. He turned and walked the other way, leaving her to stand by herself in the dark. She wiped her nose with the back of her hand and shuddered with the cold, watching him until he disappeared back into the shadows. Then she turned around and went back home.

Alyssa sat next to Joel on the dusty threadbare velvet seats of the downtown theater and watched the screen as she shifted in her seat. Joel had one arm around her and his other hand submerged in a bucket of popcorn in his lap. When he'd asked if she wanted any, she'd said no and he'd shrugged and ordered the biggest size anyway. *You have to have popcorn with a movie* he said, and then added that his mother had always told him that every time they went to the movies. Alyssa had nodded but didn't say anything. She'd heard a lot about Joel's mom by this point. She knew that next he would say that his mom also always told him that he had to get butter—*Because if you're going to get popcorn*, she always said, *you have to get it with butter*—and then Joel said those exact words a few seconds later, just as she had silently predicted. She had nodded again, only half listening, and went back to scanning the lobby. She didn't recognize anyone there.

After they'd taken their seats, Joel went back to talking about his mom again. She would *not* have approved of this movie, he said, chuckling and digging into his popcorn. She had railed against Freddy Krueger and the Nightmare on Elm Street movies, and also Jason, and Michael Myers, and every other killer villain in "that kind" of entertainment. Joel's mom was into the Bible. Like, *really* into it, he said. He couldn't remember a day when he hadn't seen her reading it, and she also wanted to talk about it all the time. She specifically liked to point out what she thought someone was doing wrong and then point to some passage in the Bible and explain why that passage showed that the person shouldn't be doing that thing. Of course, he loved his mom, he wasn't saying that he didn't love her, but that didn't change the fact that he felt like maybe the Bible was just a bunch of bullshit and if it *wasn't*—if it truly was all mystical and magical and everything—well, he doubted his mom understood it very much then anyway. His mom didn't have a mysterious bone in her body. She worried all the time and was always fretting, always trying to be in control. Always trying to pin things down between the pages of her precious Bible, he said, looking grimly off into space, as if he might be seeing her there, right in front of him, snapping her Bible open and shut like a trap, hoping to catch something and make it one less thing to worry about.

Alyssa had heard all these details before too. She twisted around to look behind her, looking over the audience and checking the doors where they had come in. No one looked familiar. Then the lights went down and the murmur of the crowd softened into whispers as the movie started.

Joel got absorbed in the movie from the moment it started, seeming to forget that his huge bucket of popcorn was even there. Alyssa had the opposite problem. She couldn't concentrate on what was going on in front of her on the screen. She kept getting lost in her own thoughts and replaying the scene that had happened earlier with Alex. How she had hit him, and how she hadn't felt like herself when it happened. She felt like she'd lost control in some way, like something had taken her over that was too powerful to resist. Now, all she felt was shame, and a deep horrible sadness that felt like it might cut her in two. She replayed how Alex had held her, and how she'd seen him—the *real* him—come back for just a second, before he was gone again.

When she finally pulled herself out of her own dark thoughts, she realized that so much time had passed that the movie was about half over. On the screen, a teenage girl moved slowly toward a flickering TV set, as if mesmerized by what was on the screen. When she banged on it, sinister robotic arms broke through the sides of it and then Freddy Krueger's head—complete with rabbit ears antenna—popped out of the top. "Welcome to prime time, bitch!" he yelled, and then shoved the girl's head through the front of the TV in an explosion of shattered glass. Another character dressed in hospital scrubs burst through the door at that moment and found the girl—now dead, Alyssa assumed—hanging out of the TV, as if the TV itself had killed her.

Joel laughed. Alyssa looked at him and then back at the screen. She tried to focus, but after a few seconds her mind wandered again. She couldn't understand why Joel and Alex loved all these horror movies so much. They weren't scary, just stupid. How could anyone really be afraid of Freddy Krueger? He was like a rock star. A bunch of false parts put together by other people. She looked back at the doorway behind her again. The exit sign glowed above it, but no one appeared. Joel looked over at her and squeezed his arm tighter around her shoulders. When she shrugged him off, he didn't appear to notice. He went back to his bucket of popcorn, avidly watching the screen as Freddy chased another doomed teenager down another final corridor.

Just as she was about to turn around and make one last attempt at watching the movie, the exit sign flickered as someone pushed through the door into the theater. Light from the lobby momentarily flooded in, and then the door swished shut again. She saw a shadow walking down the rows, pausing here and there as if looking for someone, until it made its way over to her and Joel, and then Alex's pale face came swimming out of the darkness. When he saw her, she reached over and took his hand and squeezed it. He sat down next to her and then Joel looked over and saw him and smiled wide. He pumped his fist in the air, once, briefly, and then ducked his hand back into the popcorn in front of him. Within moments, he was immersed in the movie again.

Alex looked over at Alyssa once, holding her gaze, and in the flickering light from the screen she saw the haunted quality of his eyes and the way he pressed his lips together in a thin line. He looked like he was barely holding himself together, like he was drowning inside. But still, he was here, and she knew he had come for her, and for Joel.

Resurrect the Dead

Then he looked away. He didn't look at her again for the rest of the movie.

Chapter 23
October 1987

The next morning, Alyssa woke up and heard the rattle of raindrops on the roof. She opened her eyes to gray light seeping through the windows, and caught a glimpse of the slick and shiny side of her neighbor's trailer showing through a large hole in one of the ragged curtains of the bedroom she shared with Joel. She looked around the mostly bare room, letting her eyes rest on the pile of Joel's work clothes on the floor. Then she turned and looked at Joel where he lay sleeping, breathing deeply, his face creased and untroubled, almost innocent. He looked younger when he was sleeping. She considered this for a moment, and then pushed on his shoulder.

"Joel."

She waited and then pushed again.

"*Joel*."

He smacked his lips and his eyelids fluttered. He rolled over.

"Joel, wake up."

He gave a deep sigh and then she heard him mumble.

"What..."

"I want to get out of here."

He rolled over again and then finally opened his eyes and looked at her.

"What? What time is it?" He laid his head back and closed his eyes again.

"I don't know..." She got out of bed and walked over to the window, flicking back the curtain. She stared at the rain coming down for a few seconds and then turned back to him, impatient.

"*Please* Joel, let's just go."

He blew air out of his nose and stared at the ceiling, his eyes wide and glassy. A few moments later, he sat up and swung his legs over the side of the bed and she heard the clank of his belt as he pulled his pants off the floor and fumbled in the pocket for his cigarettes. He lit one and took a deep, thoughtful drag from it. Then he said:

"Where do you want to go, Alyssa?"

She started shimmying into her jeans.

"I don't care. Anywhere. South or—east—no—how about west? We could drive to California, go to the very end...the very edge of everything..." She grabbed a sweatshirt off the floor and pulled it on. Joel was silent. "Well?" She stood and stared at him and waited.

"Why? Why we would do that Alyssa?" He said it calmly, but when he looked up at her his eyebrows were knit together, and his eyes were serious, concerned. He flicked the ash off his cigarette into the plastic ashtray next to their bed. It chattered against the little side table, a hollow sound that suddenly deflated her. This room, the rain outside, this *life*. She suddenly saw the truth of it. There was no getting away.

"It would be better than here," she said quietly, but she had already lost hope.

"How?" Only Joel's fingers moved, almost imperceptibly, as he tapped his cigarette again on the lip of the ashtray. The rest of him remained still, bent into the shadows of the weak gray light of the room.

"Because..." As she searched for the words, all that lay between them rushed in and filled the space. Last fall, the whole year that had gone by, the memory of the truck stop where they'd stumbled into each other's lives, the next day driving with all three of them in that little car and all three of them so tired...it had been raining then too, and it had been Greg's car...but it had been Alex's decision. Alyssa sank slowly down onto the edge of the bed and stared at her hands. Joel couldn't take her away from any of this. She remembered Alex's grim, determined face as he gripped the steering wheel of Greg's car. She remembered him saying, *Get your stuff. Not too much. Just basic things. Important things. We need to go. Now.* She sat frozen on the edge of the bed, unable to look at Joel. He was right, he didn't need to say it out loud. There was no point in trying to go anywhere, they would never get out of here.

Joel ended up going back to sleep. Alyssa laid down again too, keeping quiet until she heard him breathing slow and deep, and then she got up and left the bedroom, clicking the door shut softly behind her. Once outside, she started for the woods.

It had stopped raining but the air was still chilly. Alyssa trained her eyes on the trees overhead as she entered the path. Most of them had lost nearly all their leaves and looked like bare, black skeletons. Her tennis shoes slipped on the wet grass in places, but she was careful and took her time getting to the clearing. When she got there, she pulled out the plastic tarp that contained all the supplies Alex had put together so long ago. It was still in its place under the pile of branches at the edge of the trees. She couldn't remember when they had last gotten into it and used anything. She unpacked the sleeping bag and draped half of it over the log so she would have somewhere dry to sit. Then she sat down and crossed her ankles, hunching into herself to keep warm. She could wait for quite some time, if she had to.

But then, only a few minutes later, Alex showed up.

When he came out into the clearing, he didn't look surprised to see her. He walked over to where she was sitting as if they had planned to meet at exactly this time. He sat down on the sleeping bag next to her.

"Hi."

"Hey," he said, He turned and gave her a slight smile when he spoke. As small as it was, it was the first real smile she'd seen out of him in a while. For a moment she was so startled by its unexpectedness, and the familiar gentle expression in his eyes that accompanied it, she thought she might burst into tears.

"You know...Alex...I really *miss* you."

Before she could stop herself, she grabbed him around the neck and pulled him into her. She hugged him so close and hard that she could feel his heart beating under his shirt. She buried her face between his collarbone and his throat, hiding her expression. She knew she would only have these few seconds with him—he was *letting* her have them for some reason—but then he would go back to the Alex she had seen for the past year, the cold diffident person she had grown to distrust, and sometimes, to fear.

She pulled away and he offered her that sweet, shy smile again and she almost started crying a second time. "I'm such a spaz," she said, trying to laugh to cover the moment, but the expression on Alex's face didn't change. She knew he wouldn't laugh along with her, not even to relieve her embarrassment. Alex never laughed—he never did anything—unless he meant it.

"You're not a spaz," he said seriously and then put an arm

around her and hugged her to him, but she could tell his mind was already somewhere else.

"Alex...I can't stand it here."

"I know." He squeezed her tighter for a moment and then let go and turned to look at her. "But you're gonna get out. This is nothing. You won't even remember it here. It'll be like it happened to someone else...like it happened a long time ago. When you're out of all this, it'll be almost like it never happened at all." He paused and a look of wonder came over him, as if he had just realized something. "You'll be *shocked* at how much it will be like it never happened."

Then he got up and started pacing around the clearing. She watched him walk in circles, her skin tingling still from his touch, her body from the force of his words, and she was suddenly afraid it would rub off—whatever power he had momentarily blessed her with—and she would lose it. She studied his face, trying to understand what was inside him, what he was thinking and how he could affect her this way. But Alex was lost in thought and didn't look at her again. It was as if she wasn't even there. A cold wind came up and lifted one part of the old sleeping bag and it fluttered in the air before settling back to the log again, the end of it falling onto the ground. Alyssa suddenly thought how sad it looked lying there in the dirt, and for some reason it made her think of the movie they had seen last night, and how Alex had left early and now— even now, when he was right in front of her—he wasn't really there.

Later, she realized that was the last time the three of them were all together, watching a stupid movie about Freddy Krueger, and she only wished she could remember more about that night, before everything else happened and she lost Alex forever. The only thing that made her feel any better about it later was that she remembered meeting Alex that next day in the clearing. She

Resurrect the Dead

remembered how it had felt to hold him and feel his heart beat under his shirt, and the serious look on his face when he told her she wasn't a spaz. She remembered everything he said to her, every word, and she never forgot it.

Not even when every other trace of Alex was gone.

Chapter 24
November 1987

Roger had assumed that he was only able to contact Mary through the mirror after a message came through the TV. It seemed that the voice was some kind of signal that let him know that she was in the mirror and waiting for him. But then one night he went to the mirror and stood in front of it, waiting patiently, and after a while he saw that tiny little light that was so far away, like a light at the far end of a tunnel. Soon it grew brighter, just like it always had before, and then the shadow shape formed and became Mary right in front of him.

So, he didn't need to wait for messages from the TV after all, and that was good, because he hated waiting to talk to Mary. He wanted to talk to her every day. Pretty soon, he started doing just that. Then their conversations turned into something else, or rather, started happening *somewhere* else. Every time Mary showed up now, she beckoned to him and held out her hand and Roger leaned forward and took it. Then he went through the mirror.

He came out on the other side alone, standing in a clearing in the jungle. In the middle of that clearing was the mansion he had built to be his special place with Mary all those years ago. The path of flat stones that led up to the house was the same, although some of the stones were completely buried in the earth now, which gave the path the look of a gap-toothed curving smile that led up to the entrance. The steps to the porch had also partially disintegrated, with a few of them being nothing more than splintered boards, looking sharp and dangerous and ready to do serious damage to anyone who wasn't paying attention. But when he opened the front door and entered the great hall, there was Mary, waiting for him, like she always had before. The long table full of silver dishes was there, and so was the chandelier. Everything was the same. It was just like old times.

Except, a few things were different, and it wasn't just the stones that made up the path or the steps outside. Lately, Roger could have sworn the chandelier was...*almost*...moving. It never happened when he looked directly at it, only when he was looking somewhere else and caught it out of the corner of his eye. The décor in the mansion had always been strange, that hadn't changed, and Roger remembered that same chandelier from before because it resembled some sinister undersea creature. The branches of the chandelier still looked like tentacles, and in the center of it, there was still what appeared to be a sharp, black beak. Like a parrot's beak. Roger remembered all that, but he didn't remember it ever moving before. But now, sometimes, it seemed like it did, and he had a feeling that every time he turned away one of those tentacles started writhing in the shadows, and the huge beak in the center slowly opened and closed, silently biting at the air. But then, no, he was wrong. He turned and looked at it and it looked just like it always had, an odd fixture in a crumbling hall that had long ago been something grand.

At this point, Roger's attention was usually diverted by Mary, who led him out to the veranda, and he knew he had to ready himself to pay close attention. Because Mary had been giving him things to do these last few months, and each thing was very important and must be done exactly the right way. So, he tried to listen carefully, because he didn't want to miss one word, or forget anything. On this night, Mary's instructions were brief.

"Get rid of him," she said. Her dark eyes glinted like water under moonlight and it sounded like she had a throat full of gravel. He had noticed that her voice was worse every time he saw her. It had become progressively rougher and deeper, and more distorted, as if something had damaged her throat, or was slowly eating away at it.

"Who?"

"Greg," she said, and then a slow, cold smile spread across her face.

He looked at Mary for a long moment, and then nodded. If Mary wanted him to do it, it would be done. He put a hand over his face and closed his eyes. When he opened them again, he was lying on the bathroom floor and the mirror was empty, but he remembered what Mary had said.

Get rid of him.

Greg.

He would do it.

~

"That's right, you heard me," Roger said, his eyes narrowed. "I said get outta my house."

Purely out of reflex, Greg smiled. He usually did this before even processing what someone else was saying to him. He had never fought with anyone, not since Nam. In fact, confrontation in any form made him nervous. He had seen Roger get touchy on occasion, and Alex had said things in the past that led Greg to believe that Roger sometimes went into a rage at night when he was having one of his episodes, but Greg had never personally witnessed it, and he'd never before been met with this cold,

Resurrect the Dead

furious energy coming off him now. Roger's eyes were blacker than Greg had ever seen them, and his face was set in an expression of ruthless dismissal. If he hadn't known it was Roger he was talking to, he would have barely recognized him.

"Roger...I...what's going on?"

He felt the smile slipping off his face as he groped for words. The attack had come out of nowhere. He had stopped by after his shift with a load of groceries, and when he'd put everything away and popped a can of soda off the ring, turning as he shut the refrigerator door, Roger was waiting for him. His fists were clenched and a cunning snaky look moved in and out of his eyes. The Roger he had grown used to over the past few years was slow and a little soft, like a small child who needed to be led places. The Roger who stood in front of him now was a massive black-bearded man built like a lumberjack. He looked like he wanted to hurt someone, and he didn't much care if it happened to be Greg who had stumbled into his path. No, he really didn't look like himself.

"What's going on?" he finally managed, trying the smile again.

"What's going on is that you need to get the fuck out of my house." Roger's voice sounded like a growl coming from the back of his throat.

Greg stared at him, dumbstruck, and then Roger started toward him.

"Okay, okay. Okay, Roger!" He backed up fast and hit the refrigerator. He clutched his soda and squeezed it too hard. Cold foam drenched his hand as it spilled out of the top of the can. Roger halted, watching the drops of liquid as they spread across the linoleum at their feet. "Okay, Roger. I'll go." He reached behind him and deposited the soda on the counter, sidling out from underneath Roger's shadow. He walked quickly to the living room and grabbed his jacket and then made for the door, Roger following him the whole way. He had the uneasy awareness of some sort of prey animal being stalked, as if the small space between the kitchen and living room of the trailer had turned into a jungle. He got to the front door and violently jerked the handle, his mind racing. He felt like Roger might clobber him from behind at any moment, and was that really so crazy? He had seen murder in Roger's face just a few seconds ago, he could swear it. What had he done? What the fuck was going on?

Greg checked behind him again as he opened the door and scooted outside. Roger was still coming. "So long Roger..." he said, hearing a shaky voice come out of him that he barely recognized. He slammed the door behind him and jogged down the steps and into the lane, stopping there to get his breath and let his heart work through its frantic trip-hammering beat. He watched the door for a few moments, convinced Roger would come bursting out of it, but nothing happened. The door stay closed for as long as Greg stood there. Roger never came outside.

I guess I won't be seeing you anymore, Roger, he thought. And then: *I'm sorry, Alex, I tried to do the best I could for you. Dear God, I really tried.*

He took a deep breath and one last look at the door, and then he started for home.

Chapter 25
November 1987

On the nights that he went out, Telly still started by driving around the park and blasting the message through the TVs of his neighbors. He figured that repeated exposure to the information most likely increased the chances of getting through to some people and so it was a strategy worth pursuing. But as time went on, he also started branching out and traveling farther away because he didn't feel like he was doing enough, limiting himself to the one little town he happened to live in. He could reach more people in a larger, more urban area.

Some nights he drove two hours all the way to Detroit. He drove up and down the streets of derelict neighborhoods with crumbling sidewalks and a lot of different houses that had boards nailed across at least one window—like a patched-up blind eye in the middle of a scarred face—and he slowed his car to a crawl and looked for the telltale white glow through a window that said someone was sitting up late watching TV. When he found it, he stopped in front of the target house for a few moments, sent the message through, and then moved on to the next one.

He wheat-pasted his fliers all around town too. Since he saw lots of other fliers pasted up on the wood panels of the construction hoarding walls around different building sites, he started there, but he also pasted them on telephone poles, electric boxes, newspaper boxes, and dumpsters. He tried to think about places that people would not only see them, but also wouldn't be able to escape them, like intersections where maybe someone might be stuck sitting in traffic, or near city benches where a person might hang out for a while. Because he had limited space on the fliers, he'd had to streamline the message. He had carefully cut it down to what he felt were the briefest—and yet still the most informative—parts of the text.

Flier number one read:

You are going to hear of wars
These things are a beginning
people will kill you
You will be objects of hatred

Flier number one was done in plain simple text, with no decoration at all. On flier number two he had added the illustration of a watch, which he had drawn himself and he quite liked. It went well with the message, which was the shortest out of the entire set:

Keep on the watch
You know neither the day nor the hour

On flier number three, he'd gotten the inspiration to use another drawing he did of skull and crossbones. He felt the skull imagery was eye-catching, and out of all of them, he expected that the most people would probably stop and give this one a closer look. Flier number three read:

I saw the dead
Hades gave up the dead

Resurrect the Dead

This means the second death
Then the end will come

Driving around downtown and throughout the different areas of Detroit all night long, looking for more places to paste up his fliers, he sometimes felt like he was on another planet. The streets were usually deserted. The pavement gleamed eerily under the streetlights and often the only sign of life he saw was the occasional neon sign in different store windows. Sometimes though, he passed small groups of young black men huddled together on a corner, but they were always silent as he drove by. If his windows were down, he heard nothing. If the windows were up, he furtively glanced at their mouths as he passed, but he never saw their mouths move. Sometimes they pretended they didn't see him —he could tell they were pretending, he didn't know how he knew that, he just did—and sometimes they stared after him with baleful eyes and he felt suddenly afraid and held his breath until he saw them disappear in his rearview mirror.

That feeling of fear had grown stronger in Telly lately. He had started to feel it not just when he saw those men on the corners, but all the time. He had never been able to trust anyone, that much wasn't new, but this feeling was different. He felt watched, that was the only way to put it. Yes, more and more lately, he felt *watched*.

At first, he tried to shrug it off, but then, the more he thought about it, the more he could see how it might actually be true. He wouldn't be surprised if there were folks out there who didn't like that he was spreading the message about the cycles, who didn't *want* him to be informing people about what was really going on. If those people knew about what he was doing, then Telly thought that, yes, very probably they would try to stop him, and maybe they wouldn't be above using extreme measures to get their way. That wasn't out of the realm of possibility.

Telly drove around the empty streets, chewing over these things in his own mind, and he thought that he had never felt so alone, which was saying a lot because, really, he'd felt alone his whole life. He wished he could rewind time and go back to just a few months ago, when he'd first started doing the work of spreading the message. He had felt like he was doing something that mattered, and the fact that he was doing something that mattered was *all* that mattered. But then as the weeks wore on, that subtle sense of following an important purpose had waned. In recent days, he'd sat tinkering in his backroom workshop or making more copies of the fliers and ended up asking himself why he was even doing it. Was he really making a difference? Were people hearing the messages he was sending out? Was anyone even taking them seriously? In his darker moments, he thought, probably not. In his very darkest moments, he figured he should give up trying.

For as long as Telly could remember, he had never been able to get through to another human being. Not ever. Not one single time. His dad had always been too drunk, his mom always locked in a prison of self-pity, and every other person he'd ever met impossible to reach for some other reason of their own that Telly had no control over and couldn't get past. That's why he was so good with machines, he thought, it wasn't hard to see that. Machines were easy to fix. They only went wrong in a certain number of different ways. All you had to do was check their parts and then find the broken one and repair or replace it. A machine wouldn't suddenly lash out at you and try to hurt you for no good reason. It wouldn't pretend to be one sort of machine when, deep down, it was really something else. Machines made sense. They were sane, and reasonable.

He didn't understand why people weren't the same way.

He supposed *that* was why he kept on with his project of spreading the message, because it gave him that same feeling of

Resurrect the Dead

fixing something. He might not believe in the Preacher's version of Armageddon, but he did believe there might be a spirit world beyond this one, some invisible realm that worked in subtle but direct correspondence with life on earth. Maybe something had gone wrong in that other world a long time ago, some part had been broken and needed to be repaired or replaced, and that's why life on earth had gone so wrong. If he could help people to wake up and look around at things so they could fix whatever was broken in this world, and in themselves, then maybe everything would line up again, and then both worlds—the invisible world of spirit and the one he lived in—would come back to harmony and order. He knew it was unrealistic, but he also couldn't get away from it. There *was* a chance that he was repairing something by doing the work he was doing. It seemed best to keep right on doing it.

It all sounded crazy if Telly really thought about it, but a lot of things sounded crazy if you said them out loud. That didn't mean they really were. But still, sometimes he remembered the glassy vacant look in his dad's eyes when he'd been drinking, and how his mom had wielded her power as the tearful martyr, and then he began to doubt again. It seemed impossible that he would ever get through to anyone with the message, no matter how urgent or important it was. But it also didn't feel like it was up to him anymore. He was beginning to think he'd been given a mission—by God or something else, he didn't know—and that was all that mattered. Even if he was being watched—even if others might try to stop him—he couldn't let that stand in his way, because he had important work to do. So, there was nothing else he *could* do, except keep trying.

With these thoughts in mind, Telly kept on driving around and blasting his message through people's TVs and pasting up his fliers whenever he saw a promising space for them, and he realized somewhere along the way that he might be doing this for many years, maybe even forever, and at some point, the deep anxiety that lived in the shadows within him began to make an uneasy peace with that.

Probably because he really had no other choice, he thought. The only alternative was to give up, and that would lead to nothing but despair.

Chapter 26
November 1987

Greg had quit drinking in 1974, and although AA had helped him get back on his feet back then, at this point he hadn't been to a meeting in years. He had never thought that he missed them either. He had nothing against the meetings, he just felt like he'd come to a place where he didn't need to go anymore, because he'd felt all right. Staying sober wasn't a challenge because he could get through life on his own, without the booze. But in the past week or so, since Roger had thrown him out of his house, he'd been dreaming about Nam again. He woke up shaking and sweating, and sometimes gasping and crying. In the dreams he saw piles of corpses, and some of them stayed laying in the piles and some of them came to life and started coming after him. All of them were gray and rotting, and falling apart like old houses caving in on themselves.

After a week or so of the nightmares, he knew that if he didn't do something to kill the dreams, he would end up going insane, and if it was between insanity and having a couple of beers, he would choose the couple of beers. There was no one around to notice that he was drinking again anyway, he thought to himself.

Not that Roger would have noticed, even if they were still speaking, but Alex sure would have. He might not actually have said anything, but he would have given him one of those Alex looks—quiet, but appraising—the kind of look that goes through you like a blade, and then you're left staring at your own secret cut open in front of you. If Alex had looked at him like that, Greg knew he probably would go back to the meetings. He would find some way to shove the nightmares outside of his head and build a padlock on his mind.

But Alex couldn't give him that look, or any kind of look, because Alex wasn't there. Greg couldn't go over to Roger's to see him and he hadn't seen him around. He couldn't remember the last time he *had* seen him, as a matter of fact, it was like he had just disappeared. So, he didn't go back to the meetings, and he didn't need to deal with the nightmares, the beer did that for him, and he kept that can of beer where it wanted to stay, right there in his hand.

He started stopping by the party store on his way home from work every evening to pick up a six-pack, and then when he got home, he sat in his recliner and watched TV and worked his way through each can, trying not to think about the past, or what might be going on down at Roger's place. As much as he tried to forget though, it all came creeping back in anyway. He remembered when Roger had first shown up at his door with Alex, and how they had stayed with him until they got their own place. He remembered what Alex's eyes had looked like when he was just a little four-year-old boy. He had known that Alex trusted him even at that time, he could sense it. Alex had needed someone—that was more than obvious, Greg thought, after all, he was a little boy who had just lost his mother—but it was more than that. There had always been something in Alex, a restless, searching sort of hunger, an untouchable loneliness that shadowed his every

Resurrect the Dead

expression, and it had remained year after year, even after Alex had grown from a little boy into a young man. Greg had never encountered anything more heartbreaking in his life than that loneliness that surrounded Alex. He'd always thought that—even though he'd had Roger—what Alex had really always needed was a dad.

And Greg had always wanted a son.

Every once in a while he caught himself thinking that it would have been better if Alex had left Roger and come to live with him. But then he immediately cringed and hated himself for that thought. How ungrateful could he be? He owed Roger so much, and here he was, secretly wishing he had been the one to end up with Alex. God knows he would have been happy to take him in all those years ago when he was still the grubby little boy with the light brown feather-fine hair and huge brown eyes—and he would be happy to take him in now, if he needed it—but he would never have taken Alex *away* from Roger. *That* was not right. Roger had saved his life. He would never, *ever* stoop so low as to take away the person Roger loved most.

Because Roger did love Alex, he was sure of that. Roger was a strange one—and he'd always been strange, it was true—but he was loyal and brave and Greg knew he considered himself to be a father to Alex. He had always taken care of Alex as best he could, even after he'd gotten so sick the past few years. He'd given up damn near everything to serve his country, and he'd saved people who maybe didn't even deserve to be saved—and here Greg inwardly cringed again without even knowing it—and he was a better man than most. As baffled and hurt as he was about how he'd been thrown out, he could only assume that Roger had his reasons. Even if he personally couldn't come up with the tiniest clue as to what those reasons possibly were, he had to trust Roger's judgment. They must be very good reasons indeed.

Greg reached down and pulled another can off the plastic ring of that night's six-pack. He was tired of thinking. He changed the channel until he found a cop show he liked, popped open the can and took a long drink, and a few moments later he was absorbed in the story.

He didn't think any more about it that night.

Chapter 27
July 1972

When the shit hit the fan that day, everything started happening really fast. Greg always thought that was funny, because in the movies when things go crazy, they always slow everything way down. You get the impression that when you're in the middle of an apocalyptic crisis you can expect that seconds will feel as long as minutes, and minutes as long as hours. That everything will happen in slow motion and you'll get to see it happening like that, and have all the time in the world to leap forward and catch something important, or fall back and dodge the bullet coming straight for you. But in real life, Greg found that it wasn't like that at all. Things just started happening and it all happened so quickly that everything was a blur. One moment he had been with his unit as they made their way through the jungle, and then there was a crack and a boom like the sky was splitting open and the ground shook like there was an earthquake, and suddenly everyone was gone and he was all alone on the jungle floor, his leg twisted underneath him at an unnatural angle. He knew his throat was filled with smoke, and that he was surrounded by fire on all sides. He didn't know how his leg had gotten twisted, or where the rest of his unit had gone.

It had been a cluster bomb, of course. It couldn't have been anything else. Just a couple of weeks before, they'd heard rumors that US forces had been scattering them over the territory in an attempt to disrupt supply lines from Laos, and apparently those rumors were true, because when that thing hit the ground the wall of heat that radiated out from it felt like an actual ocean wave passing over him, if ocean waves were made out of lava. It wasn't until afterwards that he realized his eyelashes and the hair on his arms had been singed off. He remembered lying on the ground, and he thought he was screaming but he also couldn't be sure. He seemed to be very far away from himself, and also trapped on the ground at the same time. There was fire and there was pain, and that was all his mind could register at the time.

Then there was Roger.

He had still been screaming—he thought—when Roger walked into the circle of flames, gently lifted him off the ground, and then carried him out of it. He walked with Greg slung over his shoulder, calmly moving through the brush, somehow finding a way out of the flames. Greg remembered seeing the fire in the sunlight, and thinking how clear and beautiful it was. He remembered his throat burning, and how it felt like a raw wound with salt rubbed into it. He remembered that he tried to talk, he tried to say something to Roger, anything, but he couldn't, and so he gave up talking and just let himself be carried, feeling like maybe he might die and hoping he wouldn't.

Roger walked and walked and then at some point Greg passed out. When he woke up again Roger was still walking, and still carrying him. He smelled smoke but he didn't see any fire. He didn't feel any heat. Roger was walking along the edge of a shallow gully that looked like it had maybe been a stream at one time, but now was dry. A low range of hills was to the right of them, covered in jungle brush, and long shadows fell over them. It was late in the evening.

Resurrect the Dead

Roger swerved over to a clump of trees, gently laid Greg down at the foot of one of them, and then set about making camp. Greg's leg still hurt, but he was able to sit up against the base of the tree and watch Roger. His head felt thick and fuzzy and his throat ached. He kept trying to understand what had happened and what was going on with him now, but he couldn't keep hold of a thought. Then it all came back. The explosions and the screaming and the fire. He felt like he was going to be sick. He moved down to the ground and curled up into a ball, breathing hard, his eyes wide and staring, sweat trickling into his eyes. He was hollow all the way through, just like a hollow bone, he could feel it. He was a shell, lying on the ground, forgotten and empty, and every breath he took was the wind whistling through him. He clutched his own arm and had a hard time believing it was there, it felt like an arm, but an arm that belonged to someone else. He couldn't feel himself feeling himself. It was the most disorienting feeling he'd ever had in his life.

After a while the feeling subsided, or maybe Greg just pushed past it, he was never really sure which. At any rate, he was able to lift himself off the ground and take the food Roger gave him. Swallowing was hard but he made himself do it. He had no idea where they were or what had happened to his men or how to get back to anywhere for help. He would need to make himself eat, even if it was painful.

That night Greg slept while Roger kept watch. In the morning Roger said only, "stay awake," and then promptly fell into a deep, untroubled sleep on the ground nearby. After only an hour had passed, he woke up as if he'd slept the whole night through, packed up their little camp, and then walked over to Greg and pointed at his leg. Greg knew what he meant.

"I think I can walk," he said. "I can't have you carrying me all day again."

Roger only shrugged, as if carrying Greg all day again would be no big deal. Then he helped him stand up, adjusted his pack on his shoulders, and the two of them moved on.

They were together for the next two weeks.

Greg limped alongside Roger as they made their way back into the jungle, and then his leg seemed to get better as they hiked slowly forward over the next few days. He never questioned where they were going or when they would get there. It didn't matter and he also didn't really care. They moved mostly at night and slept during the day, Roger leaving periodically to get fresh meat. Mostly he caught monkeys, but sometimes he returned with bats, or turtles, and one time even a snake. He split the animals apart with his knife and roasted them over the small fires he built. Greg dutifully ate the pieces Roger gave him, chewing them apathetically while staring into the fire. Although they must have traveled miles and miles during that time, there didn't seem to be any change in their location. Awake or asleep, Greg felt like he was caught in the same cycle of morning, afternoon, and evening, endlessly replaying itself over and over again.

He barely spoke, and Roger didn't say much either, although he did tell Greg his name when he asked. Beyond that, Roger's communication mainly consisted of grunting to himself as he went about setting up and tearing down their little camp every day. Every once in a while he would say two or three words to give Greg a direction, or he would ask how his leg felt and if he could walk any more that day. Whenever they bedded down for the night, he made sure Greg was as comfortable as he could be on the ground, and every morning when they got up, he checked Greg's eyes and skin, making sure he showed no signs of infection or illness.

Then, one night after they had made camp and had dinner, Greg felt something crumble inside him. He stared up at the stars, each one of them a slit in the flesh of the night sky, like tiny open wounds of light, and he remembered looking up at the stars when

Resurrect the Dead

he had been just a boy, and then before he knew it, he was shaking, and crying. He sat there with his arms wrapped around himself and cried violently without making a sound. He could feel his face stretching and contorting into grotesque shapes, but he couldn't stop. He wanted to scream. He wanted to open up and let go with everything he had and get this poison out of him, the explosions and the screaming and the fire, the way it had smelled —he had smelled people *cooking* and known they were his own men—the sound of the sky cracking open, the pain and the fear, all of it. But he couldn't make a sound and he knew that. Charlie was still out there, might be watching them right now for all he knew. Until they got the fuck out of this jungle and to wherever Roger was taking them, Greg would have to swallow his screams, and every last drop of poison, with them.

He felt like he had almost completely lost his mind, and he didn't know how to get a grip on himself again. He looked over to where Roger was sitting in the moonlight, still and stoic, with his face turned up to the sky, and he thought to himself that Roger looked like a very wise being, someone who knew the secrets of life, and who could bring him to the other side of this horrible, hellish journey. Roger had broken through a barricade of fire to get to him and save him, and then gotten them through miles and miles of enemy territory without getting them killed, keeping them both alive through constant foraging and hunting, and he looked as calm and serene as a man who was sitting out in own his backyard under the stars, fully at home. Every night when they camped somewhere, Roger did this. He sat and stared and said nothing, but Greg could see it in his eyes. Roger was going somewhere else, far away in his head, and Greg wanted to know how he did it, how he could look so peaceful in the middle of this nightmare, and he wanted to know how he could learn to do it too.

For the first time in many days, Greg spoke first.

"Roger...how do you...how do you do it? I-I-I'm a mess...but you...you're okay. You're *okay*." Greg let out a long exhale of breath and suddenly everything else came out too, all his fear and his pain and his worry. Everything. He couldn't stop talking. He started with how he had lost the rest of his unit and his fears that no one else had made it out alive, and then he tried to describe how his thoughts had been since then, flying everywhere at once like a spooked flock of birds rising from the trees, but then dying all at once too and leaving him with a nauseating feeling of blankness, as if his head were stuffed with cotton. He told about how confused he was. He didn't know where they were, or what day it was, or when they would get out of this, or what was coming next. He talked about all of it, and he talked for a long time. Finally, when he was done, he took a breath and then glanced over at Roger, who he had been afraid to look at the whole time he'd been talking. He probably thought he was a nutcase, the way he'd been babbling on, but still, he felt better, washed out, cleaner, and he knew at least a little of the poison had gone out of him with his words. Roger looked at him, expressionless.

"We're safe..." he said, and then he paused and looked like he was concentrating, trying to figure something out. "As long as...he doesn't come back."

Safe as long as he doesn't come back? What did that mean? What was Roger talking about? Then it hit Greg, and he understood, and couldn't believe he didn't get it before, it was so obvious.

"Jesus, Roger, you're right. We *are* safe, as long as Charlie doesn't come back. Here I am blabbing on about a lot of shit that doesn't matter when I need to see what's really important. All that matters is that I get my head on straight so I can help you however I can to get us out of here."

"The man with the bowl."

"What?" Greg wasn't sure he'd heard that correctly.

"The man with the...*bowl*." Roger looked at Greg and cupped his hands together in front of him. There was a spark of emotion in his eyes that Greg had never seen before. He sat back and tried to understand what he was saying. Then, he got that too.

"The whole world in his hands! Shit, yeah! You're right. He's got the whole world in his hands, God does. And he's holding us too. Looking out for us. We're going to be all right. God's with us. God's *with* us, Roger. Holy shit, yeah." Greg felt the tightness that had been in his chest for so many days loosen and he realized he didn't feel like crying anymore, he felt like laughing. Roger really was a wise man, and Greg had known it all along. Roger knew what he was doing and Roger would bring them out of this. All he had to do was trust him.

That night, Greg slept better than he had in a long time, and when they rose the next morning it felt like a whole new world to him, full of possibility. They were going to get out of this, someday he would get back home, and everything was going to be okay. As long as he trusted Roger. He knew now, that was the secret, that was the key. And so, from that day on, he did just that. Greg trusted Roger with his life, and he never doubted him again.

Chapter 28
June 1974

The whole time he was in the hospital, Roger thought about Mary. He had met a lot of different guys in school when he was growing up, and over in Nam, and it seemed like all those guys had a girl. Even some of the guys in the hospital had girls who visited them on weekends—Roger saw them sitting at the tables in the visiting room when he walked by with the other patients on the way to outside recreation on Saturdays—and he saw that the girls brought food and candy and magazines and cigarettes. No one ever came to visit him, and no one ever brought him anything. He'd never had a girl to call his own before Mary, and he'd never had anyone after her either. It wasn't fair.

Then, when he got out of the hospital and ended up at the bus station and Linda had walked into his life, he'd seen instantly that she was an angel and he knew that he couldn't let her get away. There was something about her that was special. He was enchanted, and also surprised at himself. Because even though he'd dreamed of having a girl of his own while he was in the hospital, he'd thought that Mary was the only woman he would ever love. Although, since getting out of Nam, he hadn't been able to go to the mansion like before. He didn't know why, he just couldn't, no matter how hard he tried to dream himself there. And that wasn't Mary's fault. He had the feeling that she was still waiting patiently for him until he could get back to her. But if he thought about it too hard, his head started to feel like someone was driving nails through it, so he tried to stop thinking about it, and after a while, he finally did. And now, he didn't want to bring those thoughts back again and risk the pain, or the heartache.

Then, suddenly, here was Linda. A woman who looked like an angel and gave him that same feeling he'd had when he was with Mary, and she had somehow materialized right in front of him at this one lonely bus stop. When he saw her, all his old longing for Mary dissolved, and when she spoke to him, every pain he had ever suffered seemed to melt away. But the very next moment he went cold with fear. He realized with near certainty that the bus was going to arrive at any second and then she would get on it and be torn away from him, just like Mary had been. He couldn't let that happen. This time he had to make sure that the woman he loved didn't slip away from him. Then, right after he had that thought, he looked over, and he realized Linda had someone with her.

It was a little boy. He was three or four—or maybe five—years old. Roger couldn't tell. He hadn't been around kids in a long time. The boy had light brown hair, and big brown eyes set in a delicate, small-boned face. He was quiet, and looked very serious, almost like a little adult who was carefully observing all that was going on with the people above him. Roger asked what his name was and Linda said, "Alex," but then she didn't say anything else about him. Instead, she returned to telling him all about the place she'd been living at out in the desert and how she'd gotten to know "some really beautiful people" there and just couldn't wait to get back. After a while, he almost forgot that the little boy was even there. It appeared at times that Linda had forgotten as well. She spoke so quickly, and in a scattered, breathless sort of way, as if she'd just finished running from somewhere and hadn't had time to pause and catch her breath. She sometimes laughed a little too loudly, or smiled a bit too widely. Alex watched her impassively, as if he had grown used to her long ago.

When Roger invited her to come with him, away from the bus stop, she gave him her hand and followed him like a small child. With her other hand she held onto her son. They walked for 30 minutes before Roger found what looked like a less traveled road and turned them down onto it, and by that time it was getting dark. She left Alex near a large tree full of leaves that glinted in the twilight. She told him to wait there, that mommy would be back. To wait and be good. She smiled down at him and said she would be back in just a few minutes. Then she kissed him, as if she didn't see his wide, terrified eyes, as if she didn't hear him whimpering, or feel his small hand pulling on her sleeve.

With Roger right behind her, she pushed through the brush that separated the strip of grass by the road from the overgrown field that lay on the other side and they made their way to a clump of trees just a few feet away. Neither of them said anything after leaving Alex, the only sound their panting breath and the swish of long weeds against their legs as they trampled through them. When they got to the trees, Linda led him to a small clearing just on the other side, and Roger wondered if she had known it was there all along. It was too perfect. She must have planned this entire thing. He remembered looking back toward the road and seeing the occasional flood of headlights coming over the hill from cars passing by. He wondered if Alex was old enough to know not to run out in front of one of them.

When they reached the clearing, Linda turned and faced him, and even in the dim light of the rising moon, Roger could see that her cheeks were flushed. Her eyes moved across his face, back and forth, more frantically than before. She stared at him with no expression at all, and then she smiled. For just a moment, there was something in that smile that made Roger feel as if she were some sort of dangerous animal, as if she might possibly bite. Then she stepped lightly into his arms, twined her hands around his waist, and kissed him.

Roger kissed her back. When he ran his hands through her hair, it felt like silk, and when he breathed in, he noticed she smelled like flowers. Then he clasped her around the throat, pushing in with both thumbs. He kept pushing until she stopped dancing in his arms, until her head lolled on her shoulder. With one hand he gently brushed her hair back and kissed her cheek. Then he pressed her to him. He drew in her smell again—roses and lilies, he thought—and savored it. Then he laid her down gently on the grass and made love to her there on the ground, by the light of the moon, and he thought he'd never experienced anything as sweet. Now that he'd found her, he didn't know how he would ever be able to let her go again.

He never saw Alex's small face peering through the bushes, watching everything that happened.

An hour or so later, Roger returned to the side of the road and retrieved Alex from where Linda had left him, by the big full tree with all the leaves. Alex had been sitting when he came back, his knees drawn up to his chest, his face pale. He looked up at him dully, evincing no surprise that Roger had returned, while his mother had not. He was such a little kid, thought Roger, he probably wouldn't even remember any of this. He could probably tell him Santa Claus had shown up and his mom had gone off with him to the North Pole and he would believe it. Not that he would do such a thing because—in some dim, far-off part of his mind—Roger did feel badly for the kid. He felt badly about what had happened but...he also couldn't have let Linda run off and leave him. He loved her too much. This way, she would stay his, at least for a little while.

Roger groped for words, trying to come up with something to say to the kid, and finally came out with, "Your mom...went somewhere." Alex nodded and that was all, and then Roger reached down and took his hand and pulled him up and led him down the road and back to the main thoroughfare. They walked for a while, and then Roger spotted a motel and decided to check them in for the night. He left Alex in the room while he crossed the road to visit the nearby Burger King for dinner. When he came back with burgers and fries, Alex wouldn't eat any of it. He still wasn't talking either.

Roger thought he would come around, eventually. Right now, though, he had to think about Linda. He had only left her a short time ago and already he missed her. He sat for a while with Alex and watched TV, and then when Alex fell asleep, he tucked him into bed and left, locking the door behind him and pocketing the key. He couldn't wait any longer, he had to see her again. He couldn't let her go on lying there all by herself in the dark.

That night he lay on the ground with Linda for a long time, making love to her again and again. He'd never had so much energy for a woman before, and he realized he was the happiest he'd been since he lost Mary. He cradled Linda in his arms and looked up at the moon, so full and white and brilliant that he could still clearly see the track through the field that they had made just a few hours ago. Lying here like this reminded him of Nam, where he'd slept outdoors every night for years, but the faint sound of cars going by on the road just a short distance away also reminded him that this wasn't Nam, and he knew there was no way he could keep Linda with him, and there was no way he could keep her here and continue to visit her every night. Sooner or later, someone would see him with her boy and get suspicious, or she would be reported missing and then there would be a search. It would be best if Roger—and Alex too—were long gone by that time, so it wouldn't be possible to trace what had happened back to him.

He held Linda closer and caressed her cold skin. She was already stiff and harder to move around. He was heartbroken that he would have to leave her, but at least he had her son, which was like having a piece of her, for always. He thought she would be happy about that, and when he looked at her, she did look happy. Her face held the faintest trace of a smile, and Roger was sure she understood that Alex was his now, and that he would be his father from this moment on. He looked at her face again. Yes, it was just what she wanted. He knew Linda and he could tell what made her happy, and this made her happy.

The next morning, he checked out of the motel with Alex and they went back to the bus station and got on a bus to Michigan. As hour after hour passed with nothing to do but stare out the window, he thought about Linda lying there abandoned in the clearing. But then he looked over at Alex sitting next to him and he remembered the promise he had made to her, that he would be a father to Alex, he would take care of her son—who was a little part of her—forever. That somehow made him feel better.

When they got to Michigan, Roger hitched a ride outside of the bus station to the address Greg had given him, which turned out to be a trailer park right outside of town. He showed up with Alex in tow, a bundle of Greg's letters, and a reminder that Greg had promised that he could get him a job. After they had settled in later that night, when Greg asked about it, he told him Linda had run off and left her little boy with him. When Greg pressed further, Roger shrugged and brushed him off. Not only could he not have anyone find out about what had happened with Linda, but it hurt too much still to even think about it. He couldn't stop seeing her on the ground in that clearing, lying there all alone.

As the years went by, Roger still thought about Linda and he still missed her, but his memories of her grew soft around the edges, almost filmy, until he had trouble remembering what she had really looked like, or what she had really said to him during the brief time they were together, until one day he realized all he remembered clearly was the story he'd told Greg, that she had boarded the bus she was supposed to get on and made her way to the back, not even looking out the window once at him and Alex, not even waving goodbye.

That memory hurt him too.

Chapter 29
December 1987

Joel ambled down the path to the clearing in the woods. For once, he was headed out there by himself. He didn't know why he'd felt like going out there today, he just did, and since Alyssa had gone to school for once and he had the day off, he figured why not. It would be better than sitting around in that back bedroom of Alyssa's mom's trailer, waiting for Alyssa to get home so they could do something.

As he walked the path, he breathed in deeply, feeling the cold dry air tickle his lungs, and he crunched over dead leaves and brush, avoiding the mud where he could. Although it hadn't snowed yet, he spotted patches of frost here and there and he knew it wouldn't be long until it did. Sometimes he really didn't get why Alyssa and Alex liked coming out here so much. It was freezing in the winter, muddy in the fall and spring, and hot and full of gnats in the summer. But then he forgot his thoughts as he came out into the clearing and saw Alex was in his habitual place, sitting on the old sleeping bag on the ground, leaned back against the log.

"Hey man," Joel gave him a short wave and then came over and sat down on the other end of the log. He shook out a cigarette from his pack and lit it and then offered the pack to Alex. When Alex shrugged, Joel tossed him the pack and Alex shook one out for himself.

"Alyssa went to school," he said, but Alex only nodded. Joel stayed silent for a few moments, smoking and looking at the ground. Then, as if deciding something within himself, he turned and stared at him curiously. "What's up with you, Alex?" he said. "I mean...for real. You're always acting strange now."

Alex looked over and then looked away again.

"Nothing."

"Yeah right," Joel snorted. "Tell that to Alyssa. She knows something's up. That something's going on with you."

Alex shook his head.

"What is it?" Joel pushed ahead, feeling stubborn now. He was tired of Alex acting so mysterious all the time. "What? What the fuck happened?"

A cold wind came up and ruffled the boys' hair, as if an unseen hand had moved over their heads. Clouds scudded across the sky, their shadows falling over the clearing, sucking the color out of Alex's face and eyes. Joel looked at him, waiting for an answer, and suddenly he felt like he was looking at some sort of wraith from another realm. Alex looked like he was wasting away, like he was almost dead. But then the clouds kept moving and the sun came back and he looked like himself again. Well, almost like himself, Joel thought. His eyes still looked off, although Joel couldn't quite say why.

"I found something."

"What do you mean?" Joel said, still trying to decipher the strange quality of Alex's eyes.

"In Pennsylvania, when we were there. I found something. An article, in the library."

Alex didn't speak for a few moments after that. He looked away again, through and beyond the trees at the edge of the clearing, as if he were lost in thought and had forgotten Joel was there. He seemed to do that a lot these days, Joel reflected, as his cigarette began to burn his fingertips. He crushed it out and tossed it away, and then went on looking at Alex, waiting for him to continue.

"In 1974...a woman was murdered. Right outside Pittsburgh. Her name was Linda Haley..." Alex paused and cleared his throat, but he didn't look at Joel. "The article said she had been living in California but she was on her way back to Philadelphia to visit her family. She'd been in some sort of commune, and her parents reported her missing after they didn't hear from her. She had drug problems and...maybe other problems. Her parents said they weren't surprised she was dead, when the police told them they found her body in a field a mile or so away from a bus station." Alex paused again, as if sorting something out in his own mind. "They found her off the side of a road," he finally said, and then fell silent again.

Joel looked around, sweeping the clearing with his gaze as if he might find this woman lying next to them now and then be able to give Alex some small, essential piece of information he needed about her before he could go on with his story. But Joel didn't end up saying anything and Alex went on anyway, and Joel noticed that his voice had changed. It almost didn't sound like Alex's voice anymore, and it gave him the chills.

"She was strangled. Some crazy person, the article said. Some crazy person did it. Strangled her until they broke her neck. When they found her, they...looked and saw...whoever did it—whoever murdered her—he *fucked* her too. He had sex with her. Not—" Alex swallowed and it sounded like a choking gulp, like he couldn't quite get enough air. "Not before, Joel...Not before."

"What? What do you mean?"

"After. He fucked her *after* he killed her."

Joel stared at Alex, trying to figure out why he was so upset, but he still didn't understand. What did this woman have to do with anything? Alex had found an article in the library about some random murder in a town they had spent less than 48 hours in over a year ago and he was getting all bent out of shape over it now? Why? He didn't get it. Alex wasn't making any sense at all, and maybe that was the real problem, Joel thought to himself. Maybe Alex was kind of going crazy.

The clouds had come back and covered the sun again and Joel shivered in the gloom that blanketed the woods. Suddenly it felt creepy in the clearing and he wanted nothing more than to get out of there. It was obvious that Alex's weird story about the murdered woman and the even weirder way he had told it—really the entire way he was acting—was contributing to him feeling more than a little spooked, but that didn't help him feel calmer about any of it at that moment. He glanced back at Alex's face and saw that faraway look in his eyes again, as if he had ceased to even notice Joel's presence. It was probably just as well, he thought, since it didn't seem like the time to try to talk any sense into him or even try to figure out what was going on. Alex looked almost robotic, totally closed off, and Joel didn't think much would be gained by debating the points of anything at all with him right now.

He stood up and brushed off his jeans and started to head back to the path. Alex didn't look at him and he didn't say goodbye. He just kept staring off into the woods with that strange expression on his face, and that cold, flat look in his eyes. Joel studied him for a moment more, and then he kept walking.

∽

When he got back to Alyssa's mom's place, Alyssa was home from school waiting for him. He found her on the bed half-heartedly flipping through a magazine.

Resurrect the Dead

"Hey," she said when he walked in. "Where've you been?"

"In the clearing, with Alex." At that, she raised her eyebrows and pulled herself into a sitting position on the bed.

"And?"

"I don't know. He's acting funny."

"Funny how?"

"I don't know. He told me this whole news story about some murder. But he didn't seem like himself."

"Alex hasn't been himself, that's what I've been saying."

"I know, but this was...weird. Like he was *really* not himself. He wasn't really making sense."

Alyssa paused and looked down, running her fingers over the bedspread.

"Do you think...Alex is losing it?"

"I don't know...maybe...no...I don't know. He could be," he said, at a loss for a better answer.

Alyssa nodded, accepting this information for what it was.

"What do we do?"

Joel sighed heavily and then sat down beside her.

"I don't know if there's anything we can do."

Alyssa nodded again, as if accepting this too.

Chapter 30
December 1987

After talking to Joel, Alex went home and sat in his room for a while, thinking. He'd had a feeling about something over the past few months and had blocked himself from following it. But his conversation with Joel had made things more real, and saying the details out loud about what he had found in Pittsburgh somehow solidified that feeling. It wasn't just some sick delusional story that was playing inside his own mind. It *happened*. And if that had happened, then he had a hunch that something else had happened too. He just hadn't been brave enough before to look where he needed to in order to prove that his hunch was true.

The last time Alex could remember opening the shed that was out back of their trailer had been at least a couple of years before, when their old lawnmower had stopped working for good and Greg had told Alex to put it in there. He remembered that the shed had been full of junk, cardboard boxes in sloppy stacks, each box crushing the one beneath it, plastic garbage bags full of stuff, car parts, and more appliances like the lawnmower that had given up the ghost and couldn't be revived. There had been nothing interesting in the shed, nothing that called him back to take a

Resurrect the Dead

second look. But if his hunch was right, there was something interesting in there now.

When he got out to the shed, he stood in front of the big double doors and the first thing he noticed was how shitty they looked. The paint was chipping and the hinges were rusty and the doors themselves looked like they might fall in at any moment. The second thing he noticed was that the shed was unlocked, and he was pretty sure it had always been locked before. That day that Greg had asked him to put the lawnmower away in there, he thought he remembered him having to ask Roger about a key. He thought he remembered unlocking a padlock that looped through the door handles and held the doors closed. But it was unlocked now, and there was no sign of any lock anywhere. It didn't matter, he guessed, he was just grateful that at least this part would be somewhat easy. He gripped one of the handles and gingerly pushed open the door, hoping that it really wouldn't fall in, and also that it wouldn't creak. He didn't know what could be heard from the house, but he didn't want to take any chances. He was in luck because the door only creaked a little. He stepped into the gloom of the shed, carefully pulled the door shut behind him, and then stood there, letting his eyes adjust to the grainy light. As soon as he could make sense of what he was seeing, he began looking around.

It was mostly how he remembered it. A mountain of junk sat in front of him, spilling out in all directions. Rusty gardening tools, broken boards, spools of wire, and towers of boxes stuffed full of old magazines with covers that were rippled and curled from water damage. He saw mouse turds in sprinklings here and there, and a thick layer of dust covered everything. But he also noticed something else. There was a path cleared through the junk to the back of the shed, as if someone had pulled random items off the floor and set them aside to get through, and then forgotten to replace each item in its original location when they made their way back out again. Alex surveyed the scene for a few moments, and then he followed the trail. He carefully picked up any objects that had fallen back into the way and then replaced those objects behind him. If someone came in after him, he wanted to make sure they didn't know that he'd been here.

When he got to the very back, he found what he'd been looking for. The shed didn't have a proper floor since it was just a few walls and a roof thrown up over a dirt plot in the backyard, and so Alex already knew that it would have been easy to dig down into the earth and hide something, and he knew that's what he was looking at now, a disturbed patch of ground that could be nothing other than a shallow grave. He didn't have to dig down into it to confirm what he saw.

He started digging anyway.

After he clawed up about half a bucketful of loose dirt, he saw fur. When he hauled the rest of Darwin's remains out of the grave, he hadn't decomposed so much that Alex couldn't identify him, or the cause of death. Whoever had buried him had also probably been the person who had broken his neck. He sat down and pulled Darwin onto his lap, holding him and stroking what was left of him. He talked to him and he cried, telling him he was sorry he had let it happen. He was sorry he hadn't been around to protect him. When he was done, he put Darwin back in the ground and covered him up again. It was as good a spot as any, and he didn't want to raise any suspicions by moving the body and burying it somewhere else.

Those were the last tears Alex cried for a very long time.

Alex didn't remember much before Roger, hardly anything at all. Besides the hazy glimpses he thought he'd had of the blonde woman who rode on the bus with him, who must have been his mom, he had never been able to remember anything else. But sometimes he got feelings that felt like memories. It wasn't that he got a flash of seeing something happen, it was more like he remembered a certain sound or a certain smell, but he couldn't link it to anything else. One of these feelings that had come back to him over and over was the feeling of hiding in the bushes. He remembered the scratchy branches on his face and the feeling of trying to look through them, trying to see something beyond the branches without being seen himself. He remembered the feeling of hiding from someone in those bushes, and that it was night, but it was also very bright and he could see the branches in front of him clearly.

But that was all there was, and he didn't even know if he could call that a memory. Maybe it was a dream he'd had over and over, and he just couldn't fully remember it when he was awake so it felt like a real memory, like his brain had mistaken it for something that had actually happened to him. But still, Alex couldn't shake the feeling that it was real, that sometime, a long time ago, he had hidden in the bushes on a night that was dark and also bright, and he had been very afraid because he had been hiding from someone and didn't want to be seen.

For some reason, after he found Darwin, that memory that was real-and-not-real at the same time kept coming back to him, and it almost seemed like it was getting clearer. It wasn't something he could nail down with his mind, but instead something he felt in his body, like his body remembered hiding in those bushes even if his mind didn't. His body remembered the way the branches of the bush had surrounded him, and the feeling of terror that someone might find him there, and also the feeling of needing to be there, of having crept into that bush because he was trying to find something very important.

He sat in his room, or out in the clearing in the woods, and he tried to remember more. Every problem he had ever solved came down to seeing what everyone else missed, and he felt that everyone else missed things because they usually didn't *want* to see whatever it was that was staring them in the face. Most people only saw what made them comfortable, and shut out the rest. He'd trained himself to see what was in front of him, whether he liked or not, and accept it. So, he pushed his brain to reach and grasp back into the past to see if there was anything there, anything at all, that matched the feelings of the memory that was real-and-not-real at the same time, but his brain retrieved nothing. He only ended up with a headache, and sometimes felt dizzy and then his stomach hurt too. There was nothing he could do but wait to see what emerged on its own. Either he would remember whatever had happened because it was real and something *had* actually happened, or it would fade out eventually because it was just something his overactive imagination was making up.

But lately, that was getting harder to do.

He considered talking to Joel and Alyssa about it and quickly scrapped that idea. Along with his gut feeling that the memory that was real-and-not-real at the same time was, in fact, *really* real, was also the feeling that it was all linked to Roger in some way. And then there was the matter of finding Darwin. No, he couldn't bring Joel or Alyssa into it. What was happening now was between him and Roger, and no one else. Because no one else had been there for all of it, for everything that had passed between them, over all these years.

No one, except for Greg.

It was possible that he could talk to Greg, and that maybe Greg could help. Maybe he would have some information that would explain the memory that was real-and-not-real at the same time. He already knew he wouldn't want to hear anything bad said against Roger—Alex had run into that odd stubborn wall inside Greg before, that huge and almost willful blind spot where Roger was concerned—but he could try to get through to him by

Resurrect the Dead

telling him about what he had found in Pennsylvania and how he had found Darwin out in the shed. He didn't have much hope of success, but he could at least try.

However, Greg had stopped coming over. He hadn't asked Roger about it, because he had already figured out that something had happened between the two of them, that much was obvious. Roger had probably flown into a rage and banned Greg from the house. Or something like that. The details didn't really matter. What did matter was that he was trapped with Roger and he felt like it was nearly impossible for him to get out. And he knew that Roger didn't want him to get out, ever. He was just waiting until the time was right, waiting to get a firm enough grip on him so that he could start squeezing, and then there would be no more Alex, just a space where he used to be. A space for Roger to fill with lies about what had happened to him, or some other sort of story that maybe Roger actually believed. Just like he'd done with his mom.

Except, Alex wasn't going to let things go that far.

Chapter 31
December 1987

About a week after Joel told her about his conversation with Alex in the clearing, Alyssa walked down to the train tracks by herself one evening. She had waited for a night she knew Joel would be working a later shift, leaving the house around sunset so that she could sit and watch the trains go by in the dusk and think about things. When she got there, she sat on the cold ground and nervously plucked up clumps of grass and shredded them between her fingers. Something horrible was happening to Alex, she could feel it. It wasn't just the way he had changed, that had been going on for so long that she had just about accepted it. This was something else. It wasn't anything she could see or explain, it was something she knew. She couldn't bring it up with Joel, he wouldn't understand. She needed to talk to someone who had known Alex before, when he had been the old Alex. Someone who had known him for a long time. Of course, the most obvious person who fit that description—Roger—was out of the question.

So, that left Greg.

She knew that, to Alex, Greg was more than a family friend, he was actually like family, although she didn't entirely understand the connection. He'd been with Roger in Vietnam or something, and Alex had known him since he was little. From what she knew, he helped out with Roger and was over at their house all the time. But lately, she hadn't seen him around, which might not mean anything, because she hadn't seen Alex around either. She knew Greg lived just a few trailers down from them though, and she knew that he lived alone. If she showed up and talked to him face-to-face, maybe he could tell her something that would explain why she had this feeling that something terrible was going on with Alex. Maybe he could even help her decide what they should do next.

It was as good a plan as any, she guessed. She got up from where she'd been sitting and dusted off the back of her pants and then walked back to the park as the final traces of light bled out of the sky. When she finally reached Greg's trailer it was full dark. She rapped at his door and waited a few seconds, hearing nothing from inside. Then she knocked again, harder this time, and finally heard footsteps.

When Greg answered the door, he looked like he'd just woken up. He seemed confused and his hair stuck out all over the place in little tufts. Although the overhead light on his porch was dim and flickering, and it was hard to see much more through the screen door between them, the impression that he'd just been ripped out of a deep sleep hit her forcefully, and stayed with her even after she came inside.

"Alyssa?" He squinted at her as if trying to decide if she was real.

"Hi. Can I come in?"

He fumbled with the door a moment and then held it open for her as she walked in. The light inside was brighter, but Greg didn't look any better. She noticed that his burgundy bathrobe was ratty and spotted with crumbs and the house had the shut-up smell that houses got when very old people lived in them and rarely traveled outside.

"What's wrong with Alex?" She shoved her hands deep in her jacket pockets and stared at him, waiting for his answer. Greg looked at her, bleary-eyed and struggling to focus. He'd made a trip to the party store a couple of hours ago and had already put away a few beers.

"What? Alex? Is he okay?"

"That's what I'm asking you. Nothing's happened to him...that I know of. But he's different. He's not Alex. He's not the Alex he used to be."

Greg slumped with relief and then smiled, although the smile looked like a sad one, Alyssa thought. He shifted his weight and belted his robe tighter.

"Oh...well, okay. Well...good. You had me scared there. For a second, I thought something was really wrong."

Alyssa continued to stare at Greg. She didn't return the smile.

"Something *is* really wrong. That's what I'm telling you. Alex is different."

Greg looked down at the ground, and then jerked his head up as if suddenly remembering something. He walked over to his recliner and bent down and got a beer off the six-pack Alyssa saw was sitting next to it. He popped the tab off the can and took a long swallow. Then he looked at Alyssa and gave her that same weak smile again.

"Is it Roger?" she asked. "Is it something going on with him? Is that why Alex is so different now?"

"They might have their problems...I don't know," he said quietly, and then sat down in the recliner and rocked back in it. "It's best to stay out of it," he said, looking away from her again.

"I'm not staying out of it."

Greg sighed. "There's nothing I can do."

Resurrect the Dead

"Why?" she asked carefully. "Did something happen with you and Roger?"

Greg took another drink from his can of beer. He kept his eyes trained away from her. "I don't know. Probably nothing's going on..." He licked his lips and finally looked at her again. "I don't know," he repeated.

Alyssa paused for a moment more, considering his semi-vacant expression, his stained bathrobe, and the empty cans of beer piled next to his chair. She'd seen this same picture too many times with her mother. Greg would be no help to her now, it wasn't worth it to keep trying.

"Okay. Thanks anyway, I guess."

When she left, she pulled the door shut behind her and Greg heard the click of the latch in the frame. He sighed to himself, downed the rest of his beer, and then reached for another one.

Alyssa stood outside her own trailer, just a few feet away from the front porch, and stared at the windows of Alex's trailer down the lane. The whole place was dark, except maybe the TV was on in the living room, because she could see a bluish glow lighting up the windows on that side. Then she noticed that weird car she saw sometimes turn down the lane and drive by real slow. It was a long dark car, a Pontiac, with a giant antenna on the roof. Her mom said the guy who owned it lived a couple rows over and that he was crazy. She used to work with him at the factory, when she had a job there a few years ago. She said he was a nut and never talked to anybody. Joel had told Alyssa that he knew who the guy was too when she pointed out the car to him one day. He worked in the machine shop and had been fine the couple of times Joel had run into him in the break room. He seems normal, he said, rolling his eyes after Alyssa told him what her mom said about the guy, and she knew what that meant. *Your mom's being a bitch...as usual.*

Well, her mom was probably being a bitch, but Alyssa also didn't think the guy was normal. There was something really creepy about his car. Why would anyone need an antenna that big? But when she'd said that to Joel he'd just shrugged and said maybe the guy got a kick out of trying to dial in radio stations from China. Who knew what he was doing, he said, and besides, he added, how could anyone do anything that bad with an antenna of all things? It wasn't like he was slouching around in a ski mask with a gun in his pocket. Alyssa had rolled *her* eyes at that point, and then largely forgotten about it.

Until now.

The car kept coasting along, doing about five miles an hour, slowing down even more every time it passed a trailer. When it got to Roger's trailer, it stopped for a moment and idled and Alyssa saw the blue light from the windows flicker wildly, almost like it was communicating with the car in some way. She grabbed her arms and hugged herself and shivered. It really was *too* fucking creepy. But—she told herself quickly—there was also a good chance that she was being totally paranoid. It was just a weird old guy with a weird old car with a huge antenna on it for some reason. Joel was right. How dangerous could an antenna be?

Still, when the car started moving again in her direction, she ducked fast into the shadows so that the guy wouldn't be able to see her. Maybe there wasn't anything to worry about, but the urge to hide was so strong and immediate she didn't even think about it. She watched as the car slowed down in front of her house—although it was too dark to see anyone inside—and then it kept going. She heard a sharp electric crackle from inside and then one of her little brothers yelled something, sounding pissed. She poked her head in and saw two of her brothers splayed out on the floor, watching TV.

Resurrect the Dead

"What's up?" she asked.

"Nothing," one of them said, not bothering to look at her. "TV shorted out for a second."

She moved back outside and shut the door behind her. Then she walked out to the lane and looked down at Alex's place. The blue light of the TV moving across the windows looked normal again. She wondered if Alex was up, or if it was only Roger asleep on the couch. She shivered as a gust of rainy wind blew against her and pushed her hands into the sleeves of her jacket. She needed to make a decision, and for some reason, it felt like it was now or never. If she showed up at Alex's place unannounced, this late, she might catch him by surprise. He might end up actually talking to her. From what Joel had said earlier, it seemed like Alex had been trying to tell him something, but Joel hadn't gotten it. So maybe she should just go over there right now and take a chance on him talking, because she knew that if anyone was going to get it—if anyone could understand Alex and make sense out of what was going on with him—it would be her.

She started walking to Alex's trailer, her heart pounding with every step. She felt like she could barely breathe. When she got there, she stopped and looked the trailer over again. No lights on inside, only those white-blue flashes coming from the TV through the cracks in the blinds, which were drawn down tight against the windows. Alex had to be home. Where else would he be at this time of night? Out in the clearing? In the dark and the cold? It didn't seem likely. She rubbed her thumb and index finger together rapidly and stared at the bright light moving across the blinds again. It was definitely the TV. That made sense, and that was normal. Ordinary. In fact, there was nothing she could see—absolutely nothing—that was *out* of the ordinary.

So why did she feel so scared?

Something was terribly wrong. She didn't know what it was, but she could feel it. Alex needed her. Something bad was going on, she knew it, and that finally decided it. She was going in. No matter what was waiting for her inside.

Chapter 32
December 1987

Alex sat out in the clearing until full dark came on and it got really cold, and then he decided to stop by Greg's to see if he could talk to him before going home. When he got there and stepped up to Greg's front door, the first thing he noticed was that the porch light had burned out. That was something Alex would have helped him take care of a month or so ago, but he didn't visit Greg's place anymore, just like Greg didn't visit him and Roger. He knocked on the door and stared up at the burned-out bulb while he waited. He should really get that fixed, he thought. You never knew who was going to show up at your front door. It was better if you didn't give them any advantages. While he was thinking about this, Greg opened the door, and Alex could immediately tell from the look on his face that he was probably the last person Greg had expected to see.

"Hey."

"Uh...hey, Alex." He glanced over Alex's shoulder as if checking to make sure he was alone.

"Can I come in?"

"Sure...oh sure. Sorry...come in, come in."

He noticed that it looked like Greg had been living in his robe for a couple of days—he hadn't shaved in a while either, from the growth of stubble on his face—and he wondered fleetingly if he'd lost his job at the factory. At the same moment he spotted the empty cans surrounding Greg's recliner. Drinking again. Well, there was nothing to be done about that now. Alex had his own problems to worry about, and they were much bigger than whether or not Greg was sitting around getting sauced.

He stood in the circle of light cast by the lamp on the living room rug and he stared at Greg, shivering slightly. Greg looked back at him and neither one of them said anything until Greg apparently realized he was still holding the edge of the open door. He looked at the door and then hurriedly closed it and turned toward Alex.

"Did you know about Roger?" Alex said quietly.

"Know what?"

"Did you know what Roger did?"

"Wha—what do you mean?"

"What Roger did. You knew him in Vietnam. Was he crazy then? Did you know? Did you know before he came here?"

Alex saw Greg's face change and in that moment he looked terrified. Then it was gone. Confusion took the place of fear in his eyes, and then even that ebbed away and his face relaxed again. He'd backed away from something in his own mind and changed direction, distracted himself from the fear with some lie he'd been telling himself for God knows how long. Alex recognized it because he'd seen him do it before. Greg didn't believe him. He couldn't.

"Well, now, Roger's struggling...he's always had a hard time of it. But he's okay Alex. He's not...*crazy*." Greg pronounced the last word as if it had been hard to say. "He's not. He's just...you don't know what we went through over there, Alex. A lot of guys never came back from it. Roger's okay. He's *okay*."

"I found Darwin."

Resurrect the Dead

"What?"

"Darwin. I found him. In the shed, Greg. Buried out in our back shed. And you don't have to think about it for very long to know who put him there, either."

"Alex, hold on," Greg cleared his throat and looked confused, and then, just as before, the confusion cleared and he looked like himself again. "Darwin probably...crawled off to die back there."

"And buried himself?" Alex's voice was cold. "He didn't run away. Greg, you must hear me. You *know*. I think you knew before I did, really. And I don't blame you. That isn't what this is about. But now...it can't go on. It just can't go on anymore."

"What do you mean?"

"How am I supposed to live?" He stepped up close to Greg, so close he could smell the beer on his breath and see the dandruff in his greasy hair. Greg hadn't had a bath in a while, was his first thought. His second was that he was a lost cause. He would be no help to him now, if he ever could have been.

"Alex, what—"

"Never mind," Alex said. He gave Greg and his bathrobe, the pile of cans by the chair, the whole dismal little room, one final dismissive glance. "It doesn't matter."

"I...I don't understand."

"Of course you don't." Alex said matter-of-factly. "You can't see it. Maybe because it's too close, it's happening to you. But I can. I *can* see it. And I'm done with it."

He suddenly remembered Greg teaching him how to drive. Greg dropping off groceries. Greg letting him pay back the money he had stolen, and choosing to forget that Alex had stolen his car too. Greg had always been there, as far back as Alex could remember, as far back as Roger. Greg—and Alyssa—were the only two people that Alex had never doubted, but now that was all over. He'd gotten what he came for, he'd made his attempt. Greg couldn't—or wouldn't—face what Roger was, what he had always been or what he had become. So, it was just Alex now, on his own. He looked at Greg one last time and then shrugged and turned toward the door. "It's okay. I know you did your best," he said, throwing the words over his shoulder.

Then he was gone, the screen door banging shut behind him.

∼

Alex walked home slowly, replaying his conversation with Greg. He was disappointed that Greg couldn't be of any help, but part of him was glad, too. That avenue was closed now, and it was a relief to know that for sure. He could stop holding out hope that help would be coming from the outside and focus instead on just doing what he needed to do to get out of Roger's house.

He'd already formed a vague plan, talking to Greg had only clarified the details and made him realize that he needed to put it into action sooner rather than later. He was thinking he'd drop out of school and get a job as soon as possible. He doubted Roger would care if he left school. If anything, he would probably think that at least he could help out with the bills if he got a job, which Alex would make sure to do—for a bit—just to make it look like he would be sticking around. But what Roger didn't know was that as soon as he'd saved enough to get himself started somewhere else, he would be on his way to that somewhere else without a backward glance. He was thinking Chicago, or maybe Cleveland. Probably Chicago because it was bigger. It would be easier to find a job there, and easier to get lost, and that's what he needed the most. Somewhere he could be sure of staying hidden.

Joel could get him a job at the factory, that was almost certain. Everyone liked him there, because everyone liked Joel in general. Alex was glad he was with Alyssa. He knew she would be taken care of, and that Joel would watch out for her. He'd known what kind of guy Joel was from the moment they met him. Good-

Resurrect the Dead

hearted and loyal. Innocent and open in a way that Alex could never be, and never had been. He couldn't tell either him or Alyssa that he was leaving. They wouldn't understand. Even worse, they might try to follow him. He could see Alyssa doing that. She never gave up. He sighed deeply, stopping to look down at her trailer for a moment. He just hoped she ended up having an all right kind of life. She deserved better than she'd had so far.

It shouldn't be that hard, he thought, as he started walking again. He would talk to Joel tomorrow and then the wheels would be set in motion. He would get the job, save the money, and then when the time was right, he would go. Just like that he would walk out of this life and into a new one.

Just like that he would be free of Roger. Forever.

Chapter 33
December 1987

When Alex got home, he found Roger in the living room with all the lights off, with the TV still on. That wasn't out of the ordinary. Roger usually sat in the dark and watched TV all night until he fell asleep on the couch. What *was* out of the ordinary was that the sound was turned all the way down on the TV and Roger wasn't watching it. He was sitting on the couch looking toward the door when Alex came in, as if he'd been waiting for him.

Alex saw his eyes first, glinting in the darkness, and in that moment, he thought of a panther crouched in a tree in a jungle, waiting to spot its prey. Fear crawled through his gut. Something was off, something was wrong, but he didn't know what it was. Roger was different. He looked more awake, more *alive*, than he had in a long time. It was in his eyes. But what could have happened between now and a couple of hours ago when Alex had last been home that would make him look like that?

"I've been waiting for you," he said, and that was when Alex noticed it in his voice too. Roger's voice was different. *Everything* about him was different. He looked nothing like the Roger he had known for the past couple of years who could barely breathe and

Resurrect the Dead

depended on Alex to get him his smokes and his food, who needed help with pretty much everything. The Roger sitting in front of him now was a different Roger, a sharp and watchful Roger. A predator. Alex could feel that. Something about the way he was sitting there—like he had been almost smugly waiting for him to get home so he could spring some sort of trap on him—triggered something deep within him. He glanced at him again and the look on his face suddenly shoved Alex past his limit. Fuck his whole plan, he might need to just take his things and get out tonight.

"I found Darwin," he said, without planning to say anything at all. "And I know about my mom."

Roger stared at him. His expression didn't change.

"I know what happened, Roger. You killed her. You killed my mom...and then you...had sex with her dead body. There was a news story on it, I read the whole thing. I know it was you. The article said her name was Linda, and it happened right outside Pittsburgh, the same year we came to live with Charlie. You kept me...You took me. Was that why you killed her? Where was I when it happened? Did you have me locked up somewhere?"

As furious as he was, Alex also felt a flooding sense of euphoria. He had so many questions. So many questions that he'd grappled with for months with no answers. The relief of speaking them out loud was almost like a physical release.

"I didn't steal you," Roger answered, as if he'd only heard the smallest part of all that Alex had said. "You came with me."

"What about my mom? You *killed* her. And you always made it out to me like you actually cared about her. What a sick joke."

Alex saw the sharpness go out of Roger's eyes for a moment. His expression softened and he looked confused, like a tired old man who wasn't quite sure where he was. He glanced around and then looked back at Alex again.

"I loved your mom," he said, sounding surprised, as if he couldn't believe that Alex didn't know that. "She was an angel. I knew it when I saw her. I loved her." He sighed and looked down at his hands, and a desperate-sounding groan came out of him. "I loved her," he went on in a broken voice. "That's the truth. I don't know why she left. I don't know why she got on the bus. She didn't even wave goodbye. I told Greg that. I don't know why she wouldn't even wave goodbye to me. I loved her."

"She didn't get on the bus," Alex said tonelessly.

Roger looked up again, suddenly fearful. "I...saw her. I told Greg. What do you mean she didn't get on the bus?"

"That may have been what you told Greg..." he said slowly. Absurdly, he felt that he and Roger had seamlessly reverted to their old roles again, where Roger was agitated over something he didn't understand and it was Alex's job to calm him down by patiently explaining it to him. "But she didn't actually get on the bus," he continued. "They found her body in a field about a mile away from the bus station." He sank down into the chair next to the couch and rubbed his temples with one hand. He had a headache, and he was so tired. He looked over at Roger again.

"You killed her Roger...and you..." Then he paused and shook his head. "Never mind. It...doesn't matter. But you have to know, you killed her." Roger didn't answer him, he only sat and stared forward, blank-faced and silent. Alex tried again. "Do you understand what I'm telling you?" Watching him carefully, Alex saw his eyes shift around the room. That feeling he'd gotten before was back, and suddenly his hands turned cold and his mouth went dry. Roger was hiding something.

"Roger? What's going on?"

"You're worried about me... you should be worried about him."

"Who should I be worried about?" Alex spoke softly now. It felt like the energy in the room had turned dangerous.

"Him."

"Who?"

Resurrect the Dead

"That guy...who says he's your friend."

"Who? Greg?"

Roger snorted and folded his arms across his chest.

"You fucking kidding? Not Greg. That kid. That kid you hang out with all the time, with the black jacket."

"Joel?"

"Yeah," Roger said. His tongue darted out, wetting his lower lip, and the way it glistened in the light made Alex's skin crawl. He was just about out of patience with Roger and his weird mind-fuck attempts.

"What *about* Joel?"

"You tell me. Where'd he come from anyway? All he wants to do is pal around with your little girlfriend. He lives with her now, yeah?"

"She's not my girlfriend," Alex said reflexively.

"But she was...she was yours."

"You don't know what you're talking about," he said, and then he realized again how tired he was. It felt like he could barely hold his head up.

"I *do* know what I'm talking about." Roger said. "I think you just don't wanna see it. That's why I had to step in. Because if it all got left up to you, you woulda done nothin'. Just let her walk away from you and straight into that other kid. That's right."

Here, Alex paused. Carefully, he began examining every fact that he knew. Because thinking was what he did best, it was also what he did the most quickly, but in these few moments he took his time. He couldn't allow himself to miss anything, he couldn't afford to make any errors, not right now. So, he thought about Alyssa, and then he thought about Joel, and then he thought about all three of them together as friends. He kept his face blank, as his brain calculated several different possibilities as to what Roger might be talking about, in the space of a few seconds. He came up with nothing. He still didn't understand what Roger was getting at with all this. There was nothing that Roger knew that he didn't.

"You know it's the truth," said Roger.

Alex stared at the carpet and thought harder. There was nothing that Roger could know—not about him, or Alyssa or Joel—that would make any bit of difference in the way Alex felt now. He knew Alyssa was safe, because she was with Joel. He had set it up that way. So why did Roger have that look on his face? What in the fuck was he talking about? He examined the front of his own dirty white Reeboks, his eyes landing on the places where the Velcro was unraveling. He imagined pulling back the torn leather from the front of his shoe, where it was already ripping open. He kept thinking, but still, he had nothing.

"You were gonna lose her, Alex," Roger said, sounding as sad as if he himself had lost something. "She was trying to run away from you, just like your mom woulda tried to run away from me. She coulda been *yours* Alex. But you let her go. And she ran right to that guy who says he's a friend of yours. But he ain't no friend." Roger took a long breath. Alex stayed silent. His eyes caught again on Roger's wet lips and how they gleamed in the light. He felt nauseous.

"I took care of it for you, Alex. I did it for you," he said. "I took care of it."

"What do you mean?"

"I helped you."

"Roger, what are you...?"

"I had to do it."

"*What* are you talking about?"

"She coulda been yours Alex."

"Roger—"

"Coulda been yours but you *fucked* it *up*."

"I—"

Resurrect the Dead

"Couldn't even see when something was being taken from you. So...I took it back. I had to because you weren't gonna."

"Roger!" Alex finally yelled *"What are you talking about?"*

"Alyssa," Roger said softly. "I got her back for you, Alex."

Then, instantly, like all the lights going on in a dark house at once, Alex knew.

Roger had Alyssa.

He froze, and sniffed the air, and then he was certain. He recognized the familiar apple scent of the shampoo she used. She had been here, in this room, not long ago. No, not so very long ago at all. Maybe ten minutes. Maybe less than that.

He turned away from Roger without a second glance, as if he had ceased to exist. He scanned the room, and then turned and walked to the closet that was in the hall between his bedroom and the kitchen. He heard himself breathing and he heard his own breath catch in his throat. It was as if he were listening to someone else breathing, someone else who happened to be trapped inside his body. When he got to the closet, he yanked open the door and Roger's duffel bag tumbled out, the big, beat-up bag he had brought back from Vietnam. Alex had tried to crawl inside it once when he was little and playing some game of his own and Roger had screamed at him and scared him so badly that he never went near it again.

Until now. He stared down at the bag, listening to the sound of someone else's ragged breath coursing through his body, and finally, when he couldn't take the sound of that horrible noise any longer, he reached down and opened the bag.

Alyssa was inside.

Suddenly, there was a screaming pressure inside his head and he couldn't breathe. He dropped to his knees and squeezed his eyes shut. It felt like something was rupturing in his brain. He *saw* it. He was in the bushes, hiding, barely breathing, so scared, but watching too, not looking away from Roger in front of him with his mom, Roger with his hands around his mom's neck. He saw Roger squeeze and shake her and he saw her flop against him and then she was still. Too still. He saw Roger put her on the ground and start pulling her clothes off and then he saw him get on top of her. He saw it all. The branches scratched at his face and he smelled the cold night air again and he watched everything happen in the bright white light of the moon. He saw everything.

He couldn't believe he had forgotten.

How could he have forgotten?

Slowly, the pressure in his head subsided to a slow, dull roar and he opened his eyes. Alyssa was still there, right in front of him. He laid a hand across her forehead, as if testing her for a fever. Her eyes were closed and duct tape was plastered across her mouth, like a shiny gray bandage plastered across a wound. The pressure in his head increased again, collecting behind his eyes until he felt like they might burst out of his skull. He felt himself trying to leave, trying to fly out of his body, to vacate his mind, but if he did, he knew he might be lost forever. He pulled himself back using every ounce of mental power he had, and then he was clear again. But that didn't change the fact that Alyssa was still lying there, halfway out of Roger's beat-to-hell old duffel bag, and he couldn't push that reality away.

Except, it didn't really look like her, now that he had gotten a hold of himself and started to examine her more closely. He *did* see blonde hair, and a delicate-boned beautiful young face, but it wasn't Alyssa. It was a girl not much older than Alyssa, but old enough to be a woman. It was his mother. His real memories of her had always been hazy, but he had imagined the details of what she looked like many times. The woman lying on the floor looked just like her. Then he heard someone else breathing through his body again, someone else that wasn't him.

Resurrect the Dead

He gently pushed Alyssa and the bag back inside the closet and shut it. Roger had killed his mother all those years ago and Roger had killed Alyssa tonight. It was all true. He stood still for a moment and looked around. His arms and legs felt heavy, like concrete blocks, and his head felt like it was full of fluid. It was hard to think. He heard some noise in the background—an insistent thumping, as if someone was pounding on the door—but that noise also seemed very far away. He shuffled forward, leaving the closet behind for now, he would come back and deal with that later. He had to get to the kitchen.

When he got there, he walked behind the eat-in counter that divided the kitchen from the living room and then he paused and stood looking toward the couch. Since the couch faced the TV, all Alex could see was the back of Roger's head and the greasy mat of his black hair. He sat motionless, but Alex somehow knew that he had been listening to him walk around, and he almost certainly was aware of where Alex was standing right now. Even though Roger had seemed to be a complete zombie for the past couple of years, Alex had a feeling that now he would hear and respond to any slight sound he might make. He wondered if Roger might actually have the ability to leap off the couch and fly at him, before he could get across the living room to the door and get out. He didn't know, and at this point it also didn't matter. Time was short. If he was going to do anything, he had to do it now. He looked around the kitchen. He would use anything in sight, as long as it did the job.

The first thing he saw was a pair of scissors.

They were a bit rusty, but they would work. He grabbed them and then he was at the couch, standing next to Roger. He didn't remember getting from one place to the other, he was just suddenly there. He had one hand buried deep in the tangle of Roger's long black hair, and as he pulled his head back, he looked into his eyes. Roger looked so tired, as if all the life had gone out of him and he couldn't hold himself up anymore. He winced, just once and only slightly, and then he looked at Alex one last time and closed his eyes.

Alex cut his throat.

Chapter 34
December 1987

When he opened the door and saw Alex standing there on the front stoop, Joel's first thought was that he wasn't looking so good. He had dark circles under his eyes, and his face was so pale that his lips looked as red as if they had been smeared with blood. Randomly, Joel thought of Snow White, the fairytale his mom had read him as a kid, before she'd laid down her judgment on all things evil and banned those kinds of stories forever. Joel remembered that Snow White had been described as having skin as white as snow and lips as red as blood. That was exactly how Alex looked right now.

Joel looked him over again and noticed a streak of dirt on his chin.

"Right here," he said, passing his thumb over his own chin. "You got something right here, buddy." For a moment Alex looked terrified, maybe even dangerous. Like a hunted wild animal. But then it was gone and he looked like himself again and Joel shook off the thought.

"Can I borrow your truck?" he asked. Joel moved outside and pulled the door shut behind him as Alyssa's mom yelled at one of the kids inside the trailer. He gave Alex a look.

"Can't even hear myself think," he said, but Alex made no sign that he had heard anything. He stood and waited, his eyes intent on Joel's face, waiting for an answer. "Sure, you can take it," he said, sighing. "I'm just waiting for Alyssa to get home..." He trailed off as Alex started shaking his head. "You haven't seen her?" he asked, misunderstanding.

"No. No, I just—I have to go now. It's important."

Joel looked at him again. Something was definitely off. He wondered if maybe Alex and Roger had gotten into it. He remembered when he and his mom would get into screaming fights. If he'd had a friend back then, or a car, things might have been a lot different. He looked at Alex for another moment and then nodded his head.

"Yeah. Yeah, sure," he said. He dug into his pocket, came out with the keys and handed them over, then smiled at Alex. "That's what friends are for, right?"

Alex didn't answer, and he didn't smile back. He just took the keys and walked away fast in the dark and a moment later he heard the truck start up and then Alex was gone.

Later, Joel played over those last moments in his mind, again and again. Why hadn't he said, *Hey Alex, where the fuck you going?* Why hadn't he said anything at all, really? But when it had been happening, it hadn't seemed like the right time. When he thought back on it, he remembered how he had almost felt Alex straining away from him, as if he wanted nothing more than to bolt out to the truck and be gone into the night. At the time, it had felt like it was no big deal. Alex just needed to borrow his truck to run out and get something, or run away for a while and get some space, and then he would be back. Besides, he had been waiting for Alyssa to get home. He'd already thought it was strange that she hadn't shown up yet and he'd been wondering if everything was okay when Alex had popped up at his door.

So, he'd had his mind on other things, and it really did feel like

Resurrect the Dead

it was no big deal. He'd had no reason to question what Alex was doing. Except for his pale face—white as snow—and blood-red lips. But how was he supposed to know the way Alex looked was a clue to anything? There was no way he could have known that, he told himself later. No way at all. So, it made sense that he didn't ask any questions, and that he hadn't tried to stop Alex. It made sense.

But later, when it was all over, that didn't change the way he felt inside, like he had somehow failed Alex. And then later, he felt like he had failed Alyssa too.

Joel went back inside and sat down on the couch with Alyssa's little brothers, only half watching the movie that was playing on the TV. He couldn't concentrate. Alyssa should have been home by now, it was getting late. And also, where could she have gone? She hadn't been there when he'd gotten home from work about an hour ago and so he'd guessed she was probably off trying to talk to Alex, but Alex said he hadn't seen her. So where was she? It was too dark and cold for her to be out in the clearing, and besides, he doubted she would go out there alone by herself at night. He knew she didn't have any other friends and her only mode of transportation was him and the truck. As he sat there and went over these things in his mind, absentmindedly listening to Alyssa's brothers fighting about changing the channel, he started to feel seriously uneasy. There wasn't really anywhere for Alyssa to go. So where in the hell was she?

"Hey!" he said suddenly, raising his voice to be heard above the two boys bickering. Both kids stopped talking and turned to stare at him. "Was Alyssa here? Have you guys seen her?"

"Yeah," said one brother, rolling his eyes, as if this were obvious. "She was here. She left."

"Where'd she go?" Joel asked. The boy shrugged.

"Don't know."

"When? When was that?"

"When the TV was being weird again."

"What?" Joel was confused. The other boy spoke up.

"The TV went all crazy. It does that sometimes. Voices come through it."

"What?" Joel looked at them and sighed heavily. "You guys are morons. Shut up. I'm being serious. I need to know where your sister went."

"We *are* being serious," the first brother whined, and then the other one punched him in the ribs and the two of them flew onto the floor, wrestling and trying to choke each other.

"Hey! HEY! Fuckin' cut it OUT. *When* did Alyssa leave? How long ago?"

The two boys froze and looked over at Joel. "An hour ago? Maybe?" One of them said, and then the other one hit him and they went rolling across the floor again.

An hour ago...and she was on foot. She couldn't have gotten far. Joel jumped up from the couch and grabbed his jacket. When he got outside, he jogged out to the lane and looked in both directions. He started walking toward Alex's place, toward the woods and the clearing down at the end of the park, and then he noticed something. He couldn't tell for sure from this distance what he was seeing, so he started jogging again. Then, as he got closer, he was sure.

The front door to Alex's trailer was open.

Joel stopped and stared. *That* was weird. Alex would never have left his house without shutting the front door and, from what he knew, Roger never went anywhere farther than the end of the driveway. So, was Roger just sitting inside with the front door wide open on a cold night like this? Unlikely.

He thought back to how Alex had looked when he'd shown up

earlier. If he and Roger had gotten into some sort of fight and Alex had taken off to get away from him for a little while, Joel was pretty sure that Alex wouldn't do anything stupid like leave the front door hanging open, which would definitely alert Roger to the fact that he was gone. *And maybe not coming back...*said a whisper that came from the back of his mind. He pushed the whisper away.

Slowly, he walked to the driveway that belonged to Alex's trailer, and then he stood there, a few feet away from the open door, and tried to peer inside, without actually going inside. It was hard to see anything. There wasn't a lamp on in the whole place, only the light of the TV flickering across the walls. Joel couldn't hear anything so he guessed the sound must be off, and that made him feel even weirder. Why would anyone be watching TV without the sound on but with the door open late at night in this cold-ass weather? His stomach twisted and suddenly he had a bad feeling, about everything. He shouldn't have let Alex leave, that was a mistake. He should have kept him talking, kept him with him, at least until he could find Alyssa and she could talk to him, then maybe she would have been able to make sense out of what was going on.

He forced himself to walk over to the steps that led up to the door and got one foot on the bottom step and then froze. He tried to move forward and couldn't. It was like there was an invisible wall of cold air pushing him away from the house. He felt himself trembling, and he couldn't stop. With one foot on the pavement and one foot on the step above it, he stood, and he watched the light from the TV quiver and flash into the part of the room that he couldn't see from where he stood. He would have to go in, that was the only way to figure out what was going on. Alex would do it, if he were in his place. Joel knew he would. And somehow, absurdly, he suddenly felt like Alex had left him in charge, and he couldn't let him down. Then he stopped thinking altogether and he made himself do it. He walked up the steps and went into the house.

The first thing he saw was Roger. He sat on the couch, his arms folded in front of him, his legs crossed, casually, at the ankle, as if he were just sitting there waiting for something good to come on TV. He looked totally normal, except for the fact that where his throat used to be was now a ragged, messy black hole, still dribbling dark blood down the front of his old t-shirt. It looked like someone had tried to saw through his neck and decapitate him but had done the worst job ever, and then had just finally given up and left everything only half done.

Things being what they were, Joel was surprised at how calm he felt. In fact, he had just started to think that he should maybe devote some serious attention to having more of a reaction, when he heard sounds coming from the back of the house. There was a rhythmic thumping noise that went on and on, punctuated by a muffled kind of yelping. It sounded like someone kicking a wall, or a trapped dog trying to get out of a closet. He paused to listen more closely to figure out what it was, and then, he realized exactly what he was hearing.

It was Alyssa.

Chapter 35
December 1987

Alyssa had gone through so many different horrible emotions between the time Roger had answered the door and let her in and the time that Joel found her and untied her that she felt like she'd lived at least a hundred lives. She also wasn't sure how much time had actually passed because she'd been unconscious somewhere in the middle of it all. She remembered Roger had grabbed her after she stepped inside the house and hit her over the head, and the next thing she knew Alex was looking down at her. She tried to talk but she could barely nod her head and Alex didn't seem to understand that she was trying to communicate with him. His face was whiter than she had ever seen it and his eyes were glassy and vacant, almost as if he weren't seeing her at all. Then the strangest look came over his face, as if he did see her, but maybe like was seeing something else too, something that wasn't her. Recognition and confusion flickered back and forth in his eyes until he pushed her back into the closet and shut the door and then she was enveloped in darkness again.

Slowly, her head began to clear, and as it did, she started kicking at the door, trying to get Alex to come back. When she paused for a moment, she heard something clatter on the kitchen counter, and she stayed still, trying to figure out what he could be doing. After a few more moments, she heard a long, wet gurgling noise that triggered such a deep terror in her—she didn't know why—that she froze stiff as a wild animal playing dead. Then she heard a gasping, wheezing sound, like maybe someone was panting and crying at the same time—she could have sworn that was Alex—and then water running in the kitchen sink, and that was when she started kicking her feet against the wall again and trying to yell through the duct tape Roger had pasted across her mouth, but Alex never came back to the closet. She paused and listened. Nothing but silence. Where had he gone? What had happened?

She tried to sit herself up but immediately got dizzy and had to lay back down again. She rested there for a while, she didn't know how long, staring down at her legs, which were bound together with duct tape too. After what seemed like hours but was probably only minutes, she heard footsteps. Had Alex come back? He wouldn't have just left her here with Roger. Maybe he had taken Roger somewhere else and called the police. Maybe he had come back to get her after getting Roger out of the house. But that gurgling noise...Alyssa remembered it and shuddered. No, something had happened. Something bad. Whoever she was hearing wasn't Alex, but she was also sure it wasn't Roger either. She started kicking and screaming through the tape again. And that was how Joel found her.

Now, she sat shivering, wrapped in a blanket and telling everything to the detective for the third time, everything except about the gurgling noise she had heard, and the person gasping and crying and how she was almost sure that had been Alex. She kept those parts to herself. She said that Roger had grabbed her and Roger had hit her. Roger had tied her up. She didn't see anyone else but Roger. After that she had lost consciousness and then Joel had found her. Over and over again, she said she didn't remember anything else. She hadn't seen anyone else. Joel sat next to her on the couch, clenching his hands together so tightly every knuckle had turned white. She thanked God that her mom had gone out for the night so she couldn't pry into all of this and say something about Alex and make everything worse. Her little brothers clustered together at the back hallway off the kitchen, taking turns peeking out to watch the whole scene. Every time Alyssa glanced back there, she felt a chill go through her. That would be where the closet was in Alex's house, all these trailers were built the same.

"So, let's go back to when you were in the closet," the detective said again and Alyssa felt a wave of nausea rise up in her. "You didn't hear anyone else come into the house before Joel? No one?"

"That's right."

"You didn't hear your friend Alex come into the house? You're sure about that?"

"I'm sure."

"The *first* person you heard come into the house was your boyfriend Joel here, when he came in and found the deceased?"

"Yes."

"And from the time between you going into that closet and Joel coming in and finding the deceased, you don't remember *anything*?"

"That's right."

He peered closer at her.

"You're sure about that?" he asked carefully.

"Yes."

"When *was* the last time you saw your friend Alex?"

"I *didn't* see him," said Alyssa, and now she looked at him steadily. "I didn't see him at all."

"And you didn't see Alex either, is what you said?" The detective turned his attention to Joel and Joel shook his head. He stared at the ground, still clenching his hands. The detective looked back at Alyssa again.

"So where were you before you went over to the deceased's residence?"

"At Greg's."

"Greg?" The detective asked.

"Yes. He lives just down the lane." Alyssa sighed and seemed to tremble. "I...I don't think I can talk about this anymore right now," she said, her voice catching. The detective smiled at her and patted her hand.

"I understand, sweetheart. You've been through a lot."

He patted her hand again and then stood up and turned away from them. Joel glanced over at Alyssa and she shot him a look. He knew she'd been lying, and she knew that he knew. They would talk about it later. For now, play it cool. When the detective looked back at them again, they both wore the same blank expressions they had just a moment ago.

"Thanks, kids. You've been a big help," he said.

They both nodded, and then looked anywhere else but at each other.

The detective didn't have any easier of a time with Greg. Much as Alyssa and Alex had, he also noted the stained bathrobe and the general fogginess of expression Greg wore when he answered the door after the detective pounded on it a few times. When he explained who he was and why he was there—giving only the briefest description of what had happened to Roger in order to spare him the particulars—Greg went pale and then began to cry in a genuine, if slightly drunken, outpouring of shocked grief.

Resurrect the Dead

Since he didn't seem to have the presence of mind to ask him inside, the detective shouldered his way through and then asked him if maybe it wouldn't be better if they both sat down.

When Greg's tears had tapered off, the detective asked him when he had last seen Alex and he said about an hour ago, no, it was two hours ago, at least. Yes, he had left upset, but Greg hadn't been sure what about. He couldn't entirely remember what they had discussed when Alex had been with him. It was all hard to piece together now. The detective tried asking the same questions in different ways, hoping to prod him into giving better answers, but Greg only repeated over and over that he didn't know. He didn't know why Alex had acted the way he did, or what he had wanted, or where he had planned to go after running out the door.

The detective looked at him for another long moment and sighed. It was impossible not to believe him. This guy wouldn't be able to lie his way out of a paper bag. He was a little more than pathetic, but he wasn't calculating. He had no choice but to conclude that Greg was exactly as he appeared to be, a sad drunk, and that any more time spent talking to him was time wasted on a dead end.

Alex's friends were a different matter, though. He had questioned them over and over but gotten nowhere. The one kid stayed mostly silent and just shook his head, and then sometimes asked if he should get a lawyer. He seemed not to understand that he wasn't actually in any trouble for stumbling across a dead body. At the same time, he almost stopped talking altogether whenever he was asked about Alex, which led the detective to believe that he knew more about what was going on than he was saying. Same with the girl. When she talked about what had happened with Roger she sounded one way, and then when he asked her about Alex, her voice changed and her eyes changed and she looked and sounded another way. And Alex himself, the one who seemed to be at the center of everything, well, he was just gone. It was like he had completely vanished.

He left Greg's trailer and walked back down to the residence of the deceased, pushing his way through the small crowd of people who had gathered in the lane around the cluster of police cars parked out front. They had cut the sirens upon arrival, but the red and blue lights still flashed across the neighboring trailers and the faces of the people in the crowd, and the squawk of the police radios intermittently traveled through the cold night air, creating an odd party-like atmosphere that was both somber and expectant. The detective had moved through many crowds like this before. An energy of excitement buzzed through them, but at the same time hardly anyone spoke.

He went inside and took one last look around, pausing again at Alex's room in the back, standing in the doorway and sweeping it with his gaze. There wasn't much to see, he thought. It was almost as bare as a motel room. Then he shook his head and walked back out to the living room, through the crime scene, past his colleagues still gathering evidence, and out the door and down the front steps. He walked over to the ambulance where the paramedics were getting ready to load the body into the back and lifted the sheet to take another look at the deceased.

His eyes were still open but—unlike so many others he'd seen—this one didn't look surprised. If anything, he looked resigned. Like whoever had come for him was someone he had been expecting for a long time. The detective's gaze traveled farther down to the deceased's throat, which hadn't been cut so much as torn open. As if someone had taken a gardening tool and dug right into his trachea like it was a stubborn rocky piece of ground that needed to be turned over. That was because the murderer had used an old rusty pair of kitchen scissors, which they'd found at the feet of the deceased and were being dusted for prints now. The detective was honestly astonished that the murderer had been able to make that much progress with them. He had seen the scissors, and he doubted if most people could have used them to cut through a tomato.

The murderer had been determined, to say the least, if not depraved. Or maybe even clinically insane. For some reason he suddenly thought about a book he'd had to read in college, about a guy who had gone crazy in the Congo. As he stood and looked down at what was left of the deceased's throat, one of the lines in that book came back to him. The main guy—the guy who'd gone crazy—he'd died at the end. And right before he died, he'd only said two words: *The horror*. It seemed like none of the characters got why he said that either. But the detective got it, which is probably why that line came back to him now. *The horror*. Yeah, that about covered it, he thought. No further discussion required. He didn't think the guy who wrote that book had been a detective, but he must have been in a similar line of work.

He covered the body back up, nodded to the paramedics that they could take it away, and then started to walk over to his car. But before he got there something caught his eye on the ground. It was a piece of paper, a leaflet or something. He bent over and grabbed it and then straightened again and angled it so he could see it in the orange glow of the streetlight. It was a little homemade flier, maybe four by five inches. He squinted at the couple of lines printed on it.

Keep on the watch
You know neither the day nor the hour

The detective chuckled to himself. What the author didn't know, apparently, was that a man could keep on the watch his whole damn life and still get attacked by some crazy nut with a pair of rusty scissors. He got in his car, rolled down the window and lit a cigarette and then sat there for a moment more staring at the paper. Then he threw it out the window. It had nothing to do with anything. *Goddamn shitty job*, he thought to himself as he started the car. *One day I have got to get out of this goddamn shitty job.*

Then he pulled away.

About the Author

Lauren Sapala is the author of the West Coast Trilogy: *Between the Shadow and Lo* (Book One), *West Is San Francisco* (Book Two), and *Enormous Forces* (Book Three). She also writes nonfiction books for writers and other creatives. To find out more visit laurensapala.com.

Made in the USA
Middletown, DE
25 January 2025